A Patient Woman

Tabitha & Wolf Historical Mystery Series

Book Nine

Sarah F. Noel

ISBN-979-8-9919192-0-3

Cover design by: HelloBriie Creative
Printed in the United States of America

ALSO BY SARAH F. NOEL

Tabitha & Wolf Historical Mystery Series

A Proud Woman

A Singular Woman

An Independent Woman

An Inexplicable Woman

An Audacious Woman

A Discerning Woman

An Indomitable Woman

An Intrepid Woman

An Enigmatic Woman

A Valiant Woman

An Anointed Woman

The Continental Capers of Melody Chesterson

A Venetian Escapade

Mischief In Morocco

The Amsterdam Enigma

Acknowledgments

I want to thank my wonderful editor, Kieran Devaney and the eagle-eyed Patricia Goulden and Mary Virginia Avery for doing a final check of the manuscript.

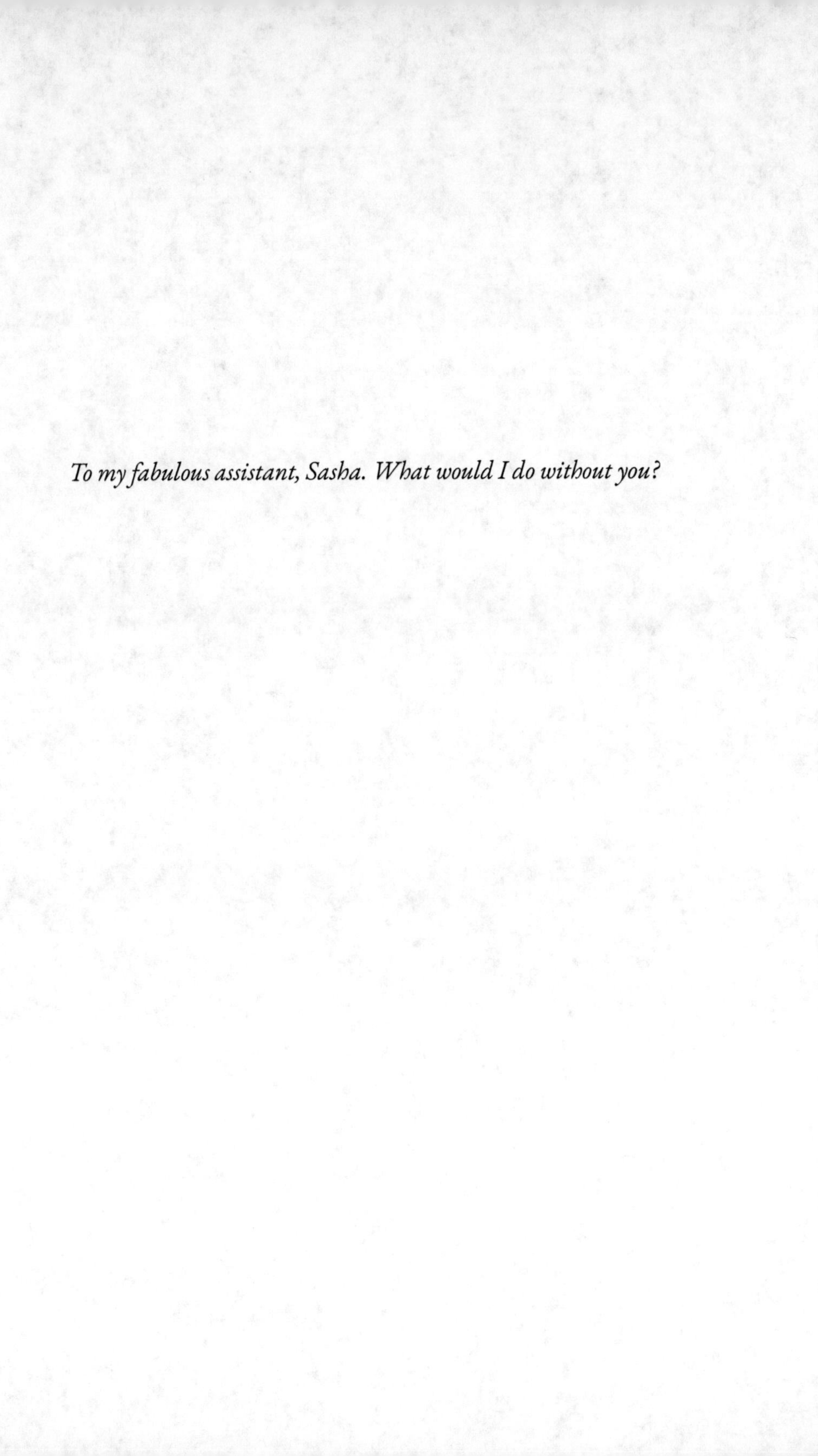

To my fabulous assistant, Sasha. What would I do without you?

Foreword

This book is written using British English spelling. e.g. dishonour instead of dishonor, realise instead of realize.

British spelling aside, while every effort has been made to proofread this thoroughly, typos do creep in. If you find any, I'd greatly appreciate a quick email to report them at sarahfnoelauthor@gmail.com

PROLOGUE

The man heard steps behind him but thought nothing of it. When he finally turned, he could barely see the person approaching him in the dark alleyway.

"Who goes there? What do you want with me? Tell me now!" he demanded in a tone that insisted on obedience.

As the person following him stepped out of the shadows, the look of disdain on the man's face was such that there was nothing more to be done than to dart forward, jamming the sharp knife between his ribs and into whatever was left of his heart.

Chapter 1

May 5, 1898

"I am not sure why this is so difficult for you to manage, Jane. You wanted a task you might make your own, and the flowers for St Paul's seemed something even you could take on without too much of a palaver. Yet here we are."

The dowager spread her hands in exasperation as if she were stating a wholly predictable yet utterly avoidable calamity. While uttering these words, the dowager assumed an expression of such disappointment that her daughter hung her head and replied in a tone of dismay and contrition, "I am so sorry, Mama. Lily loves yellow roses and so I assumed they would be a nice addition to the floral arrangements."

"Jane, I imagined I would not have to spell out such things for you, but I see I was mistaken. Yellow roses symbolise jealousy and infidelity. Because of this, I would have thought it obvious how inappropriate they are for a wedding. Orange blossoms, however, given Her Majesty's preference for them, are always acceptable. Her Majesty has also demonstrated myrtle can be charming in a bouquet. In addition, white or pink roses, Lily of the Valley, white or purple violets, and even camellias, as long as they are white or pink, are acceptable. Yellow roses are most certainly not."

Adopting the tone of voice one might use with a recalcitrant toddler who has been given and then lost their final opportunity for compliance, the dowager informed her daughter, "It is for the best if you concentrate all of your efforts on ensuring you are dressed appropriately for the wedding. After all, Jane, Lily is marrying into the aristocracy and raising your family up from the drop in status to which you chose to subject it through your marriage. The mother of a future countess should adhere to, or in your case, aim to reach, a certain baseline standard of fashionable style, at least while you are in London. Once you return to the heathen backwoods you call home, I am sure no one will care if you revert to your usual outdated, unflattering garb."

Jane hung her head even lower and allowed this one task she was hoping to perform for her daughter to be taken away from her.

Tabitha watched this scene play out, unsure whether to interject. While Hamish, Laird MacAlister, had been detained in Edinburgh for work, Jane MacAlister was staying at Chesterton House in anticipation of the impending marriage of her daughter, Lily, to Viscount Tobias. While it might be considered more appropriate for her to stay with the dowager, Tabitha had made the offer of her home, and Jane jumped at the opportunity. The dowager might have been more inclined to comment on this breach of social etiquette if not that Jane's uncle, the irascible Uncle Duncan, was also staying with Tabitha and Wolf, and the dowager did not intend to invite that uncivilised, heathen Scot to set foot over her threshold. The truth was, while she was somewhat miffed her daughter preferred to stay elsewhere, the dowager did not have an interest in hosting her.

The dowager found her daughter to be dull and insipid. She viewed her own ability to cow Jane so completely as proof of the woman's appalling timidity. Added to these sins was Jane's complete lack of style and sense of fashion. The dowager really didn't need her neighbours, particularly the very nosy Lady Davenport, judging her as Jane arrived in one of the potato sacks she deemed a dress.

And then there was Jane's husband, Laird Hamish MacAlister. It was the dowager's late son, Jonathan's, decision to allow the marriage. Jane's debut into society had been deemed a failure, at least by her mother. Despite lacking a real English title, Hamish possessed considerable land-holdings and inherited a small fortune after his father's passing. Jonathan considered Hamish's offer for his sister to be the very best she was likely to receive. Eager to get at least one sister off his hands as soon as possible, Jonathan happily gave his blessing to the union despite his mother's well-known feelings about Scotland and its people.

All in all, the dowager's relief at not having to host her daughter and her family far outweighed any grievance she was inclined to feel at their evident reciprocal disinterest in staying with her. As it was, the dowager presumed she would be obliged to offer lodging to her other daughter, Edith, over the actual wedding.

As appalling as the dowager viewed Jane's marriage to Hamish, Edith's husband couldn't even claim the pretence of a title as Hamish did as a so-called "laird". At least Jane kept the right to call herself Lady MacAlister. Edith, on the other hand, was Mrs Reginald Clutterbuck. While Mr and Mrs Clutterbuck did live within the English border, which was undoubtedly preferable to Scotland, their residence was just outside a village with the unfortunate name of Lumbfoot in West Yorkshire. Mrs Clutterbuck from Lumbfoot! The dowager looked on the bright side: Jane and Edith were never close; perhaps the Clutterbucks would choose not to leave Lumbfoot for the wedding of a niece they barely knew.

Most of the wedding planning was finished, but Tabitha had offered to host this gathering to go over the final details. The dowager arrived early, which allowed her to judge and then berate her daughter before the groom's mother, Fiona Williams, Lady Warwick, arrived. That was probably for the best, Tabitha considered. There was almost no possibility the dowager would approve of her daughter's choices, and it was better her acerbic comments not be made within earshot of their soon-to-be relatives.

As Tabitha reflected on this, the door to the drawing room opened, and Talbot announced the Countess and Dowager Countess of Warwick. While Tobias' mother was expected, his grandmother Charlotte, Lady Warwick, was an unexpected addition to the party. The dowager often referred to Charlotte as her dearest friend, and Tabitha was intrigued to discover what kind of person was worthy of such a moniker. What kind of aristocratic lady could not only win the dowager's respect, but also her affection?

Tobias' mother, Fiona, Lady Warwick, was a slim, finely boned, very pretty woman. Given her son was grown, she must have been at least in her early forties, but she might easily have passed for ten years younger. Her straw-coloured hair curled softly around a delicate face.

Charlotte, the elder Lady Warwick, seemed quite solid next to her wisp of a daughter-in-law. She possessed an open, cheerful face with a generous mouth which widened into a broad smile at the sight of the dowager. Charlotte's once black curls were now heavily peppered with white and silver. Even so, there was something very youthful about the older woman; perhaps it was the twinkle in her warm brown eyes that only seemed to increase as she looked around the room.

In a very uncharacteristic move, the dowager sprang to her feet and rushed to embrace her friend. "Charlotte, what a delightful surprise. I did not realise you were returned to civilisation from the wilds of Oxfordshire."

"Warwickshire, which I am quite certain you knew already," the other woman said in an amused voice. "But yes, I decided to come down a little early to help Fiona with whatever last-minute arrangements there might be. Though of course, given your involvement in every last detail of the wedding day, I do not doubt there is little left to be done." Charlotte, Lady Warwick, said this in a knowing tone, still full of affection.

Tabitha eyed this other dowager countess with curiosity. Charlotte seemed in no doubt who Julia Chesterton, Lady Pembroke, was, yet she was extremely fond of her anyway. It was going to be a fascinating couple of weeks, there was no doubt.

"Yes, yes, well, you know how I am," the dowager said, perhaps somewhat chastened. "However, it did not seem fair to leave it all to Fiona, and certainly Jane could not be counted on." The dowager did not clarify whether Jane's unreliability was because of geographic distance or overall incompetence. Of course, knowing the dowager, it was probably both.

After embracing the dowager, Charlotte turned towards Jane. "How well you look, Lady MacAlister."

"Please, call me Jane. I really hope you will remain my Aunt Lottie."

Charlotte laughed. "It has been far too long since anyone has called me by that moniker. I would be delighted to still be Aunt Lottie." The two women embraced, and Charlotte continued, "It seems particularly fitting now our families are to be united. I cannot thank you enough for what your darling girl has done for our rapscallion, Toby."

Undeniably, love for Lily had been pivotal in making Viscount Tobias mend his ways. Jane just smiled.

"Rapscallion is too kind a term for what the young man was when I encountered him in Brighton," the dowager said in a voice which made clear the credit she believed was due her for the young man's changed ways.

Picking up on her cue, Fiona came towards the dowager and took both her hands in hers. "Yes, thank you, Lady Pembroke, for all you have done for my son. I know I speak for Clarence when I say we nearly gave up on Tobias. His turnaround in such a short time has been nothing less than miraculous."

The dowager smiled benevolently as she accepted far more of the credit than she was due. In truth, Tobias was on his way to being a dyed-in-the-wool rake when they came upon him by chance in Brighton some months before. No amount of scolding by his godmother, the dowager, impacted the young man, and only when he took an interest in Lady Lily did his behaviour turn around.

At that moment, the young man in question and his bride-to-be entered the room. Both young people made their lack of interest in wedding planning clear early and were happy to leave all the decisions up to their elders. Instead of joining the planning party in the drawing room, they had been out in the garden enjoying the beautiful spring weather. When Talbot informed them his mother and grandmother were in the drawing room, the young lovers hurried inside to pay their respects.

"Speak of the devil and he shall appear!" the dowager said with a sniff.

CHAPTER 2

The plan was for the two Ladies Warwick to join the group in the late afternoon and for Clarence, the Earl of Warwick, to join them later for a family dinner hosted by Tabitha and Wolf. This dinner would be the first time the entire extended family, including Uncle Duncan, would be together, and Tabitha was anxious everything go smoothly. In furtherance of that end, she planned for Uncle Duncan to be seated as far away from the dowager as possible. Bear was tasked with keeping an eye on the incorrigible old man.

Sometime before they were expecting their additional guests, Talbot entered the drawing room and announced, "Mr Duncan MacAlister, milady."

Tabitha looked wide-eyed at her butler; she was sure her communications to Uncle Duncan were clear: he should time his arrival to coincide with dinner. She and Wolf agreed they needed to minimise the dowager's exposure to the man in the lead-up to the wedding.

Whatever Uncle Duncan understood, the man had decided to arrive early. The words were barely out of Talbot's mouth before the garrulous old Scot came barrelling into the room. It was immediately apparent he was three sheets to the wind. His always rather florid complexion was particularly ruddy, and he almost tripped as he crossed the threshold.

Uncle Duncan was a near-perfect physical match for his nephew, Hamish, twenty or thirty years hence and probably many bottles of whisky later. The uncle shared the same large gruffness as his nephew, but rather than red threaded through with grey, his hair was a shock of snow-white. He possessed the same twinkly blue eyes and wide, toothy grin, which was stretched particularly broad at that moment as he looked around the room, grinning from ear to ear.

"Did ye all start the party without me? I know I'm a wee bit late, but I was waylaid by an old friend. It would have been rude tae nae stop for a wee dram."

Tabitha remembered the man saying something remarkably similar when she first met him. It seemed Uncle Duncan was often waylaid by old friends who twisted his arm to have a drink or two.

"Actually, Mr MacAlister, you are not late but are actually early," Tabitha said, rising to greet him.

"Let's stop wi' this Mr MacAlister business. We're going tae be family, so it should be Uncle Duncan frae now on," he said, coming towards Tabitha and enveloping her in a bear hug, which definitely broke many rules of social etiquette. He then approached Jane and Lily, saying, "If it isn't two of my favourite lasses!"

Then he turned to Viscount Tobias, slapped him on the back and exclaimed, "Are ye ready tae be leg-shackled, laddie?" Tobias blushed to the roots of his hair and muttered something in return.

The dowager had been suspiciously quiet ever since the announcement of Uncle Duncan's arrival. However, the thunderous look on her face said all anyone might need to know about how she viewed their newest visitor. Someone more sober might have noticed and been forewarned. Uncle Duncan was not sober and, even if he were, he always seemed blissfully unaware of the contempt in which the dowager held him. Either he didn't notice, or he didn't care.

Now, he came towards her, his grin even broader if possible, and said in a booming voice, "And speakin' o' my favourite lasses, if it isnae the bonniest o' them all!"

In a tone so icy, Tabitha could have sworn the room became chillier, the dowager looked Uncle Duncan up and down and said, "Are you drunk, sir?"

"Drunk? Ha! What kind of Scot would I be if a wee dram or two got me blootered? Nae lass, I'm just happy to see ye bonny face!"

Just as the dowager's self-control was being tested to its limits, Wolf burst into the room. Tabitha suspected Talbot left the room and immediately tracked him down to warn him about the potentially volatile situation in the drawing room. "Darling, what splendid timing," Tabitha said, raising her eyebrows and widening her eyes at her husband to indicate the standoff he was walking into. "Mr MacAlister, or rather Uncle Duncan, has arrived early. Is it not wonderful?"

Correctly interpreting her expression, Wolf replied, "It is indeed, Uncle Duncan. Why do we not leave the women to their wedding planning and retreat to my study? I recently acquired a fine new Cognac. Perhaps you would care to sample some with me?"

Tabitha smiled gratefully at her husband; he knew one thing Uncle Duncan would never refuse was a drink. Even he was not so beyond the pale as to expect one in a drawing room full of women at four o'clock in the afternoon. There was no doubt he'd eagerly seize the opportunity to continue his afternoon's consumption of libations uninterruptedly.

As expected, Uncle Duncan was more than happy to follow Wolf out of the room. In fact, he left so eagerly he didn't even get the chance to meet Fiona and Charlotte, the Ladies Warwick.

As the door closed behind him, Charlotte turned to the dowager and said, "I sense there is a history there, my dear Julia." Tabitha nearly snorted with amusement; history was a mild way of putting it.

"He is the most appalling man, entirely lacking in social graces or any basic manners. And I am not sure I have ever experienced a conversation with him where he was sober."

Belatedly realising she was speaking ill of Lily's uncle, the dowager remarked, in a tone lacking the apologetic nature it perhaps should have, "Well, Lily dear, you must acknowledge the truth of my words, however harsh they may be."

"Grandmama, you are rather mean to him," Lily said. Unlike her father and uncle, Lily's Scottish accent was barely perceptible. Tabitha knew the young woman could fall back into a quite pronounced brogue when she chose, but she was wise enough rarely to do so in front of her grandmother.

Lily was a beautiful young woman. Tall with a graceful, swan-like neck, perfect alabaster skin, and bright blue eyes framed by dark, thick, long lashes, she possessed thick, curly, dark auburn hair styled fashionably.

When Tabitha first met her, the young woman shared her mother's unfortunate preference for unfashionable, unflattering clothing. Since moving to London and coming under her grandmother's tutelage, Lily's wardrobe was everything it should be for a wealthy, well-born socialite. Today, she was dressed in a simple, yet elegant navy-blue silk dress Tabitha was sure was from Worth.

Despite the dowager's insistence that clear vision wasn't necessary for a viscountess, Lily was adamant about continuing to wear her glasses. However, the large, unbecoming glasses she wore in Edinburgh were replaced with thin-wired frames which accentuated her beautiful eyes.

In response to her granddaughter's criticism, the dowager said sharply, "I am not sure one can be too harsh with Mr MacAlister; the man seems quite oblivious to my rebukes." Turning to her friend, she said sadly, "Charlotte dear, I am sorry you witnessed that scene. However, the man will now be part of your family."

Charlotte looked more amused by the situation than worried by the impending familial tie to Uncle Duncan. "Do not worry about me, Julia. Do you remember my Uncle Tom? Mr MacAlister seems quite harmless compared to him." Turning to Lily, she said kindly, "Every family seems to have an Uncle Duncan, do they not? I suspect yours is good fun, at least."

Lily smiled gratefully at her future in-law. "He is a lot of fun. And Uncle Duncan was always the only person who took my botanical studies seriously. Until Toby, of course," she added, gracing her husband-to-be with a grateful smile. He returned it with a look of utter devotion.

With Uncle Duncan safely ensconced in the study with Wolf, the work of discussing the planning for the wedding resumed. The Earl and Countess of Warwick were to host the wedding breakfast, and there seemed to be little to discuss. Certainly, even the dowager knew better than to suggest those plans needed her approval. With the task of choosing the flowers taken away from Jane, there was little left that needed to be planned.

Looking down at the list on her lap, the dowager pronounced, "It seems everything is in order. This will be a society wedding to rival any in recent memory. And in St Paul's! Not every young woman, even in the highest echelons of society, can say as much, Lily."

The look on Lily's face indicated she wasn't as overawed by this honour as her grandmother expected her to be. An observant member of the Church of Scotland, Lily had been attending the Crown Court Church of St. Andrew in Covent Garden since she moved to London. Her grandmother made it quite clear, almost from the moment the betrothal was announced, that her granddaughter would not be marrying a future peer of the realm in a "heathen hovel next to a stall selling cauliflower". While she might have been inclined to argue under normal circumstances, Lily recognised Viscount Tobias' family might well share the dowager's prejudices.

Securing St Paul's Cathedral was quite the coup. St Paul's was not made available for weddings under normal circumstances, even to members of the aristocracy. The dowager was being unusually coy about how she had managed such a feat. Her immediate family knew the woman wielded unheard-of influence and commanded surprising compliance, however reluctant and exasperated, over the Archbishop of Canterbury. So, it was presumed the honour came by way of Lambeth Palace.

The rest of the afternoon passed smoothly enough. However, when the time to gather for dinner was nearing and Clarence, the Earl of Warwick, had still not made an appearance, the dowager began to get rather antsy.

"It is one thing to consent to lower standards, such that we are not dressing for dinner to accommodate our guests – which I am happy to do, of course," she quickly added. "But I will not bend so much to push our dinner hour into the late evening. What are we, the Spanish? Heaven help us."

Fiona caught Tabitha's eye and jumped in to assure the crotchety old woman. "Lady Pembroke, I cannot imagine what is keeping my husband, but I am sure whatever it is, he would not want you to be put out in any way. Please keep to your original schedule."

Of course, it wasn't her house, and so not her schedule to direct, but such things had never stopped the dowager in the past, and she dipped her head graciously. "Thank you, Fiona." Then, turning to Tabitha, she demanded, "In which case, where is Talbot? At my age, one might expire on the spot at any moment without sufficient sustenance."

Tabitha didn't consider it worth pointing out the dowager had been drinking tea and eating shortbread biscuits all afternoon and so was in little danger of imminent starvation. Instead, she summoned Talbot to alert the butler they were ready for dinner and requested he summon Lord Pembroke and Mr MacAlister.

The group was already on their soup course when Talbot entered the dining room with the Earl of Warwick. The earl looked rather shamefaced. He bent to kiss his mother, who was nearest to the door. He nodded to his wife and then approached the dowager.

"My dear Lady Pembroke, please excuse my tardiness." By rights, this apology should have been made to Tabitha as the lady of the house, but Clarence had known the dowager his entire life and correctly assumed she would fume at his late arrival.

In a haughty tone, the dowager replied, "You may be an earl now, but please do never forget I have known you since you were in swaddling clothes. A woman of my age should not be kept waiting for her dinner." It was unclear what linked the two sentences, but no one was going to interrupt the dowager when she was in full high dudgeon. "I cannot imagine what excuse you might give to justify leaving me and your mother, of course, weak with hunger." Wisely, Clarence adopted an expression of even more abject apology.

Tabitha decided this absurd charade continued long enough and welcomed her guest. "Pray think nothing more of it, Lord Warwick. As you can see, we did not wait, and so no one," she looked pointedly at the dowager, "was forced to wait for food."

There was a noticeable harrumph in reply, but nothing else was said, and Clarence took the empty seat beside his mother. "You look a little dishevelled, my dear," Charlotte commented. Now, it was said, Tabitha looked more closely at their guest. His cravat was askew, and his waistcoat was missing a button. What on earth had happened?

"Do I, Mama? I cannot imagine why that might be," Clarence said as he tried to straighten his cravat. Even as he said this, Tabitha couldn't help but think there was an undertone to his words. What was it? It almost sounded like guilt.

Chapter 3

Later that evening, Wolf climbed into bed beside Tabitha. "I think the dinner went well, all things considered," he said, settling into the sheets.

"Hmm," she replied.

"I cannot tell if that is a good or bad sound."

"Well, we managed to keep Mama and Uncle Duncan apart, so that was a good thing. But the scene with Clarence coming late and looking so dishevelled... well, I just cannot stop thinking about it."

Wolf was lying on his back, but now he turned towards Tabitha and propped himself up on his elbow. "It was a little odd he did not offer any explanation as to what had held him up. However, I am sure he is a busy man. I know he is very active in the House of Lords, so perhaps it was because of something there."

"Is there something you are not telling me about what happens in the House of Lords to cause a peer to leave there looking as ragged as a scarecrow?" Tabitha asked with a smile.

"You may be exaggerating somewhat, my love. His cravat was somewhat askew."

Tabitha was quick to add, "And he was missing a button on his waistcoat. I am sure he did not leave the house looking like that this evening. At least not if his valet is anything like yours."

Wolf laughed. "I am sure that if I were to leave the house with a button missing from any item of clothing, Thompson would consider it nothing short of an offence for which he ought to be dismissed. In fact, he would immediately pre-empt any dismissal by resigning."

"Exactly. So, what might have occurred earlier to have Clarence looking at sixes and sevens and cause him to be late for dinner?" Wolf shook his head. Unlike his wife, he hadn't picked up on anything particularly suspicious about the Earl of Warwick's behaviour.

Instead of answering her question, he pulled her down towards him and kissed her on the lips, first gently but then more insistently. If he hoped to distract Tabitha, then he was successful. Whatever concerns she might have wafted out of her mind as she melted into her husband's embrace.

Tabitha would have liked to have lazed in bed the following morning, perhaps enjoying a repeat of the night before, but they had guests. She was far too conscientious of a hostess not to ensure she was up and at the breakfast table with more than enough time to greet them.

Surprisingly, Uncle Duncan was the first one down. Known for carousing well into the wee hours, even unaccompanied, Tabitha assumed the man stayed up late, breaking into Wolf's secret stash of fine whisky; the man possessed a sixth sense for hidden alcohol.

"Good mornin', lass. It's been a long night, and I might need some coffee."

"Uncle Duncan! Have you been out all night?" Tabitha asked in astonishment.

"Aye. I ken a fella who runs a wee place. I won a bit and lost a bit. I didnae want to come in late and wake yer staff, so I just stayed out all night." The man said this as if staying out all night gambling was a perfectly acceptable thing to do. Perhaps it was in his world, Tabitha pondered.

Uncle Duncan helped himself to a hearty plate of shirred eggs, bacon, sausages, and fried mushrooms.

"D'ye no have any kippers?" the man asked in a very disappointed voice.

"Uncle Duncan, I apologise. I will ensure they are available at breakfast from now on," Tabitha promised. "Is there anything else you would like?"

"Aye. A bit o' porridge wid go down well," he volunteered.

Her housekeeper, Mrs Jenkins, and cook, Mrs Smith, were loyal servants of many years and Tabitha did not doubt they could and would rise to the occasion. Even so, she wondered how much Uncle Duncan's stay might stretch the patience and goodwill of everyone at Chesterton House before the wedding was over.

Not long after Uncle Duncan took his seat and began to tuck into his overloaded plate, Wolf entered the breakfast room. From his surprised look, Tabitha assumed he was equally shocked at Uncle Duncan's appearance at the breakfast table. As soon as she could, she'd enlighten him why.

Jane was next. Lily remained at the dowager's, where she'd been staying since they came to London from Scotland. Viscount Tobias was staying at his family home, also in Mayfair.

They were all tucking into breakfast when Talbot entered the room with Fiona and Charlotte close on his heel. Both women looked as if they might start crying at any moment.

Instinctively, Tabitha rose to greet them. "What has happened? I can see from your faces something is wrong. Please, take a seat. Talbot, please get both Ladies Warwick cups of tea."

Neither woman disputed Tabitha's intuition that something was amiss. They took seats, but they both remained on edge. When Talbot placed full teacups in front of them, Fiona, Lady Warwick, merely fiddled with the cup without even taking a sip.

Finally, the tension was too much to bear, and Tabitha asked, "Lady Warwick, Fiona, what has happened?"

The younger Lady Warwick looked at the older, who nodded almost imperceptibly. "Clarence has been arrested. For murder."

Whatever Tabitha and Wolf expected her to say, this wasn't it. Apart from anything else, it was so unusual for a high-ranking member of the aristocracy to be held accountable for any crime, even murder, that it was shocking to hear the Earl of Warwick had actually been arrested, no matter what he might be accused of doing.

In fact, Tabitha was so shocked, she barely restrained herself from commenting on the rarity of such an event. Instead, she composed herself and asked, "Who is he accused of murdering?"

"Lord Redding," Fiona replied as if it was all the explanation needed.

"Who is Lord Redding?" Wolf asked, clearly as bewildered as his wife.

"He is my son's archenemy," Charlotte, Lady Warwick, explained.

Tabitha tried to control her face so as not to laugh at the rather melodramatic explanation. Instead, she asked, "Archenemy? What has Lord Redding done to deserve such a moniker?"

Fiona and Charlotte exchanged glances. "It goes back a very long way," the elder Lady Warwick explained, taking a seat at the table. "It started at Eton some forty years ago. Redding, who is now a baron, is a year older than Clarence and bullied him incessantly. My darling Clarence was quite a sensitive soul as a child. He really did not fit in well with the cricket or rowing crowds. He was not the heir back then."

Charlotte's face took on a look of great melancholy as she continued, "Clarence was my second son. His brother, Edward, died of dropsy at age twenty-four. Clarence was twenty-two at the time and was suddenly thrust into the role of viscount. It was all quite overwhelming for him." Her face softened as she relived the long-ago memories. "Clarence was always the sensitive one. Edward fit in at Eton perfectly: captain of the cricket team, head boy, destined for glory."

She paused and took a deep breath. "Of course, I knew none of this back then, but from what I learned many years later, this Redding character hated my Clarence almost from day one. Who knows why? He tortured my son for three years. Then, just as my darling boy thought he was finally free of this fiend, he left Eton for Oxford, and there this Redding was again."

Tabitha sympathised with the woman as she recounted her child's pain, but surely a murder charge had to do with more than boyhood bullying decades before. She wanted to be sensitive and not rush Charlotte along. However, they needed to know all the pertinent details of what happened, and this walk through the past was unlikely to provide them with the information most likely to help the Earl of Warwick.

Wolf must have felt similarly because, in a gentle yet firm voice, he said, "Lady Warwick, can you bring us a little more up-to-date and tell us why your son has been accused of Lord Redding's murder?"

Tears started rolling down Charlotte's cheeks. Fiona was sitting next to her mother-in-law and reached over to take her hand. After giving her mother-in-law's hand a sympathetic squeeze, Fiona picked up the story. The younger Lady Warwick explained, "My husband's loathing for Lord Redding has followed him through his adult life. He tried his best to avoid the man, but they seemed to be thrown together despite his best efforts. They belonged to the same clubs and served on the same government committees. From what I heard years ago, they even shared a mistress."

Neither Tabitha nor Wolf could hide their shock at her statement. While it was hardly unusual for the men of the aristocracy to keep mistresses, it was hardly the done thing for their wives to acknowledge such relationships. It was unheard of for a woman such as Fiona not only to know about the women her husband kept but to speak of one of them so blithely. To speak thus in the company of her husband's mother was perhaps the most shocking thing of all.

Perhaps guessing at their reaction, Fiona explained, "My husband and I did not marry for love, nor did it develop over the years. There is some mutual affection of a kind, at least on my side. However, once Tobias was born and it became clear he would be the only child, I always expected we would eventually develop mutually agreeably separate lives."

Tabitha wasn't entirely sure she knew what this meant and wasn't sure she wanted to be illuminated. If any of this shocked Charlotte, she certainly didn't show it.

Fiona continued, "In many ways, my husband has been far more considerate of my feelings than many other men in society. As far as I know, he has never taken a mistress from amongst ladies I would then have to sit opposite at a society dinner. There are no by-blows in Tobias' shadow. I have never found cause for complaint."

This was all said with such cool detachment, but Tabitha wondered if Fiona was as nonchalant about her husband's extramarital activities as she claimed. Regardless, none of this explained the matter at hand.

Finally, deciding to cut to the heart of the issue, Tabitha asked, "Fiona, why has your husband been accused of murdering Lord Redding?"

At these words, Fiona's well-controlled exterior finally cracked. "It seems my husband and Lord Redding had a very public disagreement yesterday at White's. At some point, Clarence threatened Redding's life.

Very early this morning, Lord Redding was discovered dead in an alleyway not far from White's. He was stabbed multiple times."

Wolf interjected, "Surely such a disagreement is not enough to accuse a peer of the realm. Certainly, it is far more likely Lord Redding was set upon by footpads. Just because heated words were spoken between two men earlier in the evening cannot be sufficient for Scotland Yard to arrest someone of Lord Warwick's status."

As it happened, Wolf bemoaned on multiple occasions that his inherited earldom granted him such privilege he could likely kill a man and still escape the gallows. Of course, killing a fellow peer was quite a different matter than killing someone of far lesser status. Again, something which appalled Wolf, but of which he was quite cognisant.

Fiona shrugged her shoulders at Wolf's question. "I know very little. When the police arrived this morning, Clarence told me to telephone his solicitor, Sir Harry Wells. I did so and he promised he would attend Clarence immediately and petition the court for bail." She paused, "They will not keep him in prison, will they? I cannot abide the thought of him in a dank jail cell full of low-life criminals." As she said this, Fiona began to weep.

Wolf was unsure what to say to console the woman. He didn't want to give her false hope. While a man of the earl's standing would usually have no trouble obtaining bail and even persuading the authorities to keep him under house arrest, Wolf wasn't sure if such courtesies would be extended under these circumstances.

"You need not have come here this morning," Tabitha told the distraught woman. "Perhaps you should be at home in case Sir Harry has news."

"I told my butler to telephone here if there is any news." Fiona exchanged looks with Charlotte, and some unspoken message passed between them.

"Toby has told us of the investigative work which you both take on occasionally," Charlotte said.

Tabitha formed a pretty good idea of what was coming next. "Have you come here to ask us to take on your son's case?" she asked.

"I know, well, we both know Clarence is innocent of this crime they have arrested him for. My son is no angel, but he is not a killer. I would stake my life on this truth."

As Charlotte finished speaking, there was the sound of the telephone bell ringing. Fiona jumped to her feet. "It must be Sir Harry," she exclaimed.

Tabitha and Wolf didn't know many people with telephones installed. While the dowager usually called every morning to speak to Melody, she rarely bothered on days when she would see the child. This was one of the days when Melody spent the afternoon with the dowager, and so she would have little reason to telephone.

A few moments later, the door to the breakfast room opened, and Talbot appeared in the doorway. "Lady Warwick," he said, addressing Fiona, "there is a Sir Harry Wells on the telephone for you. He said that you would know what it is about, milady." Talbot barely finished speaking when Fiona dashed past him to talk to the solicitor.

Fiona was gone for some minutes. Tabitha hoped Sir Harry was telling her the arrest was a big misunderstanding and Clarence was being released. Of course, she wanted this because he was Tobias' father and because it was terrible that it had happened during what was supposed to be a joyful time of anticipation for the young betrothed couple. However, Tabitha realised she also wanted it because she was not ready to return to investigating gruesome murders.

The time she and Wolf spent in Corfu with Melody was idyllic. If it wasn't for the impending wedding, they might have stayed even longer. The joy of being newlyweds, of being a family with Melody, of living a simple life with minimal servants had been intoxicating. Tabitha did relish the intellectual challenge the investigations brought and the sense of purpose they gave her. Even so, she wasn't sure she was quite ready to dive back in. There was no doubt if the telephone call wasn't to inform them Clarence was absolved of any blame in the murder, then she and Wolf would have to agree to take on the investigation.

Tabitha stole a glance at Wolf. He was always more reticent than she about taking on investigations; it felt a little too close to his previous life as a thief-taker for his liking. It was Lord Langley who finally persuaded Wolf he could do more good in the world using his investigative talents than by following the more traditional path for someone of his rank and taking up his seat in the House of Lords. Finally, Wolf relented and agreed to continue taking on investigations, but with the caveat that he would only do so when he could help to right a miscarriage of justice. He would not help pampered aristocrats find their jewels or their estranged spouses.

So, what was he feeling about Fiona's request? What if Clarence turned out to be guilty? Was this a conclusion his wife was prepared to accept? These people were about to become family. Tabitha realised how fraught this might all become.

Tabitha's musings were interrupted by Fiona's return. All eyes turned to her expectantly. By the grim look on Fiona's face, it didn't seem as if she had just been given the good news her husband was a free man.

"They are refusing Clarence bail and house arrest. He is being moved to Pentonville Prison." As she said this, she burst into tears.

Tabitha rose and gathered the woman in her arms, attempting to comfort her.

"But why did they refuse bail?" Charlotte wailed plaintively. "He is an earl, for goodness sake and as upstanding a member of the community as one might hope to find in England."

Pulling away from Tabitha's embrace and wiping the tears from her cheeks, Fiona answered, "Apparently, there have been various pieces written in the newspapers recently claiming the aristocracy has unreasonable privileges. These articles have stirred up the populace sufficiently for it to be felt by the government that giving Clarence special treatment is a politically sensitive thing to do at the moment."

"What poppycock!" Charlotte pronounced.

Wolf had read some of those articles. In fact, they were written by his newspaper journalist contact, Andrews. As far as newshounds went, Andrews was a decent, honest man. More than this, he was an excellent journalist. The articles were well-researched and compelling, which was more than could be said for the rather hysterical pieces in the Illustrated Police News, which gave a more populist twist to a similar theme.

Wolf's sympathies leaned towards treating all men equally, no matter their birth or rank, and so he needed little persuading. Even so, he found Andrews did an excellent job of crystallising precisely what the injustice was, which made Wolf even more convinced of the profound unfairness in the current system.

Given his feelings on the matter, Wolf found himself unable to answer Charlotte's outrage with any sympathy. Regardless of whether her son was guilty or innocent, why should he not wait for his day in court in a prison cell, as most other men or women would have to do? More to the point, Clarence was a man of wealth and influence. If the system of justice needed reform, it was within his power to help effect change. Perhaps it wasn't such a terrible thing if men in power got a taste of how life was for the men and women they ruled over.

Of course, his personal feelings about Clarence's continued imprisonment aside, the fact that he was not absolved meant he and Tabitha must decide whether to investigate.

Wolf looked at the two distraught women in front of him and couldn't imagine what excuse he could give for not doing all he could to help them. And then there was Lily. If Clarence wasn't released from prison soon, it was inconceivable the wedding would go ahead. Jane stayed silent during this entire scene, but from the look on her face, it was clear the idea of her daughter marrying into this family had suddenly lost some of its charm.

This last consideration made his mind up: "I believe I speak for my wife when I say we will, of course, take on Clarence's case." At his words, both women's faces lit up. Wolf raised a warning hand: "However, I cannot guarantee we will prove his innocence." What he left hanging in the air was the fact that they could not prove the innocence of a guilty man if that were indeed what Clarence was.

Chapter 4

Thirty minutes later, a very grateful Charlotte and Fiona returned home. Uncle Duncan, who had fallen asleep at the breakfast table, woke up long enough to mumble something about needing his bed, and Jane insisted she head to the dowager's home to comfort her daughter. Tabitha tried to prevent her from going. After all, they didn't even know if Lily knew yet about Tobias' father. However, Jane could not be dissuaded. In the end, Tabitha realised the young woman was going to hear the news soon enough. Better she be told by her mother than see the news plastered across the front pages of one of the dailies.

After seeing Jane off in the carriage, Tabitha requested Talbot set up their corkboard in the parlour, where she and Wolf were headed to discuss the investigation they now seemed to be undertaking.

"I should have asked you before I agreed to take on this case," Wolf said apologetically.

"There was no graceful way of getting out of it, so you had no choice but to say yes. Even if you had talked it over with me, it would have changed nothing," Tabitha said kindly as she took a stack of notecards and sat with them in her lap.

She looked up at the blank corkboard. Soon enough, it would be covered with clues and hypotheses, but for now, it was disturbingly empty; they knew next to nothing about the case. They met Clarence for the first time a few weeks before. He seemed like a pleasant, even-tempered man who laughed easily. Of course, none of this precluded the possibility he was also a murderer. Perhaps the crime hadn't been premeditated. Perhaps it had even been an accident. Though it was hard to imagine how someone was stabbed in an alleyway accidentally.

As she considered this, Tabitha had a thought. "I wonder if this murder might have been a spur-of-the-moment act."

Wolf considered her words. "You are correct. I would like to hear more from the coroner on the nature of the wounds and the weapon they believe was used."

His words were rather gruesome, but Tabitha refused to flinch from the most gruesome parts of their investigations. If she wanted to be treated as a fully equal investigative partner, then she couldn't pick and choose when she wanted to be prone to fits of the vapours.

Tabitha considered how little they knew at that point. "Our first step should be to attempt to talk with Clarence. I know you were successful in talking with Manning when he was imprisoned at Pentonville. Do you think you might gain access again?"

Wolf thought back to his visit to the prison the previous year. The warden, Mr Featherstone, was an obsequious man who hoped the Earl of Pembroke was visiting Pentonville in his capacity as a member of the House of Lords to observe the prison's conditions. Featherstone was sure of a glowing report back and disappointed to learn the true reason for the visit. However, not one to be put off, he had gladly complied with Wolf's request to meet with Manning, hoping word of his compliancy would still make its way back to the House of Lords.

"Assuming Mr Featherstone is still the warden, I do not doubt I can meet with Clarence." But what if there were a new warden? Wolf wondered. It was because of Anthony, the Duke of Somerset, that Wolf previously received a letter from Sir Matthew granting him access. Did he need such a letter this time and, more to the point, given an example was being made of the Earl of Warwick, would he be granted it?

As if reading his thoughts, Tabitha asked, "Do you believe it might be better to take the chance the same warden is still there rather than making another request of the Home Secretary?"

"I do. Until we understand more about what happened, or at least what the police believe happened, we should exercise discretion about our intention to investigate."

An unspoken question hung in the air as he used the word "we": would Tabitha be accompanying Wolf? On his earlier visit, Wolf insisted a prison was no place for a woman. However, this was very early in their investigative relationship, when Wolf still insisted on seeing Tabitha as someone who needed to be shielded from the harsher realities of life. Moreover, he didn't know at the time he would be able to talk with Manning in the comfort of the warden's office. If Featherstone remained in charge, there was no reason to believe he wouldn't receive a similar courtesy again. And even if he wasn't, Wolf had long accepted the fact that Tabitha needed his respect as an equal partner, not his protection.

Wolf answered this unspoken question. "There is no time like the present. Let us both change into clothes appropriately aristocratic to inspire acquiescence and make our way to Pentonville."

Tabitha rose from the sofa and crossed to the armchair Wolf always sat in. She climbed onto his lap, placed her arms around his neck, and kissed him.

"I am not complaining, but what did I do to deserve this?" he asked in pleasant surprise.

"You included me without hesitation."

"Well, I would not say without hesitation," he admitted. "However, I immediately realised the wrongness of the hesitation and left the thought behind."

Tabitha kissed Wolf again, and he considered himself well compensated. While it was tempting to linger in the parlour, cuddling in the comfy armchair, they both realised there would be time enough for such things once Clarence was free. Reluctantly, Tabitha climbed off Wolf's lap, and they both made their way upstairs to change their clothes.

While Wolf was often still uncomfortable with the deference paid to him merely because of his title, he now appreciated the doors an earldom opened for him. The more he dressed, walked, and talked with the arrogance that came so naturally to many in the aristocracy, the easier it usually was to persuade those in the lower orders to oblige his every wish. As much as he loathed to take advantage of this, there was no doubt it could be very useful. Persuading the warden of a prison to grant him a private audience with one of his prisoners without orders from Whitehall definitely counted as one of those times.

Wolf's valet, Thompson, was a fastidious man who considered it a personal reflection on him if his master's cravat appeared anything other than perfectly tied and his cuffs anything other than crisply ironed and starched. Given this, his patience was often sorely tried by a master who was far more comfortable without a jacket on and with rolled-up shirtsleeves than decked out in sartorial splendour. Wolf realised nothing would make Thompson happier than to be tasked with dressing him in aristocratic finery.

Thirty minutes later, Tabitha and Wolf met in the drawing room. On Ginny's suggestion, Tabitha wore a very smart new wine-coloured silk dress with a matching bolero jacket trimmed in black velvet. Tabitha wore a three-strand pearl necklace from which hung a ruby pendant. Her hat matched the dress with three black feathers tucked into a satin band. The outfit was restrained elegance, style, and good taste. While it was quite simple, the opulence of the material and the tailoring would leave no one in doubt as to the wealth and status of the wearer.

As Wolf expected, Thompson was positively gleeful at the opportunity to dress him. So often, Wolf found himself arguing with his valet as he attempted to stuff him into a stiff jacket, which, while it might be cut in the height of fashion, wasn't at all comfortable. Wolf didn't understand why fashionable must equate to form-fitting, but be it boots, a shirt, or a suit, comfort never seemed the guiding principle.

Tabitha found Wolf standing by the mantlepiece, fidgeting with his shirt cuffs.

"Remind me again why dressing the part of an earl means I have to be trussed up like a pig?" he complained.

Laughing, Tabitha approached him with an approving smile. "Well, you look very handsome. Is that a new jacket?"

"How would I know? I may be master of this house, but Thompson is master in my dressing room," Wolf complained.

"And you are better dressed for it!"

Five minutes later, they sat in the carriage, making their way through the busy streets of London.

"I swear the traffic congestion is getting worse," Wolf complained as they came to a standstill on Oxford Street. What should have been a forty-minute trip took over an hour, but eventually, they arrived in Islington.

Tabitha's expectations for Pentonville Prison were vague. She looked out of the window eagerly as they pulled up. The building, while modern, was quite imposing, with its fortress-like design and grey brick utilitarian construction. Not constructed to be welcoming, with its watchtowers and small, high-set windows covered with iron bars, just the sight of Pentonville made Tabitha shudder.

Wolf noticed her reaction and took her hand. "You could wait in the carriage. I would not think any the less of you."

For a moment, Tabitha considered taking him up on this offer. However, even if Wolf did not, she would think less of herself if she gave into this apprehension. "I will accompany you," she said in a determined voice.

When Wolf visited previously, he gave the guard Sir Matthew's letter, and this provided him access. This time, he braced himself to embody his Earl of Pembroke persona fully. On the occasions he did this, Wolf would channel his late grandfather. The old man had been arrogant and conde-scending: he always behaved as if authority and rank would get him what he wanted, and he was rarely disappointed. He made it known his time was precious and not to be wasted on petty concerns. Wolf hated mimic-king the man but couldn't deny its effectiveness.

As they approached the guard, Tabitha sensed Wolf standing just a little straighter and throwing his shoulders back enough to change his posture just enough. A tall man to begin with, these subtle shifts enabled Wolf to do what his grandfather did so effectively: look down his nose at people. Luckily, the guard wasn't nearly as tall as Wolf and thus was suit-ably awed by the imposing toff bearing down on him.

CHAPTER 5

With no greeting or preamble, Wolf said in his most imperious voice, "Tell Warden Featherstone the Countess and Earl of Pembroke wish to have an audience with him." Wolf hoped his tone sounded sufficiently authoritative to gain them access into the warden's presence even if Mr Featherstone no longer held the role.

For one brief moment, it seemed as if the guard would question their right to turn up at the prison and insist on seeing the warden. But then he looked at their clothes and Tabitha's jewels and realised it was not for the likes of him to question these toffs. Instead, if the warden didn't wish to see them, he might come down himself and tell them so. This decision made, he nodded and left to deliver the message.

Not even five minutes later, the guard returned with the small, wiry man who Wolf remembered from his previous visit. As he did then, he thought Warden Featherstone's demeanour more fitting for a law clerk than a prison director.

"Your lordship, it is once again an honour to have my lowly prison graced by your eminent presence," the man said in the snivelling, obsequious voice Wolf remembered so well. "May I be so bold as to hope this visit in on behalf of the House of Lords?" The warden was very proud of how efficiently he ran Pentonville Prison and longed for his excellent work to come to the attention of his betters.

Wolf hated to disappoint the man again. "Warden Featherstone, while I must admit it is not my primary purpose in coming here today, please be assured I intend to return at a later date for a tour of the prison in order to write a report for the House of Lords." Tabitha gave him a quick sideways glance; this came as news to her. Wolf answered her look with a quick shrug of his shoulders. It wouldn't hurt to keep the warden pleased, as it seemed they might require prison access in the future.

Warden Featherstone seemed happy enough with this answer, so Wolf then requested a private interview with the Earl of Warwick. As it happened, Clarence found himself imprisoned in the prison in London, where his rank assured he was most likely to be treated with deference. Warden Featherstone happily extended this deference to the earl's equally illustrious visitors.

"Would it be acceptable for you to talk to his lordship in my office?" the warden asked in his most ingratiating voice. Wolf saw no need to parade Tabitha through the prison and gratefully received the offer. The warden led the way to his office with its solid oak door indicated by a well-polished brass nameplate bearing his name.

Inside, the office appeared to Wolf as he remembered it, featuring an imposing mahogany desk and a comfortable-looking leather chair behind it. Wolf indicated Tabitha should take this seat, and he took the less comfortable chair in front of the desk.

"I will send a guard in with an extra chair," the warden promised. "Would you like some tea sent up while you wait for his lordship to be brought in?"

Wolf recalled his previous visit and replied that tea would be appreciated, but he also asked for an additional cup for the Earl of Warwick.

The last time Tabitha saw Clarence, Earl of Warwick, he was a vigorous man whose hearty good looks belied an age which must be at least in his late fifties. The man who shuffled into the warden's office seemed to have aged ten years. His skin appeared grey, and dark circles were under his eyes. As she greeted him, Tabitha considered the man hadn't even been in prison for twenty-four hours. What would he look like if they couldn't secure his release soon?

Tabitha was so shocked by the change in the man, she couldn't help but exclaim, "Your lordship, have they ill-treated you?"

Two guards accompanied Clarence. One led him in, wearing shackles on his wrists and ankles, while the other brought the extra chair.

When it seemed they planned to leave the earl in the shackles during the interview, Wolf demanded, "Take his lordship out of those things immediately."

The guard, a sullen-looking fellow, said insolently, "He's a prisoner. Prisoners wear shackles when they leave the secure part of the prison. We can't have him roaming free now, can we?"

Wolf summoned his grandfather and replied in an approximation of the old earl's voice, "He is the Earl of Warwick. A member of the House of Lords and a gentleman. You might leave the door to the prison open, and he would do his duty and remain."

The guard snickered, but he removed the iron shackles and said, "We'll be outside the door, so don't try nuffink."

Clarence slumped into the chair with relief. Wolf wondered if the guard might refuse to leave, but eventually, with a backward glare at them all, he left and closed the door behind him.

"What are you doing here?" Clarence asked in wonder. "Pembroke, how do you and Lady Pembroke come to be sitting in the warden's office?"

"First, please, it is Wolf and Tabitha. We are to be family soon." Even as Wolf said this, he wondered about the truth of his statement. How could the wedding go ahead under the current circumstances?

Whether the Earl of Warwick shared his doubts, the man nodded his head and said, "Then please call me Clarence. But my question stands."

Briefly, Wolf explained Fiona's request that he and Tabitha investigate. He then related his own history with Warden Featherstone.

"Are they treating you well?" Tabitha asked anxiously. The guard's attitude didn't give her hope.

"Well enough. I have my own cell, and Featherstone has done his best to ensure I have certain comforts. Nevertheless, it is a prison, and I am a prisoner." As he said this, Clarence waved his hand over his prison uniform of a plain white shirt and ill-fitting trousers made of a coarse, heavy material.

Tabitha looked closely at the now prisoner. One thing stood out: a bruise bloomed on his cheek. Tabitha remembered Clarence's unkempt appearance at dinner and considered if the punch to his cheek had been delivered since he arrived at Pentonville or the prior evening.

She decided there was no point in beating around the bush and asked in a kind yet firm voice, "Clarence, when you arrived late for dinner last night, where had you been?"

While he looked rather uncomfortable at the question, Clarence nevertheless tried to adopt a nonchalant tone. "Did I not give an excuse last night?"

"No, you did not. The dowager countess berated you, but no reason was given."

"Well, it was nothing really. I just got a little held up at my club."

"White's?" Wolf asked, mentioning the club every aristocrat belonged to, even if he also frequented other places in addition.

"Yes, White's. I got into a debate and lost track of time."

Recalling the askew cravat and missing button, Tabitha inquired, "Did this heated debate devolve into a fistfight, perhaps?"

"It was a heated debate. Nothing more," the earl said defensively.

"Yet, you have a rather nasty-looking bruise coming up on your cheek. How did you come by it?" Wolf asked, having also noticed the injury.

Clarence touched his face, as if only just realising he had a visible injury. "Well, I am in a prison."

"Are you saying another prisoner attacked you? Because, if so, we should get Warden Featherstone in here immediately," Wolf said.

At Wolf's words, Clarence sat up straight, his eyes wide. "No, there is no need for concern," he stammered.

Tabitha was losing patience quickly with this conversation. "Your lordship, I suspect you are not being candid with us. Do you not realise the trouble you are in? Murder is a capital offence."

Suddenly, looking less downtrodden prisoner and more arrogant earl, Clarence said in a dismissive tone, "I am the Earl of Warwick. I will not hang. I am sure this will all be sorted out in a few hours, and I will be free to go."

Tabitha glanced over at Wolf. Did Clarence really believe this?

"Clarence, it seems you do not realise the seriousness of the situation.

Yes, while it has long been the case that aristocrats are afforded extraordinary respite from the legal consequences of their actions, there has been quite the populist outrage about such things recently. Your very presence in this prison is proof the authorities have decided to make an example of you."

"Pfff, what stuff and nonsense," Clarence exclaimed. "I do not doubt Sir Matthew will intervene before the day is out. Heaven help the fool who sent me here without consulting the Home Secretary." With these words, Clarence crossed his arms in front of him in a show of defiance.

The man might be correct. But what if he wasn't? Perhaps his best tack was to persuade Clarence not to put all his eggs in one basket. Wolf pointed out, "You may indeed be correct, but what if you are not? Would it not be wise to allow us to investigate on the off-chance Sir Matthew does not intervene?"

As sensible as this suggestion seemed to Tabitha's ears, the haughty look on Clarence's face was evidence he could not imagine a scenario in which he would be required to spend even one night at Her Majesty's pleasure.

Tabitha and Wolf accepted the reality of the situation. With a sigh and a shake of his head, Wolf stood. "If this is your final decision, then we will leave you now and hope and pray you are correct." Taking her cue from her husband, Tabitha stood as well. They had not even been in the office long enough for the tea tray to arrive.

Wolf moved toward the door, and Tabitha followed. "I will tell the guard we are leaving," he informed Clarence, who didn't seem sure what to do next. Just as Wolf placed his hand on the doorknob, he turned and said in a solemn voice, "If and when you change your mind about your situation, Tabitha and I will be happy to help you in any way we can."

Clarence acknowledged this kindness with a stubborn raising of his chin and a grunt.

Chapter 6

Neither Tabitha nor Wolf said much during the carriage ride back to Chesterton House; both were far too absorbed in their thoughts about their interview with Clarence, Earl of Warwick. Tabitha hoped Clarence's assessment held true and Sir Matthew would intervene before the day was out. Wolf felt otherwise. Unlike most others in the aristocracy, he read newspapers beyond The Times. He understood the anti-elite sentiments playing out daily across the pages of the publications popular with the average working man.

Society was shifting, and while the changes weren't seismic yet, the undercurrents occasionally sent rumbles even to Mayfair. Wolf worried this situation with Clarence might be one of those occasions. As the Labour Party and various socialist factions became more popular, and as the women's suffrage movement used increasingly high-profile, sometimes even rather extreme tactics, the economic and social disparity enjoyed by Wolf and his class faced increasing attacks in the press.

Men like Clarence didn't realise the days of one system of justice for a few men of wealth and rank and another for every other man, woman, and child were coming to an end. However, their wilful blindness or perhaps denial of the changes the end of the century brought didn't make them less likely to happen.

His rank and fortune didn't sit comfortably with Wolf, and he welcomed what he imagined the future would bring. How far those changes would reach during his life, he could not say, but when he considered his ward, Melody, and her brother, Rat, and the world awaiting them as adults, he felt both envy and apprehension.

The technological innovations seemed not only to be coming at a faster pace and volume, but they were increasingly accessible to those in the lower classes. Wolf noticed the greater ubiquity of telephones in the almost year since one was installed at Chesterton House. Would there come a time when there was one in every home in Great Britain? Perhaps in Europe and then throughout the world. What would it mean when any person on earth could pick up a telephone receiver in his or her home and talk to someone in another country or even across an ocean?

Beyond technology like the telephone, he could not imagine what else the future held. Wolf often reflected on a Shakespearean line his father used to like to quote, "There are more things in Heaven and Earth, Horatio, than are dreamt of in your philosophy." Wolf believed the line was from *Macbeth* or perhaps *Hamlet*. Either way, Wolf thought of this line more and more these days. His father liked to use the line to berate Wolf on the many occasions when the son seemed to fall short of his parental expectations. As a young man, the quote's meaning eluded him, but now, older and possibly wiser, Wolf interpreted it as his father's caution about a world far harsher and more complex than he'd anticipated.

Finally, Wolf had stormed out of his father's house with only the clothes on his back and no actual plan, determined to make his own way in the world without following his father's wishes and entering the legal profession. As he looked back, Wolf realised his father's attempt to warn him against hubris was maybe the wisest counsel the late Colin Chesterton ever offered his wayward son.

While his father probably meant the words as a rebuke, Wolf now considered them in a more positive light. They offered an insight into the limits of human knowledge and imagination and the greater possibilities which existed beyond those current limits. Science was propelling society forward at an exponential velocity. If men such as Clarence, Earl of Warwick, didn't learn to adapt, they risked being left behind or even run over.

Tabitha saw Wolf was deep in contemplation and wondered what caused her husband to be so pensive. As the carriage pulled up outside Chesterton House, Wolf said in a sombre tone, "The world is changing, Tabitha. We must be sure to keep up and change with it."

She smiled. "What an awfully profound thought, my love."

"Are you saying I am normally incapable of such profundity?" he teased.

"I mean only you are not given to such philosophical musings, at least not until you have at least two brandies." Tabitha changed her light-hearted tone. "I assume this comment is not apropos of nothing but is rather a comment on our conversation with Clarence."

"Indeed. He imagines we are living in the world of twenty, even ten or five years ago, when an aristocrat could be assured the authorities would overlook any crime, however serious. However, the people are demanding greater equality across all dimensions of life, particularly justice."

Tabitha just bit her lip and nodded her head in agreement; there was nothing else to add. Wolf was correct. For the last few minutes of the trip, she reflected on the various investigations she and Wolf had undertaken together. In hindsight, so many of them seemed to involve or be a reaction to some great social injustice. Their very first investigation involved a duke with unnatural impulses who paid poor families in the East End for their very young daughters so that he could install them in a brothel for his perverted pleasure. Their investigations opened her eyes to how harsh life was for those not lucky enough to be born into the right family. They also made her aware the days of the masses just accepting their brutal lot in life and kowtowing to her class might be coming to an end.

As Talbot opened the front door for them, Tabitha realised immediately that something was amiss. While her butler was always appropriately inscrutable, as his profession demanded, nevertheless, a very slight raising of one eyebrow and a pursing of his lips warned his mistress sufficiently.

Talbot usually made this face when the Dowager Countess of Pembroke graced them with her presence and was in high dudgeon. "Is her ladyship waiting for us?" Tabitha guessed.

"Indeed, milady. The dowager countess has been here for quite some time, in fact."

Oh heavens, Tabitha thought. What now?

Quickly discharging their outerwear, Tabitha and Wolf made their way to the drawing room. Before they even got into the room, they heard a very familiar voice exclaim, "I am sorry to say it, Lily, but I see no other way!"

Pausing for a moment to brace themselves, Tabitha and Wolf then entered, encountering faces with a variety of emotions displayed on them: the dowager was in the anticipated state of high dudgeon and turned an irritated gaze on them, which made clear this was at least in part their fault; Lily seemed on the verge of tears; Jane looked as if she wished to be anywhere but in the room with her daughter and mother, and finally, Uncle Duncan sat in the most comfortable armchair in the room, oblivious to any tension and sipping on something alcoholic, even though it was only just midday.

"Finally!" the dowager, her tone laced with sarcasm.

"Did we have an appointment which I forgot?" Tabitha asked, sure they did not.

"Do I need an appointment to visit my family home?" the old woman asked, wilfully missing Tabitha's point.

Tabitha decided this line of discussion would get them nowhere and instead turned to Lily and asked, "Whatever is the matter, my dear?" Of course, looking at the larger picture, the matter was obvious: her betrothed's father stood accused of murder barely two weeks before her wedding day.

"Grandmama says the wedding must be called off," Lily wailed, showing far more enthusiasm for marriage to Viscount Tobias than Tabitha previously credited her with.

The dowager's next words indicated why Lily was so distraught at the prospect of her betrothal being broken. "Well, Lily dear, in many ways, the timing is most fortunate; the Season is just beginning, and if we make a concerted effort, it is possible you could have a new marriage proposal before May is out. After all, you are so much more presentable than you were before I rescued you from your mother's clutches last year."

The woman's callousness took Tabitha's breath away. She took a deep breath to compose herself before speaking. Then, Tabitha said in as even a tone as possible, "Mama, the earl has not even spent one night in prison. Surely, it is a little early to determine that he will not attend the wedding.

And, if and when such a fact becomes clear, we will merely postpone the date." Tabitha could see it would be unacceptable to continue with the wedding if Clarence's situation did not get resolved satisfactorily.

The dowager gave Tabitha a look one might give a foolish child. "There will be no postponing; regardless of the outcome, I cannot allow Lily to associate herself willingly with the inevitable scandal. No one will judge her poorly if she breaks things off now. In fact, they will expect it. She will come out of this an object of pity but in the best possible sense. We will ride this sentiment into the best drawing rooms and ballrooms in London, where it will give Lily a certain allure and mystique which, to be quite candid, she has been lacking. I would not be surprised if we cannot snag a marquis or duke if we are focused and disciplined!"

If Tabitha was shocked at the dowager's callousness a few moments before, now she found it appalling. Still, she acknowledged a valid argument existed within the insensitive, harsh language. Though Viscount Tobias desperately loved Lily, the extent of Lily's reciprocal feelings remained unclear to Tabitha. She did not doubt Lily's fondness for the young man. However, it always seemed to Tabitha Tobias represented Lily's least poor option. Marrying him saved her from having her grandmother drag her through the Season and parading her before every eligible young man in London. In addition, Lily felt sure Tobias would allow, even encourage, her to continue her botanical studies.

Though Tabitha always entertained some doubts about whether all of this formed a sufficient basis for a happy marriage, it was undoubtedly the way of her class, where love was usually the least of considerations in most betrothals.

This rationale made perfect sense while Viscount Tobias was a highly eligible young man from a family of impeccable social standing. But now, with a murder charge hanging over Tobias' father, regardless of whether his rank somehow got him out of any consequences for it, even Tabitha questioned if this was really the best match Lily might make. If the young woman were deeply in love with her betrothed, it would be one thing, but perhaps the marriage made little sense under the current circumstances. Given this, perhaps the pragmatic move might be to call off the wedding. After all, as much as Tabitha hated to admit it, the dowager made a sound point; the stench of this scandal would likely hang over the Williams family, no matter the outcome.

Just as Tabitha was poised to pour oil on troubled waters, she sensed a sudden shift in the room's energy as the dowager narrowed her eyes and asked, "And where have you and Jeremy been, Tabitha? I hope you have not been investigating without me!"

Chapter 7

Tabitha's first instinct was to glance over at Wolf and silently agree on what they would say. However, she stifled such an instinct immediately; the old woman was far too canny and perceptive and would pounce on any attempt at collusion.

Her momentary pause gave Wolf a chance to jump in and answer for them both. "Lady Pembroke, dear Lady Pembroke, let us ring for a fresh pot of tea and we can ensure you are brought up to date on all the details, at least to the full extent of our knowledge."

"Jeremy, as I have mentioned previously, as fond of you as I am, I realise when I am being placated, one might even say hoodwinked. I am fully aware Fiona and Charlotte visited this morning and requested we take on Clarence's case. I am also aware you have been out for some hours and can only imagine this was in furtherance of the investigation. Yet, at no point this morning did I receive an invitation to join you."

How did the woman learn all this? Wolf wondered. Then, he remembered Jane going from the breakfast table to the dowager's home to speak with Lily. One glance at Jane hanging her head in shame told him all he needed to know.

Wolf realised nothing would be gained by continuing to deny what the dowager clearly already intuited. "Yes, Lady Pembroke, Fiona asked the two of us to take on Clarence's case." Wolf said, "The two of us", pointedly, even if he sensed this folly would immediately come back to haunt him. Deciding he had dug himself too deep a hole already, Wolf continued, "And yes, we visited Pentonville Prison to talk with Clarence this morning."

As he said these words, Tabitha swore the temperature in the room dropped precipitously. This impression was amplified as the dowager answered in the iciest of tones, "And when were you planning to tell me all this, Jeremy?"

Wolf glanced over at Tabitha for a moment, but it wasn't quick enough to be missed. "Do not attempt some unspoken connivance with your wife," the dowager warned Wolf.

Finally, with a sigh, Wolf said in a pleading tone, "Lady Pembroke, I can say, in all honesty, there was no attempt to exclude you from anything. You were not here when Fiona and Charlotte came to speak with us, and then Tabitha and I left for the prison almost immediately."

"Almost immediately," the dowager pointed out sharply. "But not immediately." As she gestured towards Tabitha's dress, the woman continued, "I assume Tabitha did not come down to breakfast attired in this outfit, and I am certain you did not. So, you both found time to change your clothes and, therefore, could have found ample time to telephone me and request I join you."

Of course, the dowager's statement was correct; they did have time. It was also true neither Tabitha nor Wolf considered including the woman voluntarily.

Thinking quickly on her feet, Tabitha considered their timeline earlier that day. They ate breakfast quite early and departed for Pentonville by nine-thirty. "We did not want to wake you at such an ungodly hour," Tabitha claimed. "It goes without saying we planned to telephone you on our arrival home and suggest you come to Chesterton House so we could inform you of what we learned. How wonderful you anticipated this request and are here already."

In a mocking tone, with scepticism dripping from every syllable, the dowager said, "It goes without saying such was your plan, does it? I am no greenhorn and do not appreciate being talked to as if I am." She paused, gave one final sniff of outrage, then continued in a more conciliatory tone,

"Still, it matters not because I am now here and ready to be made aware of all the particulars. The sooner you put me in possession of all the facts, the sooner I can clear Clarence's name."

At this, Lily perked up. "Does this mean Toby and I may still be wed once the earl's name is cleared?"

"Unfortunately, Lily, it is sometimes incontrovertible that Jane is your mother. For all your supposed scientific smarts, you can be shockingly dense. No, it is not what this means. I wish to clear Clarence's name for Charlotte's sake. As I thought I made quite clear, even when I am able to do so, there will still be a stain on the Warwick name I will not allow to taint my family."

At these words, Lily started sobbing. Jane went across the room to comfort her daughter. The dowager was less moved by the display of emotion. "Lily, if you are going to make such an awful wailing noise, please leave the room. I need to confer with Jeremy and Tabitha."

Jane made the wise decision to take Lily by the arm and encourage her to follow the dowager's orders.

As the two women left the drawing room, the dowager said, "Now sit down and tell me everything."

There was no escaping the inevitability of involving the dowager, so Tabitha and Wolf did as she commanded.

They gave as complete a description as possible of their conversation with Fiona and Charlotte and, later, with Clarence. Surprisingly, the dowager said nothing during the entire rendition. In fact, she seemed quite absorbed by their story.

Finally, when they came to the end of the description of their visit to the prison and Clarence's refusal of help, the dowager exclaimed, "Ha! He was never the sharpest tack. A sweet child, but it was a good thing he became the heir and didn't remain a second son with the need for the acuity to make his way in the world."

What an interesting reflection on inherited titles, Tabitha thought. Did the dowager really believe their utility was to occupy men of lesser intelligence and skills? Shaking off all the ideas such a thought might lead to, Tabitha asked, "What do you know of this Lord Redding?"

"Well, the man is only a baron, of course," the dowager answered, as if this were explanation enough. "Barely a step above landed gentry." She then added, "However, I know of him. It is rather difficult not to, as it happens."

Now Tabitha's curiosity was peaked. "Why would you say so, Mama? I do not know him."

The dowager cocked her head and gave Tabitha such a dismissive look there was no need for her to explain further what she thought of such a statement. Instead, she elaborated, "The man is a prig and a prude, constantly on a rather public soapbox railing against the wages of sin. He is frequently published in The Times, writing editorials on the sanctity of marriage and the duty of noble families to uphold their bloodlines. It has long been my belief anyone who is so intent on wagging a finger at the rest of us probably has the darkest heart and adds hypocrisy to his crimes."

Tabitha remembered Dr Richard Trent's moralising during an investigation the previous year, in which he turned out to be the killer, and agreed. However, did Lord Redding's actions go beyond finger-wagging?

When Tabitha asked this question, the dowager made a face of such disgust it was almost as if she smelled a rotting fish under her nose. "The man was not content to support one sanctimonious group; from what I understand, he claimed membership of two: the Church of England Purity Society and the White Cross League. Given this, he continuously lobbied for stricter social laws."

Wolf knew of neither group and so the dowager explained further, "Well, the Purity Society promotes chastity and sexual morality. Not that there is anything wrong with those things, of course. But they have made it their business to push for the censorship of books and plays, something I find distasteful."

Tabitha found it interesting to hear the dowager espouse such progressive views, but she knew better than to voice this thought.

The dowager continued, "And then there is the White Cross League. I find everything about this group to be unpleasant. It comprises men who claim they are promoting chivalry, self-control, and moral purity. All you need to understand is that my husband, Philip, was a member before he died, and the very last thing he could be accused of was self-control and moral purity."

From everything Tabitha and Wolf knew of the dowager's late husband, she couldn't imagine why he would have any interest in joining such a group. Correctly interpreting the confusion on their faces, the dowager explained, "Philip was a hedonist, a libertine in every way. However, such vices never stopped him from sermonising to the lower classes. Of course, his views on the importance of women's chastity disappeared the moment he saw an apple-cheeked dairymaid he wished to bed."

Tabitha had never known her former father-in-law, and based on everything she had heard about him, she had long considered that a good thing. She hadn't thought the man could sink lower in her esteem, but now it seemed possible.

"Did ah hear ye say, apple-cheeked dairymaid?"

All three of them spun around to where the voice was coming from in the far corner. They had totally forgotten Uncle Duncan was still in the room. As it happened, he'd dozed off a while back with the glass of whisky in his hand. However, all the talk of debauching pastoral maidenhood penetrated even his drunken stupor. Luckily, in the surprised pause which followed his question, there was time for Uncle Duncan's eyelids to flutter as he fell back into his nap.

When Uncle Duncan was soundly asleep once more, Wolf indicated that Tabitha and the dowager should follow him out of the drawing room as he made his way to the more comfortable parlour where they kept the corkboard. Tabitha took a stack of empty notecards and began to write up the dowager's intelligence about Lord Redding.

"Do you have any idea why such enmity existed between Lord Redding and Clarence? Was it truly nothing more than the childhood animosity that Fiona described?" Wolf asked.

"I know nothing about that of which Fiona spoke. However, I can make an educated guess why Clarence did not care for the baron: because the Earl of Warwick is a sensible man and a voice of reason for the most part, and Redding is a dogmatic, puritanical bore."

While this might indeed be true, Fiona's dislike sounded far more personal. Tabitha wrote up a notecard, reflecting on this: "Why did Clarence and Lord Redding hate each other so much?" Then she pinned it to the top of the corkboard.

Tabitha considered the discussion with Fiona and Charlotte that morning. "We were told the two men shared a mistress at some point." She suggested that, putting aside the apparent hypocrisy of taking a lover out of wedlock, given Redding's public moral stance, this seemed like something which might have led to discord between the two men.

As she stated this premise, the dowager said dismissively, "If sharing a doxy were good enough reason for hostility, most of the men in society would be at each other's throats."

While the dowager might have a point, Tabitha thought it a thread worth pulling on and made a notecard saying as much.

When it became apparent there was little else to put on the corkboard, Wolf said, "I will go to White's after lunch and see what I can learn about the disagreement between Clarence and Redding."

White's did not allow women into its hallowed premises, so it was futile for Tabitha or the dowager to insist on joining Wolf. On his way to the dining room, Wolf stopped in his study for a brief perusal of the morning newspapers. As he feared, Clarence's arrest for the murder of Lord Redding was splashed across the front pages of every newspaper, from the most high to low brow. The Times seemed to adopt an appropriate attitude of innocent until proven guilty. Still, the more populist publications, particularly the Illustrated Police News, were almost gleeful in their melodramatic descriptions of one of the elite finally held accountable.

As he put the newspapers aside, Wolf sighed; it was no more than they expected, but even so, he realised this attitude by the dailies would not help Clarence's case. If his arrest continued to be so loudly cast as equal treatment under the law a long time coming, the Home Secretary would be even more loath to be seen giving the Earl of Warwick preferential treatment.

Chapter 8

After a light luncheon, Wolf headed out to White's. Despite inheriting membership to the storied club, he never felt comfortable there and rarely attended for mere social reasons. Given this, Wolf wasn't familiar with the staff, and so, at Tabitha's suggestion, he telephoned Anthony Rowley, the Duke of Somerset, and asked to meet him there. Anthony was a childhood friend of Tabitha's and deeply indebted to both Tabitha and Wolf. The man didn't even ask why Wolf suddenly wanted his companionship at White's and instead said he would meet him there within the hour.

Lily stayed for luncheon but remained subdued through the entire meal. When it was over, she indicated she wished to take the carriage back to the dowager's home. Rather than joining her, the dowager remained at Chesterton House and indicated to Tabitha they should retire back to the parlour to continue to discuss the investigation. Tabitha wasn't sure what there was to talk about, but didn't have the energy to argue.

Settled back in the parlour with a pile of empty notecards in front of her, Tabitha asked, "What would you have us discuss, Mama?"

"Tut tut, Tabitha. Are you really so incapable of continuing to investigate without Jeremy's presence?"

As she tried not to take umbrage at this insinuation, Tabitha said in a measured voice, "That is hardly the case, as you well know. However, I am not sure we have enough information to consider at this point."

"Then you are not thinking logically!" the dowager said in an annoyingly triumphant tone. Without waiting for Tabitha to protest, the woman asked, "Why do you imagine Clarence was so reluctant to tell you any more about what happened between him and Lord Redding?"

Tabitha reflected on their visit to Pentonville Prison. "It is a hubristic belief his title will save him."

The dowager shook her head in amazement. "It is shocking how lacking in imagination you are, Tabitha. The man has a public falling out with his nemesis, who then turns up dead. Under normal circumstances, would you not imagine he would be keen to enumerate all the many reasons he might imagine someone would want Redding dead? And yet, Clarence said not a word against the man, at least if your account of the conversation is complete."

As infuriating as the woman's condescending tone was, Tabitha conceded the validity of her statement; she might have expected Clarence to be all too eager to tell them all the many enemies that Lord Redding must have. Yet he said nothing.

Reluctant to feed the woman's belief in her own superiority but also unable to imagine where she was taking this line of reasoning, Tabitha finally asked the dowager what she considered the reason.

With an infuriating self-satisfaction Tabitha might have anticipated, the dowager said smugly, "Because Clarence believes he knows who killed Redding and is attempting to protect them."

As soon as the dowager said this, Tabitha was sure the woman was correct. Such a realisation left her dumbstruck at how she and Wolf missed such an obvious conclusion. She made a mental note to share this insight with Wolf as soon as possible.

Tabitha thought through their conversation with Clarence but using this new lens, Tabitha said thoughtfully, "He is confident whoever this person is will not benefit from the protection of wealth and rank he is sure will shield him, and so he is taking the guilt upon himself."

"Exactly! I cannot believe how long it took you to catch up to me."

With a sigh, Tabitha acknowledged, at least to herself, that she couldn't believe it either.

The dowager stood up suddenly and dowager said in a no-nonsense voice, "I have some enquiries to make. I will not require your company." As she said this, the dowager's face took on a pensive look, and then she continued, "I will be taking that good-for-nothing Mr MacAlister with me."

Tabitha couldn't imagine a more shocking sentence coming out of the dowager's mouth. Her distaste for Uncle Duncan was well known. That she might choose to spend time in his company and out in public was quite incredible. In fact, it so shocked Tabitha, she didn't even ask why she was not to accompany the dowager instead.

Noting the younger woman's surprise, the dowager said as a parting salvo before she left the room, "Do close your mouth, Tabitha. You look like the rather mediocre salmon we were just served for luncheon." And with those parting words, the dowager swept out of the room.

She had stated she would take Uncle Duncan with her, but the dowager now faced the dilemma of where to find him. It never occurred to her that persuading the man to join her would be any kind of obstacle. Luckily, as she left the parlour, the dowager ran into Talbot, who mentioned Uncle Duncan had retired back to the peace and quiet of the drawing room for a post-prandial drink and perhaps a nap.

On hearing this news, the dowager hurried off toward the drawing room. While she didn't need Uncle Duncan entirely sober in order for her plan to work – in fact, the dowager wasn't sure if she'd ever witnessed him so – she needed him to stand upright and speak in semi-coherent sentences.

Ten minutes later, the dowager sat in her carriage opposite a sober-enough Uncle Duncan. While the impish Scotsman was surprised at the invitation to join the dowager in paying a social call, he merely waggled his shaggy eyebrows and gave a mischievous wink, which the dowager chose to ignore.

"Ah, and where is it I find myself bein' spirited away tae this time, lass?" he said, smiling lasciviously.

Typically, the dowager's response to Uncle Duncan saying such a thing would have been to express outrage and then storm out. However, she knew it was her choice to be in his company and did her best to control her grimace and tone.

"As I mentioned, Mr MacAlister, I have need of your help." There wasn't much time to consider whether she wanted to take Uncle Duncan into her confidence. On the one hand, the man was a drunken fool. On the other hand, in order for him to be both believable and effective, he must have some idea of her aims for the afternoon.

Finally, deciding on a compromise of telling him enough but not too much, the dowager explained, "We are going to Lady Hartley's at-home. I need some information she is likely privy to. However, the woman is a shrew and the most outrageous gossip in London. She cannot glean I want this information; I can only imagine what hay she would make of such intelligence. Instead, she must be lured into revealing it organically. That is where you come in."

Uncle Duncan's faculties were dulled by quite a few glasses of Wolf's finest whisky in addition to a bottle of claret with luncheon, but even he could see the flaw in the dowager's plan. "Would I be right in thinkin' it's no' the usual practice for men tae attend such gatherings?"

As surprising as it might be, Uncle Duncan had hit on the exact problem. While it wasn't unheard of for men to accompany their wives to afternoon social calls occasionally, this was usually reserved for close family friends. The dowager was renowned for refusing to conform to the social rules of afternoon social calls, whether it be attending or hosting them. Certainly, she did not desire the hoi polloi of so-called good society to believe they possessed an open invitation to call upon her. When she desired someone's company, she summoned them. Beyond the unusual behaviour of bringing a man who wasn't even a family member with her to an at-home loomed a bigger question of why she would lower herself to attend one at all.

The last time the dowager deigned to call on Lady Hartley, it had also been with an ulterior motive: the dowager previously charged Lady Hartley with keeping an ear out for any scandals where the dowager might offer her investigative services. The woman was quite useless, of course. In fact, the one piece of gossip she'd managed to pull out from her inventory proved entirely fruitless.

Could she use this same ploy this time? The dowager wondered. However, she immediately dismissed such an idea. She caught sight of a newsstand as they drove down Grosvenor Street and realised news of

Clarence was on the front page of every newspaper. It was too much to hope Lady Hartley hadn't at least got a whiff of the scandal. While the woman lacked what the dowager would call intelligence, she was like a bloodhound when she caught the scent of juicy gossip. And gossip in any way connected to the dowager would be far too tempting to ignore. It was far too much to hope that Lady Hartley wouldn't connect Uncle Duncan to Lily and, therefore, ultimately to the disgraced Clarence.

As all these concerns ran through her mind, the dowager wondered if she had done the right thing in bringing Uncle Duncan with her. Perhaps this would attract more attention rather than less. Second-guessing her decisions felt very alien and uncomfortable. Was she losing her hold over affairs?

Just thinking such a thing about her own abilities shocked the dowager into battlefield mode. She knew a good commander of forces made the most of the situation in which he found himself rather than looking backwards at what might have been. She was now in a carriage with this absurd Scotsman. How might she best make use of him to achieve her ends?

The dowager considered what she knew about Uncle Duncan. She wouldn't give him credit for much, but he seemed genuinely fond of Lily. Of course, he was in the room when the dowager told her granddaughter she could not marry Tobias, regardless of the outcome of his father's current incarceration. The dowager cast her mind back to the conversation. She swore the ridiculous man was either asleep or too inebriated to have followed along.

Crossing her fingers and hoping this was the case, the dowager said cautiously, "Mr MacAlister, I am sure you wish to do whatever you can to ensure Lily's wedding to Viscount Tobias can go ahead as planned and must have heard of the troubles in the path of the betrothed couple."

Though Uncle Duncan paid little attention to the breakfast conversation, he'd heard enough to be dimly aware of the importance of the matter. His only response was, "Aye, lass. I ken."

Despite his words, the dowager wasn't sure she trusted he really knew, but she forged ahead anyway. However, she lacked the time, patience, and trust in Uncle Duncan's intellectual faculties to put all the details they understood so far before him. Instead, she opted for simplicity and said,

"It seems the victim, the late Lord Redding, and Clarence, Tobias' father, shared a mistress. I want to discover her identity and believe the woman we are about to visit, Lady Hartley, may be privy to such information."

"She's fond o' the clishmaclaver, is she?"

"I have no idea what clishmaclaver is, but if you are asking if she is a gossip, then the answer is a resounding yes!"

Uncle Duncan hadn't got nearly enough sleep the previous night, and his afternoon nap was interrupted by the dowager's demand that he join her for this outing. It briefly flickered through his head to ask why the dowager needed him along for the extraction of this information, but one look at the diminutive harridan's face and he thought better of such foolishness.

While Uncle Duncan avoided this question, he did ask with a twinkle in his eye, "And what's my place in this wee pantomime, then?"

The dowager forced herself to ignore his amused tone and answered, "I would prefer Lady Hartley not associate me too closely with the request for this information." She wondered if she would have to elaborate on such a statement, but luckily, Uncle Duncan merely nodded.

The dowager paused, hoping for inspiration to strike. During this pause, Uncle Duncan asked in his most lascivious tone, "Am I to be graced by the company of more bonnie lasses at this wee tea-drinkin' affair o' yours?"

With her patience almost at its breaking point, the dowager forced her mouth into what she hoped approximated a pleasant smile and answered in a strained tone which was entirely lost on Uncle Duncan: "I have no idea who else may be there, Mr MacAlister."

However, Uncle Duncan's question raised yet another concern: he could hardly ask about a man's mistress in a room full of society matrons. What if other ladies of the aristocracy were present? Lady Hartley was always so ready to give and receive gossip, she would hardly notice the impropriety of such a question, but others surely would.

"Stop the carriage!" the dowager commanded, banging on its roof. She needed a moment to strategise.

"There's a shadow in yer eyes – what's vexin' ye, lass?"

Before considering the wisdom of showing any cracks in her armour, the dowager admitted, "I am now questioning the wisdom of attempting to discover the required information in this manner. However, I find myself at a loss as to what other route to take." Suddenly, in a flash of inspiration, the dowager asked, "Mr MacAlister, are you by chance a member of any of the London gentlemen's clubs?"

Uncle Duncan chuckled, "Ye might not take me for a gentleman, but I assure ye, I have my moments. I belong to Boodles," he explained, surprising the dowager by naming the very conservative club with a distinctly rural, country-focused membership.

Correctly interpreting the dowager's reaction, Uncle Duncan explained, "I'd take talk of hounds and rifles over cards and politics any day, lass."

The dowager decided it sufficed to learn Uncle Duncan was a member of Boodles without diving too deeply into the details of why or how. Even as she instructed her driver to make his way to the elegant Georgian townhouse on St James's Street, which housed the exclusive club, she once again questioned her choices; Wolf had gone to White's anyway. In hindsight, wouldn't it have made more sense to add discovering the mistress's name to his to-do list?

However, if she'd done so, where would it have left her in the investigation? Whether through benign oversight or wilful exclusion, Tabitha and Wolf had set off for Pentonville Prison with nary a thought for including her. If she did not claw back as much as possible of this investigation, she might as well resign herself to no longer being The Investigative Countess, Rapier Sharp Logic paired with Great Insight and Boldness. A Private Inquiry Agent.

As she considered this dire choice, the dowager realised as much as Uncle Duncan was not the perfect vessel through which to act, he possessed one very worthy trait: pliability. In fact, once the carriage came to a standstill and Uncle Duncan rolled out and up the steps into Boodles, she wondered whether she was missing a trick when it came to the old sot. It was not lost on her that, for all her command of society, she could not enter White's, Boodles, or any of the similar clubs in London merely because of her gender.

It was outrageous, but Uncle Duncan might waltz into such places and be accepted by the other members. He might ask questions, even lewd questions, and no heads would turn. She might rail against the fact, but it was still a man's world. Given this, didn't it make sense to have one of them tightly under her control? Indeed, dear Jeremy, no matter how adoring, would always put Tabitha first. Of course, she had Little Ian, but the man was more suited for physical altercations. Indeed, the more she sat outside Boodles and thought about it, the more the dowager realised she had allowed personal animosity and perhaps even pride to impair her judgment when it came to Mr MacAlister.

This recognition that Uncle Duncan might be an untapped resource lasted for at least forty-five minutes before she began to regret having ever started on this fool's errand. Before letting Uncle Duncan leave the carriage, the dowager explained multiple times the task at hand. She commanded him to moderate his alcohol intake and to make as much haste as possible. It occurred to the dowager she might return home and pick him up in an hour or two. However, almost as soon as this thought crossed the dowager's mind, she envisioned an entirely inebriated Uncle Duncan stumbling out of Boodles and disappearing into the night. As it was, the dowager almost missed him as he almost did exactly this.

There was always a novel stowed away in the carriage, just in case a ride proved particularly long and tedious. The dowager became so absorbed in the one she found in the usual pocket by the seat, she almost missed the drunken Scotsman stumbling out of the club almost two hours later. The dowager was alerted to his exit only because he stumbled down the last two steps and swore like a sailor. The dowager quickly alerted her driver to grab the man with all speed.

As the driver shoved Uncle Duncan rather unceremoniously into the carriage, the dowager looked at his bloodshot eyes and vacant stare and feared her afternoon had been a waste of time. As if to confirm this, Uncle Duncan immediately curled up in the corner of the carriage and fell asleep. The dowager sighed; perhaps she should have known better.

CHAPTER 9

With Wolf and the dowager both out pursuing different investigative strands, Tabitha decided her afternoon would be best spent catching up with her new private secretary, Mrs O'Leary. While Rose O'Leary was a recent and unplanned addition to their household, she quickly proved herself highly efficient and organised. Already, Tabitha couldn't remember how she managed without her. Not only did Mrs O'Leary take over many of the more mundane tasks involved with running a house as large and grand as Chesterton House, but more importantly, she took over the day-to-day oversight of the Dulwich house.

During their first investigation, Tabitha and Wolf rescued a large number of young girls sold into prostitution by their destitute parents. Along with Anthony Rowley, whose father, the late duke, had been the purveyor of such young flesh, they created the Dulwich House as a refuge and school for these girls. The house ran under the motherly, watchful eye of Bear's mother, Mrs Elizabeth Caruthers, known as Mother Lizzy. Still, there was enough other work involved in running it and ensuring the girls received a good education. Tabitha was happy to hand all of this over into Mrs O'Leary's very capable hands.

Mrs O'Leary was recently widowed. Her twin toddler sons, Liam and Willy, now resided in the nursery with Melody, who ruled them as a usually benevolent dictator. Wolf repurposed a small room at the back of the house for Mrs O'Leary's office, and Tabitha made her way there now.

On knocking on the door and then entering the office, Tabitha was surprised to find Bear sitting in one of the two armchairs in front of the fireplace. More worrying was the guilty look on Mrs O'Leary's face as she jumped out of the other armchair and to her feet. What was going on here? Tabitha made a mental note to mention this to Wolf. Bear was a kind, gentle man, and Tabitha knew he would never knowingly lead a woman on. However, Mrs O'Leary was still somewhat fragile from her many years in an abusive marriage. Tabitha wanted to ensure Bear showed caution about raising any expectations he wasn't ready to meet.

The sight of Bear gave Tabitha an idea, though. "Please, do not get up on my account. In fact, Bear, there is a task I would like you to take on this afternoon."

Bear made his way to the less comfortable chair in front of the desk for himself, and Tabitha took the chair he had vacated. "I assume that either from the newspapers or servants' gossip, you are aware of the situation with the Earl of Warwick?" Bear nodded his head, and so she continued. "I remember you are familiar with Mr Andrews, the newspaper man who Wolf sometimes interacts with."

"I've known the man as long as Wolf has," Bear confirmed.

"Good. I would like you to go to the offices of his newspaper and find out everything he knows." Bear's face showed doubt. Tabitha assured him, "I know it is unlikely there is anything he has not already printed, but I would like to be sure."

Bear cautioned, "Andrews is a decent man as these hacks go, but he's no saint; he's going to want something in return."

"Tell him we will ensure he has the full story of whatever we uncover before anyone else," Tabitha replied.

Bear raised his eyebrows. "The full story? Are you sure you want to promise such a thing? You have no idea what you are going to find."

Tabitha considered his words; it was wise counsel. "You are right. Tell him we will tell him as much as we are able before any other newspaper. Or something similar. I trust you to use your best judgement about how to gild the offer appropriately." Bear nodded, rose and left with just a quick half-smile towards Mrs O'Leary. Inwardly, Tabitha sighed at what she had witnessed; she hoped this wasn't doomed to get messy.

The next hour involved reviewing the account books for both houses. This kind of work was not something Tabitha enjoyed or excelled at. Mostly, she was happy to leave as much of the running of Chesterton House to her excellent housekeeper, Mrs Jenkins. However, she knew it was an unfair burden to lay entirely on the woman who had more than enough to do. Given this, Tabitha was thrilled to find that not only was the lion's share of the bookkeeping now taken off Mrs Jenkin's shoulders but it was now being performed with an efficiency Tabitha knew she could never have come close to.

While Tabitha and Wolf vacationed in Corfu, Mrs O'Leary took it upon herself to go to Dulwich to inspect the house and meet with Mrs Caruthers. Based on this inspection, she suggested a variety of improvements, from redoing some chimneys to hiring a second tutor to help with the older girls who were now coming to the age when they might consider taking up a profession.

When the girls first moved into Dulwich House, Tabitha assured them that there was no time limit on how long they might enjoy its safety and security. However, she realised that the idea of a group of girls locked in amber was not reality and that the girls needed to be prepared for productive lives. Some might choose to go into service, but she encouraged the girls to dream more expansively than a life as servants.

To that end, Mrs O'Leary suggested that the school might benefit from a tutor to teach the girls more practical skills, such as shorthand and bookkeeping. Tabitha's heart sang at the possibility these girls might be equipped to lead lives far beyond the ones that would have likely been their destiny even before their horrific interlude as prostitutes. If she and Wolf could be part of sending these girls out into the world as women who might be secretaries, teachers, or perhaps even more, then, well, it would have all been worth it. Tabitha wasn't naive enough to believe that. However, perhaps something positive might have come from the horror that the children had been exposed to. And the thought of that made her glad.

After Mrs O'Leary took Tabitha through all her proposals and accounted for the necessary funds, Tabitha asked about the twins.

"Well, Miss Melody has whipped them into shape, that's for sure," Mrs O'Leary said with a grin.

"I want your boys to feel that they are Melody's equal in the nursery and this house. If she ever gets too much, please alert me immediately, Mrs O'Leary," Tabitha assured her. Melody's roots were no more grandiose than the twin boys. They had all found a sanctuary at Chesterton House, and Tabitha wanted to ensure that each child benefited equally from the twist of fate that brought them under the protection of an earl and a countess.

"My boys adore Miss Melody," Mrs O'Leary assured her. "She can order them about as much as she likes, and the only dispute is which of them gets to do her bidding first."

While this put Tabitha's mind somewhat at ease, she would have a word with Mary, the nursery maid. With Melody as the official ward of the Earl of Pembroke, there was the real possibility that the children would be treated differently by the servants and beyond, whether consciously or not.

By the time Tabitha and Mrs O'Leary were finished, Tabitha looked at her watch and realised that it was likely Wolf would be home soon. Eager to hear what, if anything, he had learned, she hurried to the parlour to await his return.

On entering the parlour they used when it was just family at home and they wished to be comfy, Tabitha was surprised to find Lily.

"Did you not return to your grandmama's?" Tabitha asked in surprise.

"I cannot be in the same house as that woman," Lily declared passionately. "I talked with Mama, and she agreed it was better for everyone, well at least for me, that I stay here for the time being. I hope that is acceptable, Cousin Tabitha."

In truth, Tabitha was ashamed that she hadn't considered making the offer to Lily. Given the dowager's insistence that the wedding would not be happening under any circumstances, Tabitha couldn't blame the young woman for wanting to put some distance between her and her grandmother.

"You are always welcome here, Lily," Tabitha assured her. Taking a seat in her customary armchair, Tabitha weighed saying what was on her mind. Finally, she decided she might not get any better, more private occasion than this. "Lily, I realise your grandmother can be rather harsh in her comments," Tabitha began cautiously.

"It is not for her to decide whether my wedding will go ahead," Lily declared, jutting out her chin in defiance.

"It is true, it is not. However, it is possible that your father may share the dowager countess' opinion. She is correct in saying that the stench of scandal will be attached to Tobias' family for some time to come, no matter the outcome."

With Lily about to protest, Tabitha put up a hand. "I do not condone such behaviour, but I have lived long enough in society to understand the reality of how it works. In fact, I have personal experience of such things. When Jonathan, my late husband, died, some initial suspicion attached to me." Tabitha didn't bother to say that the dowager had fanned the winds of such suspicion. "Even when my name was cleared, members of polite society shunned me. Indeed, I was only rescued, if one can see it that way, by my remarriage to Wolf. It is one thing to snub a widow, quite another the new wife of a handsome, rich earl."

"And what do I care if I am shunned?" Lily declared. "I have no interest in socialising with these people anyway. It might almost be a blessing to be relieved of the pressure of being part of society."

"Lily, you say that now, and perhaps you even believe it. But such a taint can last some time and may follow any future children you have. Do you really want that?" Lily blushed at the allusion to a future family with Tobias but said nothing. Finally, Tabitha realised she had to come to the point and speak plainly. "Lily, I do not doubt Tobias adores you, and I am sure you are fond of him. However, I have always had the impression that there is an imbalance of affection which is made up for by whatever independence you imagine marriage to him will afford you. If you truly loved him, I would say nothing, but to put yourself willingly under such a shadow where your affections are not fully engaged seems unwise."

There! She had said it. As she watched Lily processing her words, Tabitha only hoped that the advice would be taken in the spirit of love and concern in which it was intended.

What Tabitha hadn't expected was that Lily would burst into tears. Rushing to kneel by the girl's side, Tabitha said in a concerned voice, "Lily, I am so sorry to have upset you. That was not my intent, I assure you."

Sniffing and wiping the tears from her cheek, Lily asked, "Is this what you all think? That I do not really love Toby?"

How to answer? The answer was yes. That was what Tabitha and Wolf thought. Who knew what the dowager thought?

Finally, Lily saved her from having to answer and said, "It is true that I did not love Toby as much as he loved me to begin with." Then, she added quickly, "And Toby is entirely aware of that fact. The dear boy said that it would be his great honour to spend his life with me, and he would strive to do all he could to make me one day feel even half of what he does for me. Can you imagine someone loving me that much? I am not sure that I would be as magnanimous if the tables were reversed."

"Lily, I am truly glad that Toby is aware of how you feel or do not feel. However, that does not change the point that I am making; you would not be breaking your heart if you called the wedding off. I understand what getting married to someone who would encourage your studies means, but other men might feel similarly."

Tabitha regretted having to say this; she was very fond of Viscount Tobias, who had really matured and grown for the better over the past months. Nevertheless, she felt that someone other than the dowager should make the case for breaking off the betrothal.

As soon as Tabitha talked of other men, Lily began to cry again. "You do not understand; I do love Toby now. Perhaps I will never love him as he loves me, or perhaps I will. But I love him, and I do not want any other man."

This put a different complexion on the situation, Tabitha acknowledged. "If you love him, Lily, then that is very different. I should add that if I did not realise that you feel this way, I can almost guarantee that your grandmother does not either. Even she might react differently if she did." Actually, Tabitha wasn't entirely sure of the truth of such a statement, but it made Lily perk up and the crying stop.

Worried that she had now given the girl too much hope, Tabitha followed up with, "But this is all premature. If the earl is not released from prison, then there cannot be a wedding any time soon regardless." Reluctantly, Lily acknowledged this truth.

CHAPTER 10

Tabitha and Lily sat together for some time in the parlour. Tabitha carried the faint hope that if she talked to Lily about Tobias' family, it might turn out that she knew something that would be useful. However, after almost an hour, it became clear that Lily knew nothing more than that Clarence was a rather exacting and stern father, at least by his son's telling. This hadn't been Tabitha's impression of Clarence from their various interactions so far. He seemed to have developed from an awkward and quiet young man into a much more self-assured yet good-humoured adult. Such a change in his confidence was hardly surprising given the decades he had been an earl. Still, Tabitha recognised that a man might present one face to the world and quite another to his wayward son.

Finally, Lily decided to go for a walk in the garden. She left Tabitha alone, contemplating the very little information they had gathered so far. Suddenly, she heard a commotion out in the hallway. Leaving the parlour to investigate the sound, she saw the dowager's carriage driver propping up a very inebriated Uncle Duncan, who seemed inclined to slide down and lie on the marble by the front door. The dowager, looking as if her patience was worn threadbare, brought up the rear.

Tabitha's surprised expression caused the dowager to exclaim, "What possessed me to believe this man could be counted on for anything except drinking to excess."

'Where did you take him that he managed to do so?"

"Well, I intended to take him to Lady Hartley's at-home," the dowager acknowledged.

"He got this drunk in Lady Hartley's drawing room?" Tabitha exclaimed, equal parts horrified and amused.

"I reconsidered such a plan at the last moment," the dowager explained. "And so, I sent him into Boodles to see what he could find out. What in the world possessed me?"

She took the words out of Tabitha's mouth.

"Take him upstairs," Tabitha told the carriage driver. "Talbot, can you call one of the footmen to help?"

With Uncle Duncan taken care of, Tabitha returned to the parlour, the dowager in tow. Talbot promised to see that Uncle Duncan was settled and then bring in a tea tray.

Ten minutes later, the dowager attempted to restore her composure with a cup of Earl Grey and a ginger biscuit. It had been quite a trying afternoon in the end. Uncle Duncan might be pliable, but that didn't translate to useful.

As the two women sipped their tea, the door opened, and Wolf entered.

"Well, Jeremy, I hope you have had a more productive afternoon than I have!" the dowager said with such force that Wolf glanced at Tabitha to see what he'd missed. She shook her head to indicate that she would tell him later.

Wolf took a cup of tea and sat in his customary armchair. "Well, thanks to Somerset, I was able to interview the staff who witnessed the altercation that evening."

He paused and took a sip of tea, causing the dowager to exclaim, "Then what are you waiting for, Jeremy? Heavens. As it is, I feel as if I have aged years this afternoon with Mr MacAlister."

Now Wolf was even more curious about what he had missed. However, he understood the folly of keeping the dowager waiting. Instead, he relayed what he had discovered. It seemed that the enmity between the Earl of Warwick and Lord Redding was well known amongst the staff of White's, and they always strived to seat the men as far apart from each other as possible. They were hardly the only members of the aristocracy with long-standing feuds, but the staff at White's had no clue about the root of the antagonism.

"Whatever it is, I do not believe that it is merely dislike from their school days," Wolf said. "Clarence must be almost sixty, and that seems too old to continue a childish distaste for another man. Anyway, that the two men cannot say two civil words to each other is as well-known as the adverse reaction Marquis of Essex has to prawns. Given this, the waiter I spoke with expressed great surprise when, last night, he saw Clarence approach Redding, who was sitting and reading the newspaper at the time."

"Did this waiter hear what they were arguing about?" Tabitha asked.

"Unfortunately, not everything. It seems that discretion and good manners prevented the man from overtly eavesdropping. However, he said that whatever the topic, Lord Redding's face became bright red with anger. He stood when Clarence approached, and the two men began pointing in each other's faces. This waiter was worried they would come to blows there and then. He did hear Clarence say one thing. Just as he turned to leave, he said, "Do you have no honour, man? I warn you now, if you will not do the right thing of your own accord, then I will have to take matters into my own hands.""

"I assume that this was the line that caused the police first to suspect Clarence," Tabitha suggested.

"Yes. At least according to the evening papers. I picked up most of them on my way back. I had Talbot put them in my study. Though I can bring them through if you would like to peruse them."

"Did you look through them already?"

"I glanced at The Times and The Illustrated Police News. I decided to see what each end of the melodrama spectrum had to say."

"And?" the dowager asked impatiently. "Do I strike you as someone who enjoys a story being dribbled out to me?"

It had been a long day, and Wolf had hoped that he wouldn't find the dowager when he returned home. All he wanted was a quiet evening with his wife. He knew that was unlikely, given their houseguests, but he wished for at least a peaceful hour before dinner.

Wolf realised he was merely postponing the inevitable and so answered resignedly, "Honestly, it all seems like utter speculation. The Times piece was less sensational, of course. There was also a very solid, even-handed piece in The Westminster Gazette written by Andrews. It spoke of the life-long animosity between the two men and of a heated argument at White's. The Illustrated Police News made as much of the supposed melodrama as one might expect. Interestingly, it did suggest that the men were fighting over a lover, but there were no details."

Tabitha had totally forgotten that she'd sent Bear to speak to Andrews. Now, she told Wolf and wondered aloud whether the newsman might have luck tracking down this mistress.

Wolf considered it worthwhile asking Andrews to share what information he uncovered, "Although, if he knew anything, you can be sure he would have published it."

"Bear said the same thing. However, perhaps he will share a piece of the puzzle that he hasn't been able quite to place yet," Tabitha said hopefully.

"Should we ask Fiona?" Wolf asked hesitantly.

"If we have no choice, we can try. However, just because she knows her husband has a mistress does not mean that she knows the woman's details. I would hate to have to resort to asking her such a question about her incarcerated husband; the woman is going through enough."

Wolf agreed, and even the dowager didn't disagree, merely adding, "It was always a given during my marriage that Philip kept mistresses, but I certainly would never have lowered myself to discover the tawdry details. I cannot imagine that Fiona feels otherwise."

"I assume the newspapers reported all the details about the actual killing," Tabitha said.

"Indeed. It seems that Lord Redding often chose to walk home from White's rather than take his carriage. That evening, when he left White's, Clarence followed him out, and they again exchanged words on the pavement. The newspapers spoke to the porter on duty that night, as well as two carriage drivers waiting outside. They all said the same thing: the men argued, and then, at one point, they came to blows and punches were exchanged. Then, Redding turned and left."

Wolf paused long enough for the dowager to exclaim impatiently,

"And then what happened? Listening to you relay a story is quite painful, Jeremy."

It was tempting to point out that this story appeared in all the newspapers, and so the dowager might have read it for herself. However, there seemed little to be gained by making such an observation. Instead, Wolf continued, "Apparently, Redding often took a shortcut home down a rather badly lit alleyway, which was where his body was found in the early hours of the morning, soaked in blood."

The question remained, why was this such damning evidence against Clarence? The group sat for some time in subdued silence as they processed the information, then Tabitha said, "Is that all there is to this? An argument? Did anyone witness Clarence following Redding?"

"No. However, Scotland Yard feels this is sufficient evidence for an arrest. One thing that the newspapers did mention was that the coroner is sure that Redding was murdered around the same time he left White's."

"That still leaves open the possibility that a footpad attacked him, does it not?" the dowager asked. Everyone agreed it did. However, it seemed the police were determined to see Clarence on trial for the murder, nonetheless.

The conversation left everyone somewhat subdued, a state that continued for the rest of the afternoon and into the evening.

The dowager decided she would stay for dinner. Tabitha had informed her that Lily had moved to Chesterton House, and she could have sworn that the septuagenarian looked quite melancholy at the news. As she watched the dowager take her seat for dinner, it occurred to Tabitha that the dowager might have enjoyed having Lily's company over the past almost nine months. Perhaps she wanted to stay for dinner because she was lonely.

No one expected to see Uncle Duncan again that night, but he surprised everyone by showing up at the dinner table, seemingly no worse for wear. The man really had an astounding constitution for near-constant inebriation.

They were halfway through their fish course when Uncle Duncan suddenly announced. "Caroline Turnbull."

All heads spun around at this seeming non sequitur. When it dawned on him that he might need to elaborate, Uncle Duncan continued, "A

Caroline Turnbull, if ye can believe it – once quite the voice on the opera stage, or so I hear. That's the mistress. Oh, he had plenty, right enough. But she was the one he took after the earl was finished with her. No, at the same time, mind ye. But close enough tae set tongues waggin'."

Uncle Duncan took another swig of claret, then continued proudly, "Took a fair few drams and a fair few men afore one of them was willin' – and sober enough – to spill the tale. Ye ken, men are just as bad as the ladies for a bit o' clishmaclaver when they've had a dram or two in them." He nodded his head sagely as if articulating quite the philosophical insight.

"And you are sure of this, Uncle Duncan?" Tabitha couldn't help but ask. Given the state that the man had arrived home in, it was hard to believe he'd achieved anything during his visit to Boodles. However, the man stood by his information.

"Then, we should make a trip to see Mr Bailey tomorrow," Wolf said. "If anyone knows where we can find Caroline Turnbull, I imagine it to be him."

"He does seem to know everyone and anyone involved with the London theatre scene," Tabitha agreed.

The dowager remained surprisingly subdued. Tabitha could guess why; the woman despised Christopher "Kit" Bailey, impresario, even more than she did Uncle Duncan. Both men shared an uncanny ability to get under the woman's armour and she did not enjoy the experience. In their last investigation, the dowager had been similarly torn between not wanting to be excluded and making every effort to avoid Kit's company.

Finally, she said through clenched teeth, "I will accompany you tomorrow."

"Are you sure, Mama? I realise you do not care for Mr Bailey."

"I do not care for broccoli; I loathe Mr Bailey. However, I refuse to exclude myself from this investigation. I assume we will make a quick stop at the theatre, learn where we can find this so-called singer and then be on our way. I can tolerate even Mr Bailey for such a brief period."

The rest of the meal continued uneventfully. After dinner, they retired to the drawing room, where Uncle Duncan promptly fell asleep again. Jane played the piano for them for some time, and Lily and the dowager made such a point of ignoring each other that Tabitha was extremely happy when the evening came to an early end.

They knew from past experience not to arrive at the theatre too early; thespians were late-night, not early-morning people. Given the dowager's distaste for leaving her boudoir before noon, Tabitha and Wolf agreed to arrive to fetch her at one o'clock.

As they got ready for bed that evening, Tabitha bemoaned their slow pace. "An entire day has passed, and I feel we are no further along in our investigation. And now Clarence will have to spend a night in a prison cell."

Wolf came and put his hands on her arm, "Tabitha, surely you never imagined we would solve this case in less than a day? We are good but even we are not that good." He said this last sentence with a gentle smile on his face and was rewarded by the slight brightening of his wife's mood. "And let us not forget that Clarence has refused to cooperate with us. Perhaps the reality of a night or two on a thin prison mattress rather than his luxurious feather bed will be just what Clarence needs to make him rethink how cooperative he wishes to be."

Tabitha hoped Wolf was right. "I assume that if the Home Secretary were inclined to intervene, he would have done so already, and we would have heard something."

"I cannot imagine otherwise. If Sir Matthew is willing to let the Earl of Warwick spend even one night in prison, then he is willing to let him spend many more. Unless something more compelling arises quickly, the press has a juicy topic that they will be disinclined to let go of any time soon. The public has been braying for aristocratic blood, and now Clarence is being thrown to the lions."

This rather gruesome metaphor did not help Tabitha's mood. Now, she contemplated a possibility she hadn't wanted even to consider earlier. "Might he hang for this?"

Wolf sighed. "I assume it is possible, though unlikely. It may feed the populist hunger merely to see a man such as Clarence even brought to trial. I cannot imagine that anyone in government wishes to execute a peer of the realm – that would set a disturbing precedent." He shook his head. "We are in uncharted waters. Only time will tell how this will play itself out. Meanwhile, we must do all we can to clear Clarence's name."

As they prepared for bed that night, Tabitha remembered she hadn't yet mentioned the dowager's surprisingly insightful observation that Clarence was trying to protect someone.

"I cannot believe we missed that," Wolf said, smacking his head.

"Indeed. I've contemplated this all day and wondered who in Redding's orbit Clarence might care enough about to protect. The only person I can come up with is this mistress that they both once had relationships with."

"It is possible. Yet Fiona made it sound as if this particular mistress was in the distant past for Clarence."

"Well, perhaps she was once. Maybe she has resurfaced," Tabitha suggested.

"Or perhaps Fiona just has limited information. It is surprising enough that she even knows what she does. If she and Clarence have the kind of relationship she claims they do, I doubt he had only one mistress many years ago. Perhaps this woman has continued to be part of his life, and he suspects she might have had reason to attack Redding."

It was possible. It was also all a lot of speculation. One thing was for sure: they needed to track this mistress down and talk to her. At this point, she was the only thread for them to tug on.

CHAPTER 11

The following morning's newspapers did not give Tabitha or Wolf cause for hope; if anything, the worst of the scandal sheets and half-penny presses, particularly the Daily Mail, seemed to treat Clarence's arrest as a win for the common people. Now they had got wind of a shared paramour in the victim and the accused's past, this was declared the motive.

"This really is the most sensationalist rubbish," Wolf declared in disgust as he read the Daily Mail headline over his toast and tea. "The Bloody Earl murdered in a jealous rage."

"The Bloody Earl? Is that what they're calling him? It is quite catchy, and the double-entendre is clever," Tabitha acknowledged. They were eating breakfast alone, probably a good thing given that Lily was now a guest at Chesterton House. These headlines were not likely to lessen her anxiety.

Tabitha considered the headline. "How did they find out about the mistress? And more to the point, do any of these newspapers seem to have any idea who she might be?"

Wolf shook his head. "Who knows how they found out. These Grub Street hacks have been known to sink low in order to rake up dirt. It is telling that The Westminster Gazette has not resorted to such tactics and merely has a story on the baron's background and how it has intersected with Clarence's over time, particularly as boys."

"Is that written by Andrews?"

"Yes. Bear came back late last night; it seemed he had to track Andrews down. He left a note in my study that confirmed that Andrews knows no more than he has written. This article seems to confirm this. It is hard to imagine he has more information on this mistress than the other newspapers and yet failed to publish it."

Tabitha sighed; while this wasn't unexpected, it was yet another dead-end in this investigation. Wolf folded up the newspapers, which was just as well because Jane and Lily joined them moments later. Talbot had informed them Uncle Duncan had left the house late the previous evening and hadn't returned home yet. This might have been cause for worry if they were talking about anyone other than Duncan MacAlister.

There were dark circles under Lily's eyes, and she didn't look as if she had slept well. Jane looked no more rested.

Tabitha realised they hadn't seen Viscount Tobias since the dinner two nights previously. "I hope Tobias does not feel unwelcome in this house?" she said to Lily. "Please know that our affection for him is unchanged, regardless of the outcome of these charges against his father."

Lily replied with a wan smile. "Toby is not staying away because of you and Cousin Jeremy," Lily assured her. The young woman's meaning was clear; Tobias was avoiding the dowager.

"While I cannot promise that he will not run into your grandmother here, I assure you that neither Wolf nor I will tolerate her talking about Tobias' family with anything less than respect."

"I do not believe that he worries about how she may speak to him but rather how he might speak to her. I spoke to him briefly on the telephone yesterday and he is furious that she has forbidden us from marrying, even if the accusations against the earl are dropped."

It was hard to argue with the wisdom of Tobias' actions; he had known the dowager all his life and was fully aware of the perils of going into battle against her.

With a morning to kill before visiting Kit Bailey, Tabitha decided to visit Melody and her two new playmates in the nursery. She was sure that spending an hour or two with the children would lighten her mood.

Given the spur-of-the-moment decision to hire Rose O'Leary and have her come and live at Chesterton House with her two young boys, no initial accommodation was made in the nursery, and Mary looked after all three children. However, despite Mary's youth, energy, and joy in being with the children, Tabitha quickly realised it the unfairness of asking the nursemaid to take on the extra responsibility without assistance.

As luck would have it, Mary had a younger sister, Kitty, who was old enough to enter service. Ever since the family's return from Corfu, Kitty had been installed as a junior nursemaid. Kitty was fourteen years old and not much more than a child herself. She was a tall, solid young woman with ruddy cheeks and brown, curly hair. All the children took to the new nursemaid immediately, but the twin boys seemed particularly attached. Perhaps that was because they somehow sensed Mary's utter devotion to Melody and decided that they needed an adult presence in the nursery who favoured them.

The two sisters seemed to be managing the rambunctious group of children very well. As Tabitha approached the nursery, she noted the sound of childish laughter and prattle that was happy but not out of control.

Tabitha stopped outside of the ajar nursery door for a moment and listened to Melody say in a scolding tone, "No, Kitty. That's an A, not a B. Mary, Kitty needs to start lessons with Mr James!"

While the precocious little girl's schoolmarm tone was quite amusing, Tabitha realised the child did have a point; Kitty needed to learn to read and to do at least basic arithmetic.

When Melody first came to live at Chesterton House and Mr James' services had been engaged, Tabitha had insisted that all the servants be given the opportunity to study with him if they wanted to. Some, if not all, had taken her up on the offer. Most had learned to read and gained some familiarity with their numbers and had then stopped. Mary, who realised that she had to keep up with her highly intelligent charge, continued to sit with Mr James at least once a week. Though sometimes Tabitha wondered whether there might be some more personal reason for the maid to continue.

Regardless of Mary's primary motivation, the nursemaid's ability to read with Melody was a good thing, and Tabitha made a mental note to include Kitty in future lessons.

When Melody and the boys saw Tabitha enter the room, they threw down the dolls they were playing with and rushed over, jostling to be the first to hug her.

Laughing, Tabitha stooped and gathered all three children into a hug. "Is everyone being good today for Mary and Kitty?"

"Liam spilled his milk this morning and then blamed Willy. I helped Mary clean it up," Melody said in a pointed tone.

"Well, that was very good of you to help Mary, Melody. But you should not be telling tales on the boys," Tabitha added.

"I spilled the milk 'cause he hit me," Liam explained in a doleful voice.

"I hit him 'cause he called me a bad name," Willy said in his defence.

"Now, now. Let us move on from this unfortunate incident. What game were you playing when I came in?"

"We were about to have a dolls' tea party, but Liam wouldn't have his doll say what I told him to," Melody complained.

"Not fair," Liam answered. "I want to be in charge of my doll. S'not fun if you boss me around."

"Children, this is not the time to bicker," Mary said authoritatively. Tabitha bit back a smile at seeing the young woman so in control of the nursery; Mary had come a long way in less than a year.

"Mary is perfectly correct," Tabitha agreed. "Perhaps I can join in with the tea party. Melody, I do not know how a doll should behave so perhaps you can help me and Willy and Liam can be in charge of their own dolls."

Melody considered the offer for a moment before accepting. They spent the next hour with Melody choreographing the dolls' tea party, including Liam and Willy's part, despite her agreement otherwise. Eventually, the boys grudgingly accepted Melody as both writer, director, and lead in the game and went along with the lines they were given.

When the game eventually ended, the boys insisted that their payback for conciliatory behaviour be a more physical game. They quickly agreed on Blind Man's Buff—and insisted that Mary and Kitty participate while Tabitha was in charge of ensuring that no one strayed too far from the group when blindfolded.

As she watched the game quickly descend into giggles, Tabitha heart swelled with gratitude. She had made her peace with never bearing a child, but she realised there was more than one way to be a parent. A nursery full of happy, loving children was so much more than she had ever dared to hope for, and she silently gave thanks for her bounty.

Finally, Tabitha forced herself to say goodbye to the children. If they were to eat an early, light lunch and then meet the dowager at the agreed-upon time, she needed to change her dress.

At one o'clock, as agreed, the Pembroke carriage pulled up outside of the dowager's home. Tabitha understood the dowager's belief that the upper class's power came from the deference and servility their status and rank inspired in the lower orders. The dowager preferred to overawe those she encountered with her finery. That she considered Kit Bailey her nemesis only amplified this preference, as evidenced when she entered the carriage bedecked in diamonds that Tabitha knew for a fact she usually saved for balls and royal occasions.

Her furs and jewels were outrageous enough that even Wolf noticed but wisely said nothing, even as he looked at Tabitha pointedly and raised his eyebrows.

Tabitha decided to wake the sleeping lion. "Mama, you are dressed grandly for a trip to Drury Lane. Do you have a social call later that you need us to drop you at?" Then she added rather naughtily, "Perhaps at Buckingham Palace?"

"Do not attempt humour, Tabitha. It does not become you. I am dressed no more regally than usual. As you well know, I always ensure the lower classes understand when someone of quality is amongst them."

Tabitha debated whether to ask whether the diamonds were for Kit Bailey's benefit but decided that she had tempted fate long enough. Soon enough, they pulled up at the large, imposing Drury Lane Theatre that was actually on Catherine Street. As its grand portico came into sight, it occurred to Tabitha that they hadn't considered the possibility that Kit might have moved on to another theatre.

Knocking on the stage door situated on Drury Lane, Tabitha whispered her concern to Wolf. The same thought occurred to him, and they were relieved when a young stagehand opened the door and assured them that Mr Bailey was in his office.

CHAPTER 12

The stagehand led them through the large, busy backstage area, which seemed full of sets lying around higgledy-piggledy. He then took them through the dark maze of corridors that Tabitha remembered from their visits in February.

The stagehand knocked on the door and was answered with, "Come hither!"

On entering the office, Tabitha was reminded that, despite its horrible, upholstered chairs, the office was far less garish than the one in Brighton had been.

Kit Bailey looked up in surprise at their entrance. His blue eyes sparkled with mischief when he saw the dowager was with them. "Ah, Lord and Lady Pembroke. How lovely to see you. And Lady Bracknell, always a pleasure."

Referring to the dowager as Oscar Wilde's infamous, imperious harridan of a character was always sure to ruffle the dowager's feathers, and this time was no exception. However, for a change, she gritted her teeth and forced her face into a simulacrum of a smile.

"Mr Bailey!" she said, stopping herself from saying more and thus giving the man more fodder for his mockery.

"What brings you all to my theatre? Surely this isn't a social call?" As he spoke, Kit indicated that the dowager and Tabitha should each take one of the ugly chairs. Wolf said he was happy to stand.

"We are here in the hope that you can help us," Wolf explained.

"Always happy to be of service, milord," Kit said with just a mildly sardonic undertone.

"For reasons that we cannot go into, we are seeking information on a woman we believe used to be on the stage, primarily in operas. Her name is Caroline Turnbull."

Kit sat back in his chair and folded his hands over his capacious stomach. "Now, there's a name I haven't heard in a long time. I knew Caroline back in the day when I first set out to tread the boards. Quite a looker she was back then. I quite fancied her myself, but she didn't have any interest in a lowly actor. She set her sights set on bigger and better things."

This was interesting! Tabitha exchanged looks with Wolf. "What kind of bigger and better things?"

"I did hear word that she had her eye on a toff. But that was a long time ago. I changed companies after that and lost sight of her. Of course, I'd see her headlining shows around town, but I had my own problems and never gave her another thought."

"So, you do not know where we might find her?" Wolf asked despondently.

"Well, I don't. But now you mention it, I think Roland mentioned her recently. It seems that he was in the ensemble for her swan song performance."

Tabitha remembered Roland Grant, the handsome, golden-haired lead actor, very well from their last investigation. Despite his lack of complete candour with them regarding all the events surrounding Genevieve Moreau's disappearance, it was hard not to like the charming thespian.

"Let's take a wander over to his dressing room and see what he has to say," Kit offered, rising from his chair.

Tabitha was glad Kit offered to accompany them; she remembered how confusing the labyrinth of dark corridors was. Finally, they rounded a corner and found themselves in a familiar-looking hallway. Kit stopped outside a plain oak door with a small, simple brass nameplate that said, Roland Grant. He rapped sharply on the door and was hailed to enter.

They entered the dressing room to find the golden-haired Adonis sprawled out on the couch to the side of the room, which looked as messy and chaotic as Tabitha remembered. Roland Grant was as mesmerising to look at as she remembered as well. Long, golden lashes framed his striking blue eyes. Taller than average height, with a slim build, the man's features seemed to be perfect. Kit told them during their previous investigation that Roland did not enjoy the company of women. However, Tabitha could imagine how adoring female fans might throw themselves at the actor, given the chance.

When he recognised his visitors, Roland sat up and attempted to tidy up some of the clothes strewn around him.

"Lord and Lady Pembroke, to what do I owe this honour?" Then suddenly, his face took on a panicked look. "Is it Gen? Has something happened to her?" Turning, he chastised Kit, "I told you that you should have given her a second chance."

Previously, Tabitha wondered whether Kit had taken Genevieve back into the theatre company after her stunt, and this suggested that he hadn't.

"Mr Grant, we are not here about Miss Moreau. We have heard nothing more of her since we discovered her on Cloth Fair."

Roland visibly relaxed. "Well, thank heavens for that. She disappeared for a while after the incident. She didn't mean any harm, you know."

Neither Tabitha nor Wolf was convinced of this, but they were not there to discuss Genevieve Moreau. Instead, Wolf said, "Mr Bailey has informed us you are acquainted with a woman we are keen to track down: Caroline Turnbull."

Roland stood with a pile of clothes in his arms. Now, he sat back down and put them next to him. "Dear old Caroline. Poor old gal."

"Why do you say that?" Wolf asked.

"I was just another face in the gaggle at the time. We were playing The Yeomen of the Guard, and she was Elsie Maynard, the young, innocent, sweetly romantic street singer female lead." He raised his eyebrows and gave a half-smile. "Of course, she was a bit long-in-the-tooth to play young and innocent, if you ask me. She still sang like an angel, and I supposed that was enough for the audience. Or at least it was while she could sing."

"What do you mean?" Tabitha asked.

"She began to have problems with her voice. At first, she thought she'd taken a chill or overstrained it. Her understudy went on for a night or two, but her voice didn't get better. She couldn't hold the notes; some days, she was so raspy she could barely speak. When it continued for two weeks, the opera director suggested she take some time off to rest and come back when her voice was improved. She never returned."

"And when would this have been?"

Roland pondered the question. "Well, it was before I met Gen, which must be seven years ago at least. That production of *A Midsummer Night's Dream* was my big break. So, I'd say it was at least eight years ago." He paused. "Yes, definitely 1890. I remember because I was in the middle of a quite melodramatic love affair at the time and Caroline was very kind to me when she found me in tears during rehearsal one day. And I know I met that particular lover in February of 1890."

"Didn't you tell me you ran into her about a year ago?" Kit interjected.

"Now that you mention it, I remember I did. Honestly, I hardly knew it was Caroline. She was exquisite in her heyday, but now she was almost disfigured beyond recognition. Her cheeks were sunken, her skin pock-marked. She walked with this odd, unsteady gait and had these tremors in her hands. It was quite horrifying."

"Where did you run into her?" Tabitha asked.

Suddenly, Roland took on a furtive, nervous look. "It was around London Bridge, Southwark area. I was there... I was there to see a friend."

Wolf suspected the kind of friend a man of Roland Grant's tastes might find around the docklands, but he kept the thought to himself. Instead, he asked, "Was she living around there?"

"Yes, she told me she lived next to The George Inn. They let her do some laundry to make a bob or two. Honestly, I couldn't get away quick enough; she was a terrifying sight. I felt terrible because I'm sure she saw the horror in my eyes. Poor old gal."

Finally, they were getting somewhere. The dowager had said nothing after entering the dressing room but sat on the dressing table chair, regarding the room with disgust.

Now, she asked, "And did this Caroline Turnbull ever speak to you of any paramours?"

Roland Grant looked at her in surprise as if he somehow hadn't noticed the diminutive yet imperious old toff dripping in diamonds in front of him.

"Paramours? Lovers, you mean?"

The dowager sniffed but acknowledged that was what she meant.

"Caroline and I were never that close. She was the leading lady, after all, and I was a nobody. But now that you mention it, when she found me crying that day, she said she understood having a broken heart. Didn't say anything else, though."

Roland Grant seemed to have nothing more useful to share. They bid the actor farewell, and Kit led them out to the stage door.

Kit took Tabitha's hand and bowed over it, intoning, "Parting is such sweet sorrow." Then, turning to the dowager, he said with a wicked grin, "And farewell to you, Lady Bracknell."

Now that they had the information they had come for, the dowager saw no reason to continue to hold back and spat back, "As your Mr Shakespeare wrote, 'Out of my sight! Thou dost infect mine eyes'."

"Touché!" Kit replied good-humouredly. Wolf thought it best to leave before the dowager became any further riled up.

Back in the carriage, the dowager said, as if there were no need for discussion, "Then let us make our way to this George Inn."

Wolf sighed; were they really having this conversation again? "You cannot visit Southwark in those diamonds or indeed in any jewellery. In fact, I believe we should all dress less ostentatiously."

"Poppycock! It has been my experience that the masses are best cowed or at least dumbstruck with awe in order to worm information out of them."

"Mama, while we have all experienced that sometimes this is the case. In other instances, a more subtle approach is more appropriate. Wolf is best placed to decide which of those two circumstances this is likely to be." Even as she said this, she thought about the last time she and Wolf donned costumes to visit one of the poorer areas in London. "I wonder whether this might be another opportunity for John Champion and his trusted photographer, Miss Smart, to be investigating a story."

"What on earth are you talking about, Tabitha?" the dowager demanded irritably. "Who on earth are John Champion and Miss Smart?"

Tabitha smiled and explained. When she and Wolf visited Battersea Park Road seeking information about Genevieve Moreau's family, he had worn some clothes from his valet, Thompson, and she had borrowed a dress from Ginny. Their story had been that they were writing a newspaper piece on the famous actress. It seemed like the kind of ruse that might work again in these circumstances. But what about the dowager? How on earth would they persuade her not to come?

Suddenly, inspiration struck. Tabitha hoped Wolf would take her lead as she said slyly, "There is one thing of which we can be sure: John and Amanda do not travel by carriage. I doubt they earn enough to travel by hackney cab either."

"Such things are of no concern. We will have Madison drop us a short way off."

It was obvious this would be the dowager's parry, and Tabitha prepared a thrust of her own. In truth, as soon as she said the words, she realised they were not only expedient under the current circumstances but true. "We do not know how broadly we might want to investigate within Southwark and the surrounding boroughs. We have been lucky in the past when the carriage dropped us off, and we walked the last quarter mile. It is only a matter of luck we have not been spotted by people who then might spread the word these so-called journalists, or whoever we are posing as, might not be all they claim."

Wolf kept silent throughout this, fascinated to see where Tabitha would go with this line of thought. For his part, when he was a thief-taker, he always walked or occasionally took the omnibus, tram, or even underground train. However, given the traffic congestion in London, he found the omnibuses and trams slow, and the underground train made him claustrophobic, so he walked when he could. He always enjoyed walking and found it conducive to problem-solving.

Not being able to get around London in any of these manners was one thing he believed he lost on inheriting the earldom. When he first moved to Mayfair, he donned his thief-taker outfit once and walked back from Whitechapel in the course of an investigation. The dowager came across him and made it quite clear that the Earl of Pembroke should not be seen walking the streets. What would people think?

Given this, he sensed what Tabitha was trying to achieve, but he was also happy if this meant he might occasionally get around using a less resplendent means of travel.

For her part, the dowager was torn; she was an elderly woman who often resorted to using a walking stick. She could neither imagine walking great distances nor abide by the idea of the Dowager Countess of Pembroke strolling the streets like a commoner. That she might be in disguise and playing the part of a character was by the by. She was an aristocrat, and she assumed that her much higher rank was always evident, even if she was dressed as a pauper. It never occurred to her that if this were true, it might diminish the effectiveness of such a disguise.

Finally, deciding to take a cautious approach to Tabitha's suggestion, the dowager asked, "If not the carriage, then what do you suggest?"

"I suggest we avail ourselves of the omnibus," Tabitha said, trying to keep her tone neutral.

"An omnibus! What do you imagine I am? Some Irish scullery maid?"

Wolf realised this was his time to speak. "What a wonderful idea, Tabitha. If I am correct, we can catch one omnibus at Piccadilly that takes us to Ludgate Hill, where we can change for another to London Bridge."

"Two! You expect me to take two of those contraptions?" The dowager's conniption reached peak hysteria. "To sit amongst the dirty, snivelling masses for who knows how long. And then to do so again in return? Have you lost your mind, Jeremy?"

Wolf knew that while Tabitha fired the first shot over the bow, he must be the one to bring this battle to its conclusion. While the dowager deferred to no one, she had slightly more respect for his word than for his wife's.

"Lady Pembroke, we do not expect you to take anything. Tabitha and I are willing to forgo your assistance if necessary. Suffice it to say, you may meet us back at Chesterton House for a full report of our activities."

Taking a deep breath, the dowager narrowed her eyes at them but said in a tone that might almost be described as ruefully admiring, "Well played, Tabitha. Well played."

Chapter 13

The dowager accepted defeat, if not gracefully, at least with a degree of resignation, and asked that she be dropped off at home before Tabitha and Wolf continued to Chesterton House to don their disguises.

"If I am to be excluded, I see no reason to wait around your drawing room listening to Mr MacAlister snore or worse. I will plan to return for dinner when you will acquaint me with all the pertinent details."

Given that they had no idea how long they might be, and it was already past two o'clock, this seemed like the best compromise they would extract from the wily old woman. Within the hour, they were dressed in their servants' clothes and on their way to Piccadilly. There seemed no reason not to take advantage of the Pembroke carriage to at least take them that far.

In fact, once they were comfortably settled in it, Tabitha said a little guiltily, "Is there any reason we should not take the carriage all the way to Ludgate Hill? Surely that far from London Bridge, it will not harm our charade to be seen descending from it."

Wolf laughed, "I am all for the expediency and comfort of such a suggestion, but might I just point out that we will rue the day the dowager countess ever gets wind of this? However, given the time, I think it is a sensible suggestion. Madison can be counted upon to keep his own counsel on this matter."

Of course, the traffic in London would be an obstacle whether they were in a horse-drawn omnibus or a carriage, but at least they did not have to stop constantly to allow passengers to ascend and descend. Given this and unusually light traffic, they reached their destination in not much more than twenty-five minutes. Wolf instructed Madison to wait there for them for three hours. If they took any longer, he should return to Mayfair, get Bear, and come to Southwark to look for them. He didn't expect that they would run into any trouble during this outing, but it was best to be prepared.

As they descended from the carriage, Tabitha felt both excited and nervous. Ever since Wolf entered her life, she had ventured further and further from the safety of her comfortable and privileged yet confining existence. A trip on public transportation was yet another step away from the proscribed, sheltered life a woman of her rank was expected to live. While she had exploited the dowager's certain unease at the idea of travelling thus, the truth was that Tabitha was hardly less discomfited.

Madison dropped them a few streets from Ludgate Hill. Wolf could only imagine the comments if they exited a fancy carriage to catch an omnibus. They didn't need that gossip following them to London Bridge.

When they arrived at the spot at Ludgate Hill where people usually hailed the omnibus, Tabitha began to look out for it eagerly. While she had seen the colourful, sturdy, box-like vehicles on the roads all the time as she travelled around London, Tabitha never gave them much thought until now. She tingled with anticipation of the new experience.

There was a group of people congregated where Wolf imagined the omnibus usually stopped, and so he and Tabitha made their way over to them. Wolf imagined it to be a good thing it was not the end of the work-day, or they might have waited for multiple omnibuses to pass before being able to get on one.

They only waited a few minutes before they spotted the rectangular wooden carriage with its large, spoked wheels, pulled by two enormous draught horses, making its way towards them. The driver pulled up beside them, and people started stepping onto the rear of the omnibus, where the conductor collected fares and helped them on and off.

As the crowd pushed them along, and it was almost their time to step up, it occurred to Tabitha that they needed to have coins on them to pay. She rarely carried small change with her. Luckily, as Wolf helped her into the omnibus, he reached into his pocket and put two pennies in the conductor's hand.

There were already quite a few people seated inside. Some of the newly boarded passengers headed up to the omnibus roof, where the seats cost only a half-penny. As they moved inside, Tabitha spotted two free seats towards the middle of the carriage.

They took their seats on the wooden benches just in time as the omnibus lurched forward. Tabitha was used to the plush, padded seating of the luxurious Pembroke carriage. However, whatever discomfort she felt sitting on the hard, unpadded benches as the omnibus rattled and bounced over the cobbled streets was barely noticed in her excitement at the new experience.

Looking around at her fellow passengers, she saw women with baskets of groceries, a young man who looked like some kind of clerk, and a collection of working-class people going about their day. There was even a vicar seated on the bench across from them. No one paid Tabitha or Wolf any mind. Their costumes must be good enough that they blended in with the rank and file of common folks, she thought.

Wolf was dressed in his valet, Thompson's, bowler hat and suit. The last time he had borrowed the clothes, he wore the man's greatcoat. However, this was a warm day in May, and he left it behind. For her part, Tabitha had again borrowed a simple navy-blue dress from Ginny and again carried Bear's pocket Kodak camera to complete her disguise. As she looked out of the window as London passed by, it crossed Tabitha's mind, not for the first time, that they really needed to get attire of their own for such adventures. They couldn't keep borrowing clothes from their servants. She made a note to ask Mrs O'Leary to arrange for a variety of suitable outfits to be purchased.

The ride took longer than it would have in the carriage because the omnibus kept stopping to let passengers on and off. Nevertheless, within twenty minutes, the conductor rang a bell and announced, "London Bridge."

Tabitha and Wolf stood and made their way to the back of the omnibus and, when it came to a stop, became part of the stream of passengers making their way off. Tabitha didn't think she had ever been to Southwark before. Even if she had driven through it in a carriage, she certainly never walked around the neighbourhood. The omnibus crossed London Bridge and then stopped next to the train station on the busy Borough High Street thoroughfare.

Borough High Street was noisy and crowded. The bustling Borough Market was off to the right, and spilling out from it, street vendors hawked their wares. There were more than the usual number of horse-drawn carts as goods were ferried to and from the nearby docks. Nearby breweries generated powerful smells of hops, beer, and grain, and these odours mixed with the decidedly less salubrious ones coming from the river to create a rather unpleasant melange.

While it was immediately apparent that the poverty here equalled the East End, the bustle of commerce with all its attendant market traders, delivery boys, shoppers, and even bowler-hatted clerks coming and going from the City, made it a less intimidating neighbourhood.

Because London Bridge Station was such a major transportation hub, there were also plenty of travellers and workers moving cargo shipments. All in all, it was a lively area where people from various backgrounds and classes mixed easily as they went about their day. It didn't have the oppressive feel of desperation Tabitha experienced in Whitechapel and its environs.

Wolf had some idea of The George Inn's location, and Tabitha stayed near as he guided them down the bustling Borough High Street. From the street, the inn looked no different from any other red-bricked public house in London. But a wrought-iron gate led to a courtyard where the full glory of the historic, galleried coaching inn, one of the last of its kind, came into view.

The three-storey, white-painted timber building, complete with galleries, ran along the length of the courtyard. For a moment, Tabitha imagined it was the end of the 16th century, and that Shakespeare and The Lord Chamberlain's Men were about to perform in the large, cobble-stoned courtyard. They made their way through a door into the main bar. Dark wooden beams on the low ceiling showed how old the building was. The air was thick with pipe smoke, and a musty, damp odour that spoke of centuries near the River Thames hung in the air.

In many ways, the inn did not differ from any other London public house or tavern; even though it was late in the afternoon, barflies still nursed tankards of ale, and the occasional dock worker wandered in who probably should have been somewhere else.

Tabitha and Wolf had discussed what fabricated story they would tell for why they were asking about Caroline Turnbull. They decided to use a version of the story they told when they undertook a similar line of questioning about Genevieve Moreau: that they were investigating a possible celebrity scandal. Instead of the story being about Caroline herself, they landed on using her past connection, however tenuous, to Roland Grant.

Clutching her Kodak camera to her, Tabitha followed Wolf as he made his way to the bar. A middle-aged, portly woman stood behind it, looking rather vacantly out at the smattering of customers. When she saw the handsome young man and his pretty companion approach, the woman, Ellie Perkins, perked up; if nothing else, they added some variety to an otherwise quite slow and boring afternoon.

"What can I get you, luv?" Ellie asked genially.

"A pint of ale for me and a small beer for the lady," Wolf replied.

"'Aven't seen you around 'ere," the woman observed as she went about getting their drinks.

Tabitha and Wolf took two seats at the bar. The woman was friendly and chatty, so she seemed the obvious place to begin their questioning.

"Actually, this is our first time in this fine establishment," Wolf said with what he hoped was a disarming smile.

"Fine establishment, is it? Well, I wouldn't go that far. But I'll let my 'Arry know. So, what brings you this way? By the sounds of you, this isn't your normal neighbourhood."

Wolf had done his best to roughen his usually round vowels and to sound somewhat less well-spoken. However, this woman possessed a good ear, so there seemed little point in denying the obvious. Instead, Wolf just shrugged his shoulders.

Rather than answering her last question, he replied to the first, "Actually, my colleague and I," as he said this, Wolf gestured towards Tabitha, "are looking for an informed local to answer some questions."

The woman looked at them suspiciously. "Folks round 'ere don't take kindly to nosy outsiders poking about."

"Of course. And we understand that. Let me start again. My name is John Champion. I'm a journalist and Miss Smart here is my photographer. We're with The News of the World." The beauty of this particular charade was that it seemed that even usually private individuals who didn't "take kindly to nosy outsiders" seemed beguiled by the idea of being quoted in a newspaper. If he correctly interpreted the change that came over Ellie's face and demeanour, she was no exception.

"From that 'alfpenny screecher, are you?" she asked in a gleeful tone that belied the somewhat derogatory term she used. "And there's someone in Southwark interesting enough to catch that rag's interest, is there? Maybe my 'Arry has a double life and is really a duke," she said, laughing at her own joke.

Tabitha and Wolf exchanged glances; now was the time to go in for the kill. "Have you heard of the actor Roland Grant?" Wolf asked. Although it seemed unlikely this barmaid patronised the theatres of the West End, Roland provided sufficient fodder for newspaper gossip that the woman might have known his name.

Ellie cocked her head to one side as she considered the question. She had learned her letters as a child, but her reading skills were not all they might be. Her "'Arry'", however, could read and would often entertain his wife at the end of an evening by reading her some of the juiciest titbits from The News of the World.

"'Aint 'e the one that sent that actress an 'undred red roses?" she asked.

Wolf didn't know, yet happily concurred.

"What's 'e gone and done now?" Ellie asked, her eyes gleaming at the thought of getting a head start on some juicy gossip.

Wolf seemed momentarily stumped, so Tabitha jumped in. "Well, as you are clearly aware, he's quite the man about town." Ellie nodded her head in fervent agreement as if the moniker "Man about town" was sufficient for both women to understand what they were talking about. Tabitha continued, "We are writing a piece on how he came to be the man he is today. What is the real story of Roland Grant?"

Ellie Perkins was utterly caught up in the narrative and leaned forward with a conspiratorial smirk. "Bit of a flash cove, is 'e?"

As it happened, Tabitha and Wolf knew Roland Grant was not interested in chasing skirt, but there was no reason for this woman to think that Roland was anything other than the lady-killer she imagined him to be. They both smiled in apparent assent.

Finally, Tabitha said, as casually as possible, "We heard a rumour that earlier in Roland Grant's career, before he made the big time, he acted in the ensemble of an operetta where the leading lady was a singer known as Caroline Turnbull." Tabitha leaned in even closer and said in a low voice, "We heard that there may have been something of a romance between Roland and this Miss Turnbull."

Tabitha felt somewhat guilty telling this lie, but she doubted Roland Grant would mind. Rumours such as these merely fuelled the falsehood that he chased women. What Caroline Turnbull might think about the story was another matter. Still, in this case, the ends justified the means.

At Caroline Turnbull's name, Ellie Perkins registered both recognition but also sadness. "Caro? Is that who 'e was mucking around with back in the day?"

"So, you know Miss Turnbull?" Wolf asked hopefully.

"Well, knew 'er more like. Popped 'er clogs a week ago, she did. She'd been poorly for a long time." She then put her hand to her mouth as if about to relay a big secret. "I 'eard rumour that it was the pox that done 'er in. Nasty business if that's true."

Then Ellie made a face as if deep in thought. "She used to tell me she'd been a famous singer and actress. Can't say I ever really believed it. Not given that she ended up living in a tenement in Southwark. Said she'd been a real looker. But again, it was 'ard to believe what with all them pocks and other nasty stuff on her face."

Chapter 14

Ellie Perkins had little more to tell. As Roland suggested, Caroline Turnbull was reduced to doing laundry for the inn. Though, Ellie confided, her health became so bad recently that her daughter had done most of it, even though she also worked around Leather Market, down the street towards Bermondsey. As far as Ellie knew, the young woman, Sally, worked in the dressing yards, sorting and preparing the raw hides. Just based on that brief description, it sounded like awful work for a young woman.

Ellie said that she hadn't seen Sally since Caroline Turnbull's death. She gave them what she believed was the address for the residence the women had shared. Ellie would have been happy to gossip to the reporters for longer. However, the bar was filling with patrons, and eventually, Tabitha and Wolf were able to slip out.

As they made their way back out to Borough High Street, Wolf pulled out his pocket watch. It was past five o'clock. He didn't know what hours the labourers worked in the leather trade, but he could imagine they'd be long and probably gruelling. However, they were in Southwark, and it would be a lost opportunity if they didn't at least knock on Sally Turnbull's door and see if she was there and willing to talk.

As they paused outside the wrought-iron gates, Tabitha pointed out, "We do not know for sure that Redding's death was anything to with Caroline Turnbull."

"No, we do not," Wolf agreed. "However, we do not have many other lines of inquiry to pursue."

After cocking her head to the side and nibbling on her lip, a sure sign of contemplation, Tabitha said, "It is interesting, and potentially meaningful, that Caroline Turnbull died last week."

"Perhaps. If nothing else, it rules her out as our murderer."

"It sounds as if poor Miss Turnbull did not have a pleasant end." Tabitha hesitated. While she didn't want to be viewed as a shrinking violet, too delicate to learn about the harsh realities of life, Tabitha was raised by a mother perhaps even more imperious and domineering than the dowager. Lady Jameson, the Dowager Marchioness of Cambridgeshire, had very decided notions of what young ladies should be exposed to, and venereal diseases were very much not on that list. As much as she longed to break free of the confining societal norms she had been raised in, old habits were hard to break.

Finally, taking a deep breath and reminding herself that she was asking this of her husband, not a stranger, Tabitha inquired, "What disease do you think Caroline Turnbull suffered from so horribly?"

Wolf had long got over any reservations about his wife's ability to hear about the harsher aspect of life. He replied without hesitation, "From what we have heard, I would imagine that she suffered from syphilis, as Mrs Perkins suggested. While the disease has many horrific symptoms, everything that has been described in terms of her physical deformities conforms to what I have heard about the illness."

Tabitha shuddered at the thought. Though her understanding of syphilis was limited, she'd heard enough to understand the disease's devastating effects, causing a slow and agonising demise for its victims. She remembered a horribly disfigured uncle who eventually went insane. At the time, her mother had refused to discuss what was making Uncle Jamie sick, but now, as an adult, Tabitha realised that it was likely it had been syphilis.

She sighed at the memory of her jovial Uncle Jamie, who always made her laugh and usually carried a peppermint humbug or two for his favourite niece. She grimaced at the pain and suffering he must have experienced.

Tabitha shook off her gloom. "When we are home, we can write up a notecard with the open question of whether her illness is in any way relevant to this case. Meanwhile, let us find Sally Turnbull's address and see if she happens to be home."

Finding the address Ellie Perkins had provided proved easy. Even in a neighbourhood of dilapidated buildings with crumbling bricks, sagging roofs, and peeling paint, the house they had been directed to was ramshackle. The front door looked as if it was barely staying on its hinges. Wolf knocked gingerly on it, unsure if the door would fall out of its frame if he weren't careful.

When no one answered, Wolf knocked again. Just as they were about to give up and leave, they heard a window opening above and a voice called down, "Wot?"

Stepping back and craning his neck, Wolf looked up and said, "Good afternoon. We are sorry to disturb you, but we are looking for Miss Sally Turnbull and were told that she lives here."

"Not 'ere," the voice snapped.

"But she lives here?" Wolf asked hopefully.

"Not 'ere, at work."

"Are you able to tell us when she might return?"

"At work. Come Sunday." And with that, the window slammed shut.

Wolf turned to Tabitha and shrugged his shoulders. "Well, so much for that. I wonder if it is worth walking to Leather Market and trying to find her."

"Well, even assuming that we can track her down, I cannot imagine we would engender much goodwill by interrupting her workday," Tabitha suggested. She was right, of course. It seemed unlikely that Sally's employer would welcome such a visit. The best thing was to return the following day, when presumably the workers were given a day to rest.

They made their way back up Borough High Street to catch the omnibus back to Ludgate Hill. They waited for some minutes for the next omnibus. As they stood in line with the other passengers, Tabitha couldn't shake the feeling they were being watched. It was the end of the workday for many people and the street was busy, and the line of people waiting was long. She tried to look around her as unobtrusively as possible, but didn't notice anyone paying them particular attention.

Perhaps they stood out more than they realised. Even Wolf's valet and Tabitha's maid clothes were of better quality than most of the people in Southwark could afford. Thompson was particularly careful about the cut of his cloth and the shine on his buttons. When Tabitha sent Mrs O'Leary to purchase suitable clothes for disguises, she should make sure to mention the status of the people they wished to impersonate. Actually, now that she thought about it, they should have different outfits to match the various personas they might want to assume.

Thinking about her instructions to her private secretary distracted Tabitha from the feeling of being watched. However, when they disembarked at Ludgate Hill and looked around for Madison and the Pembroke carriage, Tabitha once again felt sure they were being observed. As she leaned over to whisper in Wolf's ear, Tabitha alerted him to her concern.

"I feel it too," he confessed. "What do we do? If someone overheard us at the inn and became suspicious enough to follow us, what would he or she surmise when we get into our carriage? Does it matter?"

"Well, there is no way to alert Madison and have him go home without us. So, we have no choice but to get into the carriage."

It crossed Wolf's mind that they might casually speak to Madison, perhaps as if they were asking for directions while telling him to return to Piccadilly and wait for them there. But was such a charade worth it? And if someone should come to realise that they weren't John Champion and his trusty photographer, Miss Smart, did it matter?

Ludgate Hill was even busier than Borough High Street, and it was almost impossible to spot if they were being followed. Perhaps it was no more than someone particularly nosy who descended from the omnibus at the same time and then had gone their own way.

Wolf shrugged off the concern and took Tabitha's arm, leading her across the busy thoroughfare and down the street to where Madison was waiting. Once inside the carriage, they both relaxed. It had been a long day, and it would be good to get home, take nice long baths, and have a quiet family dinner.

At this thought, Tabitha remembered their promise to give the dowager a complete account of their afternoon when they returned to Chesterton House. Sighing deeply, she reminded Wolf of this.

"I hope she has not yet arrived and that we may have time to bathe and change our clothes at least," he replied.

The traffic congestion was heavy at that time of the day, and they didn't arrive back at Chesterton House until almost seven o'clock. An unusually flustered Talbot opened the front door.

With a tight smile and a weary voice, he explained, "The dowager countess has been here for quite some time and has been rather agitated by your continued absence."

So much for a relaxing bath and a quiet dinner, Tabitha's glance communicated to Wolf.

Wolf put his hand on Tabitha's arm. "Go and take that bath. I will deal with Lady Pembroke."

"Are you sure? I am certain that you would also like to wash up and change before dinner."

"Indeed. However, I can dress far more quickly than you," he said with a mischievous grin.

"Thank you," Tabitha said, kissing him lightly on the cheek.

As Tabitha climbed the stairs, feeling somewhat guilty, she heard the drawing room door open and a caustic voice say, "So, you finally deigned to return to give me an update, did you? Really, Jeremy, I would have expected better from you if not from your wife!"

Tabitha felt even guiltier, but not so much that she was inclined to turn back and brave the dowager's ire with Wolf. Instead, she went into their bedchamber, happy to see Ginny already laying out a dress for dinner.

Within a short time, Tabitha was soaking in hot, rose-scented water, trying to forget what awaited her downstairs. Although she would have liked to relax in the water for longer, she realised the sacrifice Wolf had made for her. The right thing to do, the loving thing to do, the brave thing to do, was to go downstairs and face the music.

Tabitha got out of the warm water reluctantly. She made haste to dress, hoping that Wolf had managed to escape to a bath of his own. When she was ready, Tabitha made her way down to the drawing room. Just before she entered the room, Tabitha reminded herself that she was a grown, married woman and that this was her house. No one, not even the Dowager Countess of Pembroke, had the right to berate her in front of her own hearth as if she were still in pinafores. Of course, this was easier to tell herself than to put into practice. Tabitha straightened her back, threw back her shoulders, and braced herself for hand-to-hand combat.

CHAPTER 15

As soon as Tabitha entered the drawing room, it was clear the evening would be as challenging as she'd expected. If she'd hoped that the dowager's ire at being excluded so cleverly from the afternoon's activities might have abated by now, a quick look at the woman's stony countenance confirmed those hopes were in vain.

"Nice of you to join us, finally, Tabitha," the woman said as if she were a teacher addressing a tardy child in school. Meanwhile, Tabitha noticed that, even though Uncle Duncan sat in his now customary armchair in the corner, happily sipping on a drink of something alcoholic, Lily and Jane were not yet down. Tabitha was relieved as she realised Wolf must have escaped to his bath.

Given that neither Jane nor Lily had come down from dressing yet, Tabitha was tempted to give the dowager a tart response, but one look at the woman's face made her think twice about baiting that bear. Instead, she walked to her favourite chair and sat down. There was a book on the side table by the chair, and she made a point of picking it up and reading.

"As if purposefully excluding me and then leaving me here alone for hours was not bad enough, now you choose to ignore me!" the dowager whined.

As she put the book down, Tabitha's patience broke. "Mama, you made the choice not to come with us because you did not want to take the omnibus."

"Something that you knew would be the case when you suggested that mode of transportation."

Tabitha didn't deny it. Instead, she pointed out, "And you went home. We would have telephoned you once we had returned to fill you in on what happened." Even as she said this, Tabitha wondered how much of a lie this was. It seemed the dowager was filled with a similar scepticism as she narrowed her eyes and glared. Deciding that she couldn't make the situation worse, probably, Tabitha threw her final dart, "Furthermore, you were not alone. Uncle Duncan has been company for you."

As perhaps might have been expected, this match lit the firework's fuse. "Him! You consider this drunken fool appropriate company for me?"

It seemed that Uncle Duncan had nodded off, but the dowager's waspish reply was so sharp that it jolted the man awake. "Ah, there ye are, lass. Back at last. Now, have ye cracked the case, or shall I be forced tae lend my considerable expertise again?"

This seemed to be the last straw for the dowager, and she stood, sputtering, "I will be in the parlour. When Jeremey has finished his ablutions, I expect you both, and only the two of you, to join and give me an update on your afternoon." She uttered this last sentence with a pointed look at Uncle Duncan. When the dowager was about to leave the room, she turned and said in quite a menacing voice, "I hope you uncovered sufficient information to compensate for my exclusion from the expedition!" And with that, she flounced out of the room.

Tabitha couldn't bring herself to care about the dowager's tantrum, so she returned to her book as Uncle Duncan's eyelids fluttered and then closed again.

Fifteen minutes later, Wolf returned, bathed and dressed for dinner. Jane and Lily followed him. Lily's red eyes and pale face indicated she had been crying again. Tabitha felt immense guilt at having ever doubted the young woman's feelings towards her betrothed.

As soon as Lily entered the room, she asked in a tone of heartbreaking hopefulness, "Did you find anything that would clear the earl's name?"

Tabitha considered the question. Answering as honestly as she could, she replied, "We discovered some things of interest, and we have someone we need to talk with tomorrow. However, I cannot honestly tell you we have made significant progress towards freeing Clarence."

As she said these words, the telephone rang. A few moments later, Talbot entered the room and announced, "The Countess of Warwick for you, milord."

Lily's eyes opened wide, and her face seemed frozen in fear. Was this good or bad news?

Wolf hurried to take the telephone call, and no one spoke while he was gone. Luckily, his telephone conversation ended quickly. Wolf returned to the room and said to the expectant faces before him, "There is no real news. Fiona just wanted to tell us that Sir Matthew has declined to get involved on Clarence's behalf." As Lily gasped, Wolf realised what he'd done. "I suppose that is, in fact, news. I am so sorry, Lily. However, this is not the end. It is merely a boulder in the road."

Tabitha realised that the longer they left the dowager fuming in the parlour, the worse it would be. Mentioning that the old woman was probably impatiently waiting for their report, Tabitha suggested that Jane and Lily have a glass of sherry and wait in the drawing room with Uncle Duncan.

"I would like to join you if I may," Lily said between little sobs. "While it is true that I normally do not have any interest in your investigations, my entire life and happiness depend on a successful outcome, and I feel I should be a party to your conversation."

Tabitha didn't want to upset the girl any more by pointing out that the dowager seemed set against the marriage regardless of the outcome of the investigation. Instead, she told Lily that she was welcome to join them. Of course, she and Jane were both welcome. Jane declined and settled herself into a chair with some embroidery. And so, Tabitha, Wolf, and Lily made their way to the parlour to be greeted by the dowager barely restraining her irritation.

"I see it is my fate to be abandoned and forgotten today," she said in a tight voice.

"I apologise, Lady Pembroke. The fault was all mine."

The dowager sniffed. "I expected better of you, Jeremy. When you said that you were going upstairs and would return shortly, I expected that to be a matter of minutes, not nearly half an hour! Whatever were you doing? Tying your own cravat?" She seemed amused by her own witticism, and finally, her face moulded itself into something that might almost be called a smile.

This might be as cordial as things would get that evening, Tabitha decided as she went and took a pile of blank notecards and settled herself in an armchair. Wolf took a seat, as did Lily.

"Now tell me what you discovered," the dowager demanded. And so, they did. As they explained everything from their conversation with Ellie Perkins to their failed attempt to speak with Sally Turnbull, Tabitha wrote up notecards, and the dowager tapped her fingers on her knee impatiently.

"That is all you managed to discover?" she asked in her most critical tone. "You were gone all afternoon, and this is the sum total of your findings?"

They had told her everything, even being quite explicit about Mrs Perkins' assessment of Caroline Turnbull's medical condition. Lily blushed as they spoke, but Tabitha decided that the girl no more needed coddling than she did.

If the dowager worried about her virginal granddaughter being exposed to such ideas, she didn't mention it. Instead, she said with surprising coarseness, "So she died of the pox, did she? Well, whatever one sows, that will one reap."

"Mama!" Tabitha exclaimed. "Really, that is most unfeeling of you."

"Unfeeling, is it? These doxies who have relations with other women's husbands deserve what they get."

The dowager said this with such passionate venom that Tabitha was quite taken aback. She understood that the late earl, the dowager's husband, like most men of his class, had kept mistresses, but she had always sensed that the dowager was pleased her husband's attention was diverted from her. Perhaps she was pleased, and yet that still didn't mitigate the hurt of having the person who swore an oath to love and honour you above all others take that promise so lightly.

Indicating that perhaps she knew more about such things than any of them might have imagined, Lily asked, "If not that Miss Turnbull died last week, one might almost wonder if she killed Lord Redding out of revenge for passing the disease onto her."

"He passed it to her? What an innocent you are, Lily. Given the woman's profession, it is almost certain that she gave it to Redding."

Tabitha gasped at the dowager's words. "Mama!" She exclaimed yet again. "I do not think we need to discuss such issues in front of Lily."

"I am a scientist," Lily said, as if that were all the explanation needed.

"You are also an innocent young woman, and this is not a suitable topic of conversation. Anyway, as you have observed, Caroline Turnbull's death preceded Lord Redding's, so it is a moot point. Also, she had clearly been ill for many years. Presuming she understood the cause of her sickness and believed Redding was its source, she had ample time for retribution."

This conversation was getting them nowhere, so Tabitha suggested they go in to dinner.

As they entered the dining room, the dowager moved close to Tabitha and said in a voice that would brook no dissent, "I will be joining you tomorrow on your return trip to Southwark, Tabitha. Even if it means getting on an omnibus. Now that I see how negligible your results are when I am not with you, I cannot in good conscience allow you and Jeremy to return alone and continue to achieve so little."

Resigned to this fate, Tabitha felt obliged to say, "You cannot dress as you did earlier, Mama. If you still have the dresses from your stay at the house on Villiers Street, then you should wear one of those."

This observation earned her a withering look. "Do you imagine I have no common sense, Tabitha? That I would imagine diamonds and furs to be appropriate attire to mingle with the masses?" Given how bedecked the dowager had been earlier that day for a visit to Drury Lane, that was precisely what Tabitha thought. Wisely, she kept these thoughts to herself and merely nodded noncommittally.

Chapter 16

Over dinner, the group decided to aim to arrive in Southwark before noon the following day to allow for the possibility that Sally Turnbull attended Sunday morning church services. Of course, perhaps she was extremely devout or taught Sunday school, or a host of other possibilities. Still, the most likely scenario would seem to be that, like most working-class people, if she attended Sunday services, it was for the morning prayer, which would start at approximately half past ten and last an hour.

Tabitha and Wolf discussed this as they prepared for bed and decided that if they could not find Sally at home, they would make further inquiries with Ellie Perkins. Everything about her keenness to gossip the day before suggested that she would be willing to continue the conversation.

The following morning, they donned their John Champion and Miss Smart outfits once more and went to the breakfast room. Once again, they were the first people there and helped themselves to eggs, bacon, and sausage.

"While I feel our story of being journalists is a good one, how on earth are we going to explain Mama?" Tabitha asked before taking a bite of buttered toast.

Wolf sipped his coffee as he considered the question. Before he formulated an answer, Jane, and Lily joined them. Tabitha and Wolf explained their dilemma as Jane and Lily filled their plates – or, in Lily's case, put a small amount of food on it she then pushed around while consuming very little.

As she nibbled on one tiny piece of sausage, Lily contemplated the challenge. Suddenly, she put her fork down, and her eyes lit up. "What about if you put aside the ruse of being journalists?" she exclaimed.

"Certainly, we are not wedded to that charade but cannot think of anything more plausible," Tabitha told her.

Lily turned to Jane. "Mama, do you remember Mrs Coleridge back at home?"

Jane wiped her mouth with her napkin and replied, "Yes, of course." Then, explaining to Tabitha and Wolf, Jane continued, "Mrs Coleridge was a member of our church until she died last year. She had a great spirit for reform and made it her business to catalogue many of the social ills in Edinburgh, from workhouses to child labour. She did this by capturing the stories of some victims of misfortune. Working with a local writer, she then published these stories in a book, hoping the money raised from selling it might be ploughed back into her cause and that the stories them-selves would move others in the community to stir themselves to help."

Wolf guessed where this was going and couldn't help but point out the obvious flaw in the plan. "So, Lily, if I understand you correctly, you are suggesting that your grandmother, Lady Pembroke, pose as a social reformer who cares deeply about the plight of the lower classes?" Even as he said this, Wolf couldn't help but smirk. The idea of the dowager taking on this persona was too humorous not to smile.

Tabitha saw the smirk and understood his reaction. Nevertheless, she thought that Lily might have landed on a good idea. "Wolf, the mistake you are making is to assume those in the higher ranks who claim concern for the wellbeing of those below them are tender, sympathetic spirits. After all, Lord Redding made many such protestations, yet from what we have heard so far, I would not describe him as a gentle soul. I think Mama might at least pass as a moral crusader, even if she comes across as one who advocates for reform from a high horse."

Wolf still had his doubts but no better suggestion to make. "Then let us be John Champion and Miss Smart, research assistants to Miss Julia Phillips, social reformer."

"Miss Julia Phillips?" Lily asked. "Who is that?"

"It is the nom-de-guerre your grandmother assumed in one of her more colourful instances of involving herself in an investigation," Tabitha explained obliquely. It was not her place to tell Lily that her grandmother once managed a brothel, even if she had done so in the service of an investigation.

"Phillips was Mama's maiden name," Jane added.

Wolf, mindful that the omnibus service would likely be less frequent on a Sunday, suggested to Tabitha that they make haste to pick up the dowager and make their way to Ludgate Hill. He had decided that they would retrace their steps from the previous day and not attempt to take the additional omnibus from Piccadilly. Between the likely reduced service and the thought of having to deal with the dowager on not one but two different omnibuses, he was sure that Tabitha would agree with his reasoning.

The dowager lived only a few minutes' carriage drive away. As good as her word, she had donned one of the outfits she had worn when living on Villiers Street. The dress was a plain navy blue serge, and she had matched it with a rather austere-looking black hat. The old woman had taken off all her jewellery and her hair was worn simply. While the clothes were of decent materials and tailoring, they spoke of the wife of a vicar or a solidly middle-class woman who was very active on church committees. All in all, Tabitha and Wolf were pleasantly surprised at how she had listened to their admonitions and followed their strongly worded suggestions.

As she climbed into the carriage, the dowager caught their looks of surprise and said in a tone both sharp and yet smug, "You continue to underestimate me, Tabitha. I do understand what the assignment is and why such a costume as this is necessary." She then sat back against the plush cushions, her hands folded demurely in her lap and maintained a self-satisfied silence for at least three minutes.

Finally, happy that her point was made, the dowager asked, "What is my role in this charade?" Wolf explained the backstory they had contrived with Lily and Jane over breakfast.

The dowager considered his words, then cocked her head and asked, "Did Lily come up with this plan, or did Jane?"

On hearing that the genesis of the idea of the dowager as a social reformer came from her granddaughter, the dowager looked relieved. "In that case, I am sure that it is a sensible plan. Any suggestion that might come from my daughter would be suspect; I have never heard a bit of common sense come out of Jane's mouth!"

While it was neither the time nor the place for this debate, Tabitha was unable to restrain herself. "Mama! You speak of being underestimated constantly, and yet that is exactly what you do to Jane. She is an intelligent, thoughtful woman who you have cowed to the point where she is too scared to do much but mumble in your presence."

The dowager looked quite taken aback at the criticism being levelled at her. "My point entirely! The woman needs to develop a backbone. And let me add, Tabitha, that I do not appreciate being lectured to on parenting, or indeed anything, by you."

"Lady Pembroke," Wolf said in a gentle yet firm voice. "You can hardly criticise Jane for failing to stand up to you and then complain when my wife does just that."

The dowager harrumphed in reply, a sure sign she was aware of being hoisted by her own petard. Tabitha, who was sitting next to Wolf, reached out and squeezed his hand in thanks for riding to her defence. He squeezed it back; he would always be there, right by her side, ready to take on together whatever battles they faced.

After sulking for a few minutes, the dowager realised that the carriage was driving past Piccadilly. "Are we not to get the omnibus from back there, Jeremy?" Wolf explained they would take just one from Ludgate Hill. He couched this plan as an amendment that they only considered that morning to accommodate likely Sunday delays.

Because it was a Sunday, the London traffic was light, and they quickly reached Ludgate Hill. Wolf gave Madison the same instructions a last time: if they were any later than three hours, he should return for Bear. It had occurred to Wolf that they might bring his enormous private secretary with them. However, while Bear's presence usually deterred a certain kind of trouble, it also often brought unwanted attention to their group.

As she descended from the carriage, the dowager asked, "Does one hail this omnibus in much the same way as one does a hackney cab?"

For a moment, Tabitha wondered that the dowager even knew how to hail a hackney cab. Then she remembered the woman's previous adventures as Miss Julia Phillips and assumed they involved such conveyances.

"While people often hail an omnibus, there are also major routes they are known to take where people congregate to wait for one. That is what we are going to do now, over there," Wolf explained, pointing to a small group of people waiting in the shadow of the great dome of St Paul's Cathedral that dominated the skyline. He led the way as they crossed the street to where a rather motley group of people were congregating.

On a Sunday, the waiting passengers weren't primarily workers on their way to a day's employment. Instead, there were two rather stern-looking women. Based on their very conservative attire and the fact that they were both holding bibles in front of them, they looked as if they were returning home after the early morning service at St Paul's that tended to attract only the most pious of congregants.

Standing behind the two women was a group of quite young girls. Based on their outfits and overheard conversation, they were maids returning to their families on their half day off. Tabitha, Wolf, and the dowager joined the end of the line as the girls giggled and whispered to each other.

"How long must one wait for this omnibus?" the dowager asked impatiently in too loud a voice.

"Mama!" Tabitha admonished her in a low voice, "Remember that our aim is to blend in even now."

The dowager sniffed at the rebuke but kept any other comments to herself.

Luckily, they didn't have to wait too long. Ten minutes later, the omnibus pulled up beside the group of waiting passengers. From where they stood, the omnibus appeared quite empty, and many seats were available, so boarding involved less pushing and shoving than the previous day.

Even so, it seemed that somehow the dowager was pushed, if only a little. "Excuse me!" she exclaimed. "Have you people no sense of propriety? No manners?" Yet again, Tabitha attempted to hush her.

Finally, they were on board the omnibus. Tabitha took a seat next to the dowager while Wolf sat behind them. The dowager looked around at her fellow passengers in a way that Tabitha could only think of as gawping. It was as if the old woman considered that she had a front-row seat at a particularly exotic exhibit at the zoo.

Tabitha jabbed her elbow into the dowager's side and whispered in her ear, "Stop staring at the other passengers."

"But Tabitha, it is all just so fascinating," the dowager unapologetically replied. Luckily the trip to London Bridge was quick, Tabitha thought to herself.

CHAPTER 17

Tabitha stepped off the omnibus, grateful the ride was over. She would have thought the dowager had been involved in enough investigations over the past year and exposed to enough people beyond her aristocratic sphere that an omnibus ride with a group of lower-class passengers would not have seemed like such a carnival ride. Apparently not.

Borough High Street was a very different place on a Sunday than the day before. Apart from anything else, Borough Market did not operate on the Lord's Day of rest, so the neighbourhood was much quieter without the market vendors hawking their wares and the horse-drawn carts clattering over the cobblestones as they transported goods in and out of the market.

The dowager looked about with keen interest. "And so, this is Southwark, is it? Not a very attractive place."

Tabitha was looking straight ahead, and so could roll her eyes without the worry of being observed. "Mama, this is a very poor working-class neighbourhood next to the docks. Lack of an attractive aesthetic is the least of its issues." Then, unable to hold back, she observed, "You have been involved in investigations in a variety of poor, perhaps ever poorer, areas of London. Yet you are acting as if you have never stepped foot outside of Mayfair before."

Wolf applauded his wife's courage but also worried about what she might have started and how such a confrontation might interfere with their outing's objectives.

The dowager took as much umbrage as Wolf expected her to. "I am acting in no such way, Tabitha. How dare you imply otherwise. I am merely curious about the native population."

"There you go again. You are not David Livingstone, and this is not the Congo."

"Dr Livingstone did not explore the Congo; Sir Henry Stanley did," the dowager said in the tone of a pompous, know-all ten-year-old.

Wolf realised it was time to step in. "Ladies, we need to remain in character. It is unclear who might be nearby. Please, let us remember why we are here and, more to the point, who we are supposed to be while we are here." Tabitha felt appropriately chastened at his words. The dowager merely sniffed her displeasure at the lecture.

This conversation took most of the less than ten minutes it took them to walk down Borough High Street toward The George Inn. Just before they arrived at their destination, Wolf stopped them and asked, "Is everyone clear on what our story is and what we are hoping to ask Sally Turnbull?"

"I am not in my dotage yet, Jeremy. I remember full well what our mission is."

"Good, then let us knock on the door and hope that Miss Turnbull is home."

A minute or two later, they found themselves back outside the dilapidated house, knocking once more on the front door. Once again, the window above opened, and the same voice as the previous day yelled, "Wot?"

Adopting her most polite tone, Tabitha explained, "We visited yesterday looking for Sally Turnbull. You suggested we return today." The only answer was the window being slammed shut again.

They waited for a few minutes. Finally, the threesome looked at each other. Would this journey ultimately be in vain?

Just as Wolf was about to suggest to Tabitha that they leave, the front door opened, and a young woman stood before them, perhaps eighteen or nineteen years old. She had golden hair and large, bright blue eyes that might have been quite lovely had they not been so red and inflamed. A perfect rosebud mouth, similarly, was marred by the notched, peg-shaped upper incisors that transformed the face into something that would not have been amiss in Madame Tussaud's Chamber of Horrors. A horribly protruding forehead completed this effect.

The gruesome teeth were visible as their owner attempted to approximate a smile. "I am Sally Turnbull. I hear you came looking for me yesterday. How can I help you?"

Wolf tried to compose himself and not stare at the woman's ghastly visage. Instead, he slightly averted his gaze and gave the agreed-upon story.

When he finished, Sally Turnbull asked in a perplexed tone, "So, Miss Phillips here is writing a book about the need for reform, highlighting certain stories, and plans to use the profits to help the poor?" That was a reasonable summary of what he had said, and so Wolf nodded.

"And why have you come to me?" It was a valid question.

Tabitha stepped forward. "Might we enter and talk inside, Miss Turnbull?"

For a moment, it looked as if Sally Turnbull might send them away, but finally, she stepped aside and welcomed them into the house. The inside of the house looked as ramshackle as its outside. Wallpaper peeled off the walls, which had horrible blotches of what looked like black mould all over them. The smell inside the house was appalling, and even Tabitha had a hard time not scrunching up her face in disgust. She didn't dare look over at the dowager.

Sally led them into a room on the ground floor. It matched the horrendous condition of the rest of the house, but it seemed an effort had been made to make the space into some kind of home. A bed pushed into one corner was covered by a brightly coloured patchwork quilt, and an old bottle with a few bluebells in it sat on the small table by the window.

Two chairs were next to the table, and Sally offered them to Tabitha and the dowager while she perched on the narrow bed.

"So, why do you want to interview me?"

There was another pause before Tabitha answered, "Actually, we want to write about your mother."

"My mother? Why?"

This part was pivotal but also the most sensitive part of their story. Wolf had expressed that this explanation would be better coming from Tabitha, and the dowager had reluctantly agreed to follow their lead.

"We feel, well, Miss Phillips feels, that her book will be more compelling if readers can come to understand that falling into destitution is possible for anyone."

Before Tabitha could continue, comprehension dawned on Sally Turnbull's face. "Ah, the downturn in my mother's career and life. That is why you want to speak to me?"

"We heard of her fall from the peak of stardom into abject poverty and thought it was the kind of heart-wrenching story that would make clear how necessary reform is. Miss Phillips advocates for workhouse and Poor Law reform, as well as fighting for better conditions, wages, and hours for women and child labourers. We believe it will be much easier to make the average person care about such things through the story of someone, just like them, if not more successful, who ended up laid so low."

The dowager was surprisingly quiet throughout this explanation. Now, fed up being referred to as if she wasn't in the room, she piped up, "Yes, well, in fact, the idea was mine, Miss Smart, not yours."

Tabitha bit back the sharp retort that sprung to her tongue and instead said, "Yes, of course, Miss Phillips, I misspoke. Mr Champion and I are mere vassals." Tabitha hoped that Sally Turnbull didn't detect the sarcasm she couldn't keep from her tone.

"How did you hear about my mother's story and know where to find her?"

It was a valid question and one for which Tabitha and Wolf weren't ready. Luckily, the dowager said without hesitation, "From an actor, Roland Grant. He used to perform with your mother some years ago. You were probably a child then. I met him through an acquaintance of mine, Mr Christopher Bailey, impresario. Mr Grant relayed your mother's unfortunate fall from grace." Wolf continually reminded them it was a good idea to stick as close to the truth as possible. It appeared the dowager had actually paid attention.

"Fall from grace? Is that how he told it?" Sally laughed ruefully. "Did he tell you that my mother became unable to sing?"

"He told us she faced some problems with her voice and took time off to rest and that she never returned."

"Just like that, her beautiful singing voice was gone. She struggled for years with sores on her throat that made it extremely painful to sing. I was a child at the time, but I remember her tears of agony as she gargled salt water twice a day and did whatever she could to keep her voice intact. She knew it was all that stood between us and the workhouse."

Hearing this, Tabitha couldn't help but comment at this extreme statement. "Miss Turnbull, I must ask something. From what we heard from Mr Grant, your mother had been the toast of the London stage for some years. Surely, she had money put away. She could not have imagined that her career would last forever."

Sally Turnbull sighed. "My mother had been a beautiful young woman, and men vied for her favours. In her heyday, there was always a benefactor to pay the household bills, and so my mother spent lavishly with no care for the future. By the time the last benefactor withdrew his support, we were penniless; my mother didn't own the house we lived in and had put no nest egg aside. When her voice finally failed her, we lived for some months on the proceeds of jewellery that she sold. Then, one day, that was gone as well."

Pausing as she dipped into painful memories, Sally finally continued, "I remember the day that the bailiffs came and took our furniture and forced us to leave our home. I also remember my mother taking me to a big fancy house to meet a very well-dressed, well-spoken lady who eventually gave her some banknotes."

Who was that well-dressed lady? Tabitha wondered. However, she didn't want to interrupt Sally's story.

"From that point on, our lives were somewhat stable for a few years. Of course, we lived modestly, but we survived. When I look back, I realise that the fancy lady must have continued to send money. Then, one day, maybe five years ago, everything changed. At that point, we moved every few months into increasingly dingy boarding houses until we landed here. Ma got sicker and sicker until a week ago when she finally got some blessed relief from her pain."

The dowager suddenly seemed to notice something. "Your mother died a week ago, and yet there is no sign of mourning." She said this in a rather critical, moralising tone, and Sally Turnbull hung her head.

Despite her look of shame, the young woman answered, "It is by Ma's wishes. Her last words to me were that death was welcome and that I should not mourn because she is no longer suffering."

Tabitha wondered at the agony Caroline Turnbull must have been in for death to be a release. Worried that the dowager might continue to judge Sally harshly, she said kindly, "While your mother might have welcomed death, you must feel her loss keenly. You have our condolences. All of our sincere condolences," she added pointedly, glaring at the dowager. Then, she articulated the question that seemed most pressing, "Do you have any idea who this well-dressed lady might have been?"

Sally Turnbull considered the question. "I have wondered that myself over the years. I was so overwhelmed by the splendour when we arrived that I barely noticed anything else. The woman seemed old to me at the time because I was a child. But realistically, while her hair was greying, it was only at the temples. She was perhaps in her midlife. I remember one thing. Just as we were about to leave, she came up to me, bent down and kissed my cheek and a tear was running down her cheek."

"Do you have any idea why?" Wolf asked.

"I remember asking my mother on the way home, and she said that the fancy lady never had any children of her own, and maybe I reminded her of that."

There was one more question they needed to ask, but neither Tabitha nor Wolf were sure of how to ask it delicately. As fate, or perhaps luck, would have it, they didn't need to ponder how they might ask it because the dowager said, "Was your mother familiar with a Lord Redding? And when I say 'familiar', I mean in the biblical sense."

"Miss Phillips!" Tabitha said in shock, both at the woman's vulgarity and her lack of concern for anyone's sensibilities. She only just managed to stop herself from calling the dowager Mama".

"Well, it needed to be asked, and it seemed that you would not muster up the courage."

Sally Turnbull eyed them suspiciously. "I have never heard of Lord Redding. Suddenly, it seems as if you have a very particular interest in my mother as more than merely a riches-to-rags story for your book."

Tabitha and Wolf looked at each other, and a silent communication passed between them. Thanks to the dowager's heavy-handed questioning, their charade had been exposed, anyway. Was there anything to be lost by being honest?

Wolf shrugged his shoulders in acknowledgement of the question, and so Tabitha revealed their true purpose in questioning Sally.

When Tabitha finished, Sally asked, "So, an earl has been accused of murdering this Lord Redding, and you don't believe he is guilty?" Tabitha nodded. "And how do you believe that my mother is involved?" That was the question, wasn't it?

When Tabitha didn't respond immediately, Wolf explained, "It seems there is a long history of animosity between the victim and the accused dating back to their boyhood. However, something that has come to light is that they shared a friendship with your mother. Given that she passed away a week ago and Lord Redding was killed a few days after, it appeared there may be a connection. We do not have many other clues to pursue, so it seemed worthwhile to speak with you and see what else we might learn."

Sally nodded her head but asked tersely, "And have you learned anything?"

Had they? Possibly.

Unwilling to say too much, Wolf merely gave a half smile and another little shrug of his shoulders. However, they'd already said too much. With their charade exposed, Sally Turnbull was very unwilling to share anything else with them. After a few more questions met a tight-lipped response, they excused themselves, thanked Sally for her help, and took their leave.

CHAPTER 18

It was noon by the time they left Sally Turnbull. While it was on the early side for lunch, they did not know how long they would have to wait for the return omnibus, and everyone was hungry. Mindful that they shouldn't be too long, or Madison would have cause to worry and fetch Bear, Wolf suggested they stop for something to eat at The George Inn. Apart from anything else, he was curious to hear what other gossip Ellie Perkins might be persuaded to part with.

The dowager professed herself thrilled to have an opportunity to add to her experiences of public houses, and so the decision was made. As she entered the low-ceilinged main saloon bar, she looked around her with interest.

"Well, this is certainly more charming than Mr One-eye's establishment," she murmured. Given that Wolf didn't imagine charming was what Old One-eye was aiming for with his public house, The Cock, he didn't bother to answer.

Tabitha and Wolf were happy to see Ellie Perkins behind the bar again, filling tankards. However, on catching sight of them, she didn't seem at all happy. In fact, she almost looked nervous.

The George was much busier than the previous day, and Tabitha wondered if they'd find a table to sit at. Looking around, she finally spotted one in the corner of the room. She indicated to Wolf that she and the dowager would claim the table while he ordered drinks and food.

"You know my tipple, Jeremy," the dowager said, referring to the small beer she took quite a shine to during their trip to Brighton.

As Tabitha and the dowager made their way over to the table, Wolf approached the bar. Ellie eyed him warily. Wolf couldn't imagine what had changed in twenty-four hours to make the gregarious and friendly barmaid suddenly look so guarded and uneasy. It could be simply that the bar was so much busier than on their last visit.

Wolf decided to put aside his concerns and gave Ellie a friendly hail. "Mrs Perkins, we decided to return to your excellent establishment and bring our friend this time," he said, gesturing over to the dowager and Tabitha.

"Welcome to you all," Ellie said in a clipped tone with none of the friendliness of the day before. Wolf couldn't shake the feeling that there was something more going on here than mere busyness but couldn't imagine what it might be. He decided not to worry about it now and instead ordered three pies, a tankard of ale, and two small beers. "I'll send the pies over," Ellie replied brusquely as she drew the draughts. A few minutes later, Wolf was seated with the dowager and Tabitha in the corner of the busy inn.

As the dowager took her first sip of small beer, it occurred to Wolf that he was about to be castigated, yet again, for failing to ensure a regular supply of the beverage in the dowager's cellar. It seemed not to have occurred to the woman that this might be an inappropriate job to task an earl with. As it happened, Wolf's reason for not procuring the beer wasn't that the task felt below him, but rather that he kept forgetting.

Now, the dowager took her first sip, and Wolf waited for the recriminations to begin. Instead, she savoured the drink and then remarked, "It is good but not up to the standards of the small beer that Mr Doherty procures for me."

Tabitha and Wolf were amazed that the East End gang leader, Mickey D, had taken on this chore. Seeing the surprise on their faces, the dowager continued in a tone filled with disappointed resignation, "Yes, did I forget to mention that in the face of your continued, one might almost say determined, insistence on not performing this service for me, Mr

Doherty kindly offered to ensure that my cellar has a regular supply of small beer?"

Wolf did not doubt that Mickey D wasn't doing this merely out of the goodness of his heart. He did not doubt that the dowager was paying a hefty delivery charge on top of whatever Mickey D was buying the beer for. However, he possessed enough sense of self-preservation to refrain from mentioning this and instead chose to be grateful that this errand no longer rested on his shoulders.

A few minutes later, the pies emerged. During their investigations over the past year, the dowager discovered a surprising appreciation for the unsophisticated yet comforting food of the lower orders. In particular, she found the meat pies at The Cock to be delicious. Today, Wolf had ordered three chicken and ham pies. The meat was smothered in a delicious creamy sauce.

After enjoying another mouthful, the dowager proclaimed, "Unlike the small beer, this may be better than Mr One-eye's. I must make a point of suggesting that he put something like this on his menu."

Wolf ignored this comment and said, "Let us hurry so that we can get back to Ludgate Hill promptly before Madison becomes concerned."

"Really, Jeremy. I cannot imagine why you believe it is for you to accommodate your servants rather than the other way around." This was said in a rather loud voice.

Tabitha realised that such a conversation, and at that volume, might give them. "Mama!" she whispered. "Remember our roles. We do not know who might overhear." The dowager sniffed at the rebuke but said no more.

As they finished the last mouthfuls of pie, the dowager leaned over to Tabitha and whispered something. Wolf couldn't imagine what the old woman had said, but from the look on his wife's face, she now faced a conundrum. Tabitha wiped her mouth and stood. She went to the bar and, as discreetly as possible, asked Ellie Perkins something. Wolf watched as the woman pointed to a door to the side of the bar. Tabitha then came back and whispered something back to the dowager, who rose and went in the direction that Ellie pointed in.

With the dowager out of earshot, Tabitha said in a low voice, "She asked if they have facilities she might use."

"She is planning to use whatever outdoor privy they have?" Wolf asked in amazement. "Does she realise how primitive it is likely to be?"

"Needs must when the devil drives," was his wife's only reply. Wolf imagined the harsh commentary awaiting them on the dowager's return from what was almost certainly an outdoor, very basic privy.

When five minutes had passed, Wolf wondered what was keeping the dowager. Then he considered the intricacies of women's wear and the likely cramped conditions of whatever structure the woman found herself in. When another five minutes elapsed, he saw from Tabitha's expression that she was getting worried.

"Should I go and make sure nothing untoward has happened?" Tabitha asked, rising even as she said this.

"It may be for the best," Wolf answered.

Tabitha left in the direction that the dowager had disappeared. She returned a few minutes later to speak with Ellie Perkins, then left again out of the same door. By this point, Wolf was getting genuinely worried and felt that his concern warranted throwing delicacy to the wind, so he rose and went after Tabitha.

The door led to a lane so narrow it was really no more than an alley-way. Some wooden barrels were stacked up against a wall and a basic wooden structure that must be the privy against the other. Wolf was unable to see Tabitha anywhere. He assumed that the lane, Talbot Yard, led to Borough High Street at one end and did not know where the other end led.

Just as Wolf was deciding in which direction Tabitha might have gone, she appeared from the Borough High Street end with a perturbed look on her face. "Mama has disappeared," she told him. "I came out and knocked on the privy door and received no reply. I wondered if she thought the door to the inn had locked behind her for some reason and had gone back around through the front, but I looked, and there was no sign of her."

Wolf considered the old woman's arrogance and inquisitiveness and asked, "Is it possible she has taken it upon herself to wander up the high street?"

"I thought that myself, particularly after her comment of not caring if servants had to wait longer. However, while the woman might be reckless at times, I doubt that even she would wander off without a word.

It was a terrible thing to say or even think, and indeed, he would have been scolded for ever daring to say so in front of the dowager; however, Wolf thought the thought had to be vocalised. "She is getting older. Perhaps, instead of recklessness, it was confusion."

Tabitha just stared at him in amazement. "Surely you are not claiming that Mama has senile decay that somehow came on in between when she sat with us and ventured out here?" While she didn't mean her voice to be as shrill as it sounded even to her ears, Tabitha was too worried to take care to modulate her tone.

Wolf understood his wife's feelings and crossed to take her in his arms. "Tabitha, my love, you must admit that it is possible. While there is no doubt that Lady Pembroke is as wily and sharp as ever most of the time, she is slowing down physically. It would not be surprising if she experienced some accompanying mental deterioration."

As comforting as Wolf's embrace was, Tabitha pushed back out of it. "No. That is not what happened here. I am sure Mama has been taken against her will."

"Well, if she has, I doubt her abductor went towards Borough High Street. It is far too busy, even on a Sunday, and I doubt that her ladyship went quietly. He must have taken her this way," Wolf concluded, pointing in the other direction. As he considered what to do next, Wolf said, "Tabitha, I want you to go back into the inn and tell Mrs Perkins that our elderly friend has gone missing. For the sake of our charade, say that we worry it is an instance of senile decay. Ask her to keep her ladyship here if she returns."

"And how is she supposed to inform us?" Tabitha asked. It was a good question. Even if The George Inn had access to a telephone, which it almost certainly didn't, they could hardly ask Ellie to telephone to Chesterton House. The same was true of asking her to send a message in a less advanced modern manner.

Finally, deciding this was the least of their concerns, Wolf answered, "Just ask her to keep her ladyship here until we return. Once you have done that, I want you to return to Ludgate Hill and then to Chesterton House."

Wolf could see that Tabitha was about to argue and said in a firm voice, "This is not about excluding you. I want you to return and bring

Bear with you." Then, considering the neighbourhood they were in and the likely challenges in tracking whoever had taken the dowager, he added, "Before you do that, telephone Langley House and have Rat take a message to Mickey D. He has a surprising fondness for the dowager countess and is likely to be willing, even eager to help. We are going to need some of his boys to help us search. Oh, and telephone to her ladyship's home and send Little Ian as well. We will need as much manpower as possible."

"And what will you be doing in the meantime?" Tabitha asked. "Do you plan to start to search?"

"I think this lane leads into Bermondsey, which is a warren of tanneries, warehouses and crime-ridden alleys. I am sure that whoever has taken her is long gone."

At these words, Tabitha's hand flew to her mouth in fear. "Then what does that mean? How will we ever find her?"

Wolf considered how to answer. "It is broad daylight, and we can be sure that Lady Pembroke did not go willingly or easily. Whoever took her must have threatened her with a weapon. Someone must have seen something. And then there is the question of why take her at all."

"Is it possible it is a robbery attempt?" Tabitha said, almost hopefully.

"To rob her of what? Luckily, her ladyship removed all her jewels, and her outfit hardly screams money." Even as he said this, Wolf considered whether their disguises were as believable as they'd hoped. His love for Tabitha might bias him, but Wolf considered her natural grace and sophistication difficult for even the plainest dress to mask. And what about him? Anyone taking a close look at his hands would realise that his nails were clean and well-groomed in a way that the average working man would never bother with.

As he reflected on this reality, Wolf said, "Perhaps someone saw through our ruse, and this is an attempt to extort a ransom." The frightened look on Tabitha's face made clear her deepest fears. Wolf added hurriedly, "This would be a good thing. That means that we will receive a communication from her abductor at some point soon."

Tabitha wasn't as relieved by Wolf's words as he'd hoped she would be. However, this consideration was moot for the time being. The important thing was to return to Mayfair and enlist reinforcements to help search.

Wolf continued to explain, "I am going to wander up this lane just to make sure that whoever took her hasn't realised that her ladyship has no coin on her and has left her somewhere." Of course, this implied that the dowager was left injured, or worse. "Then, I will return to The George and talk to Ellie Perkins. Her behaviour today was odd, and I would like to understand why."

"Is that where everyone should meet you?" Tabitha asked.

"No. It is too conspicuous. Whoever took Lady Pembroke is likely a local. They might even have been in the inn and followed her out. It is very possible that the place is filled with friends, family, or at least associates of our abductor. I do not want to give them a warning about the size of our search party."

Wolf considered what little he knew of the area. He realised that there were a variety of good hiding places spread around Bermondsey and Southwark. It was even possible that whoever had taken the dowager was headed towards Horselydown, south of Tower Bridge.

Finally, Wolf decided they needed to aim for maximum efficiency. "Tell Langley everything for Rat to share with Mickey D. I am sure that Langley will send the boy in his carriage, but you might mention it anyway. Have Rat tell Mickey D to head to Shad Thames and Jacob's Island. We will meet him by the new bridge. The entire area around the docks is full of smugglers and other thugs. I would be shocked if Mickey D does not have contacts with fellow criminals in the area. The warehouses around the wharves would be an excellent spot in which to hide someone. And I am sure they are quite empty on a Sunday."

"And what about Bear and Little Ian?"

"Tell Bear to meet me outside the Leather Market. He knows where it is. If our man is a local, then it is also possible he works in the leather trade around here. Those streets are also full of warehouses and factories where someone might hide, at least for the short term."

"And Little Ian?" Tabitha asked. The enormous man was as big as Bear but did not share the other man's mental acumen. What was the best use of his brute strength?

"Have him liaise with Mickey D. If the dowager countess has been taken to the wharves, it is a labyrinth of an area, and the more men looking, the better."

Chapter 19

I t all happened so quickly. One minute, the dowager was exiting the disgusting privy, ready to re-enter the inn and complain loudly about the facilities, and the next, a filthy hand was clamped over her mouth, and foul breath was in her face as a rough, threatening voice said, "One squeak out of you and you'll be gone to Davy Jones' Locker."

While the dowager wasn't sure who this Davy Jones was and why one might not want to visit his locker, the gun jabbed into her side made the man's general message clear enough.

"Now listen, old woman. I'm gonna take my hand off your mouth, but if I hear a squeak out of you, you'll be biting the dust before anyone responds. Do we understand each other?"

Answering was impossible with the man's grimy hand over her mouth, and anyway, the dowager worried that any answer might be viewed as the forbidden squeak. Instead, she gave a little nod of her head. The only other time the dowager had been threatened with a gun was when Maxwell Sandworth, Earl of Langley, took her and Tabitha hostage. Of course, in that situation, she felt no fear. Not only wasn't Lord Langley an even remotely intimidating personage, but the dowager had clear memories of boxing his ears when he was a boy in short trousers, something she had been quick to remind him of.

This situation was very different.

Wait, now that she thought about it, there was the time in the Villiers Street house when Jason Bono, the Rascal, and his sister, Lou, took her hostage at gunpoint. However, that also hadn't felt very serious. The dowager had too much disdain for Bono and had spent too many days making that disdain known to take his threats to heart.

This situation was very different.

The dowager initially thought this was some kind of robbery. However, she couldn't imagine what her character, Miss Julia Phillips, looked to have that was worth stealing. She considered speaking up and pointing this out but was worried that the man would shoot at the first sound out of her mouth. Because, of course, that was the very real possibility; that as soon as he realised she had nothing of worth on her, he'd consider an old woman a liability most easily silenced for good.

The man took his hand off her mouth and pushed the dowager ahead of him; the gun jammed in her lower back. Even so, she had seen enough of him to form an opinion. The man was young, with greasy dark hair. He had broad shoulders and a thick neck. The arm held against her was muscular with a drawing of a heart with something written across it on the forearm. The hand that had been clamped over her mouth was very calloused, and it was a great relief to be free of it.

The narrow lane was deserted. Surely, they would eventually see people, the dowager wondered. Perhaps she could communicate her predicament with her eyes and facial expression. However, even if a passerby intuited the elderly woman was being held against her will, what would they do? Even the dowager didn't imagine that anyone would threaten her burly captor on behalf of a random stranger, but might they contact the police?

The dowager had spent enough time amongst the lower orders over the past year to realise that while she usually saw the authorities as just another group to bring to heel, people in the working class usually saw them as a group to fear and avoid, even when they hadn't committed a crime. The dowager found it difficult to imagine a leather worker or even a tradesman approaching the police on her behalf. And even if they did, what could they do? Her abductor would have her squirrelled away in some dank basement by then.

As the dowager had this disheartening realisation, the end of the alleyway came into view. How long before Tabitha and Wolf noticed she was missing? Because they really were her only hope at this point. However, they needed to know in which direction she had been taken. Suddenly, the dowager remembered Melody's favourite story, Hansel and Gretel. While the little girl loved all the Brothers Grimm stories in her illustrated book of their stories, there was something about that story that had captured the child's imagination.

Now, the dowager remembered Hansel and Gretel leaving a trail of breadcrumbs to find their way back out of the forest. While this hadn't worked out very well for the children in the story when birds ate the breadcrumbs, it gave the dowager an idea. That only left one question: what could she drop?

As discreetly as possible, the dowager slipped her hand into the pocket of her dress' skirt. Perhaps she'd find a handkerchief there. She didn't, but there was something perhaps more useful: little paper-wrapped cubes of fudge. The dowager had a sweet tooth and would often carry these delicious morsels with her for sustenance when the high teas served in society drawing rooms didn't meet her high standards. Now, she remembered that when she had left her Mayfair home to travel to Villiers Street months before, she had made a point of taking a batch of these delicacies with her just in case she found herself unable to eat whatever coarse foodstuff was served to prostitutes.

Even as she realised that the fudge might be dropped as a trail, the dowager reflected that wherever she was being taken, it might be wise to leave some to sustain her until she was rescued. The dowager pondered her dilemma. Strategically dropping the fudge might shorten her capture but keeping it would provide nourishment during it. Finally, realising there were quite a few of the fudge in her dress pocket, the dowager decided to drop them strategically and carefully.

When they exited the alley, her captor - the dowager decided to call him Bob - pushed her to turn left. At this point, the dowager slipped her hand into her pocket, brought out one piece of fudge, and dropped it as inconspicuously as possible. The dowager was worried that "Bob" might notice, but the man seemed to have other things on his mind. From the only semi-coherent muttering she could hear behind her, the dowager surmised that her capture was a spur-of-the-moment action and that the man was unsure what to do next and which way to go. Perhaps he was uncertain of who might be tempted to come to her aid if they were observed.

"Best way to Shad Thames?" the man muttered to himself. "What's the best way?"

Whatever street they were walking on was narrow and twisting, but on their next turn, they found themselves outside a public house, The Bell and Whistle, that seemed to be bustling with lunchtime patrons. The dowager surreptitiously dropped another sweet. Now, she looked at how busy The Bell and Whistle seemed to be and rested all her hopes that someone coming in or out would notice and care that she was being held against her will.

One burly man wearing a similar flat cap to Bob's was leaving The Bell as they walked by. He took notice of the unusual sight of the young, working man pushing the elderly woman ahead of him but made a point of looking away. It wasn't for him to question what another working man might feel he needed to force his mother to do. Wives, mothers, sisters, they all needed a firm hand from time to time. In fact, the burly man nodded to Bob in solidarity as he passed.

As the dowager noticed the other man's willingness to ignore whatever trouble she was in, her heart sank. Still, the dowager was not one to give in to despair. While her hopes of being saved by a passerby seemed less likely to materialise, she still had her plan to leave a trail for Tabitha and Wolf. Of course, she had a limited number of pieces of fudge in her pocket, particularly if she hoped to keep some of them for later. She had to drop them strategically. The dowager counted seven of them left in the rather capacious skirt pocket, but she also did not know how much further they might be going.

After passing the public house, they came to a much broader street with some light traffic on it. The dowager looked left and right to see if any of the drivers of the coal carts or hackney cabs might be inclined to stop and come to her assistance. No one did. Bob pushed her across this street as quickly as possible, and they slipped down a very narrow lane that reeked from the nearby tanneries. The dowager dropped another fudge at the end of this lane. It occurred to her she'd be lucky if stray dogs or street urchins didn't pick up the sweets before anyone could follow her train. She just had to hope that Tabitha and Wolf would follow her quickly enough to prevent that from happening.

Another turn, and suddenly, they seemed to be in a far dingier, more dangerous part of London. The dowager was unaccustomed to regular walking and hadn't brought her walking stick with her that day. However long Bob pushed her along, it felt like an eternity. The dowager doubted her ability to keep going but was sure there was little point in appealing to the man's humanity.

What would happen if she collapsed into a pile right where she was? Would he shoot her? Abandon her? Was she willing to take the risk? The dowager decided she was exhausted enough at least to experiment with what might happen. She came to a standstill and reached out to lean against a nearby building.

"Oy! No stopping. Keep going," Bob said in a surly voice.

The dowager decided she had at least to try pleading her case. In a calm, low voice, she pleaded, "You must allow me a moment to rest. I am an old woman."

While the gun was once again jammed into her ribs, Bob didn't stop her from leaning against the wall for a few more moments. Eventually, his patience wore out, and he snarled, "Rest time is over. Get moving, Your Royal Highness."

These last words caught the dowager's attention. Was this merely meant as a sarcastic aside, or did the man have some actual clue that she might be more than Miss Julia Phillips, middle-class social reformer? Perhaps five minutes and four more dropped pieces of fudge later, the dowager caught sight of the River Thames ahead. Painted on the side of a building, she saw the name Shad Thames. It seemed they'd arrived at their destination.

The area was full of warehouses, presumably used to house goods taken off the docks. Like the rest of the area, it remained mostly deserted that Sunday afternoon. Narrow wrought-iron, latticed walkways connected the buildings on both sides of the narrow lane they were now walking down, crisscrossing in an almost charming pattern. The dowager decided she would drop one last piece of fudge at the door of whichever building Bob ended up taking her into.

As that crossed her mind, Bob jabbed her in the back with the gun and muttered, "To the left." Suddenly, the dowager no longer felt the revolver jammed into her back. "I'm moving my hand, but if you make even a squeak or a sudden move, I'll shoot."

Then, Bob went about jimmying the lock on the door. Or perhaps he had a key? The dowager was unable to tell. Either way, before long, the door was open, and Bob had ordered her to enter the building. For a moment, it occurred to the dowager that this was her best chance of escape. Once she was in the building, likely tied up, there would be no opportunity. But Bob was young and strong. He knew his way around these streets, and he had a gun. The dowager may have had an inflated sense of self when it came to most aspects of life, but she had a realistic sense of her physical limitations, even if she kept these thoughts to herself. She couldn't outrun or outmanoeuvre her captor. The dowager knew she could outsmart him, given the chance, and so decided, for now, she would have to allow herself to be forced into this warehouse.

The warehouse had small, dirty windows that let in little light. Inside, it smelled of a not-unpleasant mix of tea, coffee, spices, and something else the dowager was unable to identify. However, underlying the aromas of the goods being stored was another less pleasant smell: a combination of rotten wood, mould, and stagnant water. This close to the Thames, a river mist hung in the air, making the dowager shiver as its cool, damp fingers caressed her skin.

The warehouse was silent. The only sound was the occasional pitter-patter of tiny feet scurrying across the cement floor. The dowager shivered again at the prospect of sharing space with the owners of those feet. Bob pushed her forward into the warehouse and then told her to stop. Before she knew what was happening, he must have found some rope on the floor and had bound her hands. He forced her into a corner and down onto the ground, where he then bound her feet. The final humiliation was when he took a handkerchief from around his neck and tied it around her mouth.

The cloth smelled of sweat and tobacco, and the dowager barely suppressed a gag reflex. From where she was sitting, the sound of what she could only imagine were rats running around the warehouse seemed louder.

Julia Chesterton, the Dowager Countess of Pembroke, prided herself on her courage and fortitude. Even during the more dire days of her marriage, when her husband had used her as his punching bag, she had remained strong and had refused to be cowed. Now, for one of the first times in her life, she was terrified. She was scared for her life, but she was also scared to be left in this warehouse, trussed up like a pig, with rodents scurrying around her.

Yet, that's what happened. Bob muttered a few more words to himself. "Got to think. Got to think. What to do?" And with that, he turned and left her alone in the dark.

Chapter 20

Once Tabitha left, Wolf returned inside and went to the bar. Before he even asked, he could tell that Ellie Perkins knew something was wrong; her unwillingness to make eye contact with him and her nervous energy spoke volumes.

As he considered the woman's apparent anxiety since the moment they entered The George, Wolf realised she wasn't anxious; she was scared. He reconsidered the feeling both he and Tabitha had experienced the day before that they were being followed. Now, it seemed even more likely this had been the case and that someone, perhaps someone who had followed them from The George, realised they were not who they said they were. Had that person communicated to the barmaid to be on the watch for their group returning? It would certainly explain the change in the woman's attitude. However, if she had been intimidated by the person who had trailed them, what were the chances that Ellie would give up information easily now?

After Ellie Perkins finished serving the customer in front of her, she had no choice but to turn to Wolf. Still avoiding his eye, she asked in a tone that tried but failed to be breezy, "How can I help you, sir?"

Wolf made a split-second decision. He was certain their ruse had been exposed. Given that, there seemed no reason to pretend to keep it up. One thing of which he was sure: the average working-class Londoner had a good sense of the unequal justice that his class received compared to theirs - the newspapers' singular focus on Clarence was evidence of that.

Speaking in a low voice, Wolf said, "Mrs Perkins, the elderly woman who was with us has disappeared. She went to avail herself of your facilities but never returned."

"Don't know nuffink about that," Ellie said defensively.

"But I believe you do," Wolf replied forcefully. "I also believe you have guessed I'm not a journalist and that my companion isn't Miss Smart, a photographer. Or, if you have not guessed it, someone has suggested that our stories are a ruse. Is that not true?"

Ellie Perkins didn't answer, but she seemed even more uncomfortable than she already was, if such a thing were possible. She looked around the room as if trying to find an escape.

Wolf decided now was the right time to shock the woman into answering. He pulled himself up to his full height and modulated his voice from the more middle-class tones he had been using. "In fact, I am the Earl of Pembroke, and my companion is my wife, Lady Pembroke. The elderly woman who has been abducted, if I am not mistaken, is the Dowager Countess of Pembroke."

It seemed whatever Ellie Perkins expected the man in front of her to say, this wasn't it. She looked as shocked and as worried as Wolf had expected her to. Under normal circumstances, someone standing at her bar, claiming to be a toff, would have received all the derision he deserved. However, what she'd already been told about Wolf not being who he claimed, and an indefinable something in the manner and voice of the so-called journalist and photographer, meant that Wolf's story had the ring of truth.

The lunchtime rush had petered off somewhat. Ellie looked around her, then gestured to Wolf to go back out to Talbot Yard. "I'll meet you back there in a jiffy."

Less than five minutes later, Ellie joined Wolf in the lane. Before he said anything, she insisted, "I don't know nuffink about where this dowager countess 'as been taken. And it's more than my life's worth to say I do," the woman said in a stubborn voice and with a determined jilt of her chin that intimated she would not be budged from this position. "We don't like snitches around 'ere."

Wolf considered his position and softened his voice. "Mrs. Perkins, a frail, elderly woman is in danger, and I am certain you know who is behind her disappearance. Think about your own parents and help me."

Apparently, this was the wrong thing to say. "Pa was a drunk, and Ma wasn't much better. They both died years ago, and good riddance to them."

Deciding to pivot once more, Wolf tried a harsher tone. "Mrs Perkins, you must realise that the police will care about someone of Lady Pembroke's rank being abducted. And I am not talking of your local bobby but of Scotland Yard. You can answer my questions, or you can answer theirs, but you will be answering questions."

Finally, he seemed to have said something with some impact; the fear on the woman's face told him he had finally struck a nerve. Ellie took a deep breath and said, "It was all the poking around that spooked 'im. And then you not being what you said you were. Ain't no one to blame but yourselves. Pretending to be one thing and then getting in some fancy carriage."

Well, if nothing else, that confirmed that they'd been followed the day before and spotted getting into the Pembroke carriage at Ludgate Hill.

Unwilling to give up too much information to Ellie Perkins, Wolf realised he needed to give some explanation if he were to have any hope of gaining her assistance. "You are correct, Mrs Perkins. We came to Southwark in disguise and misled you. However, it was for a good reason: to save an innocent man from the gallows."

Wolf hoped to gloss over the fact that this innocent man was another aristocrat, but Ellie Perkins was too quick on the uptake for him. "You trying to save that other toff, the one in the newspapers? My 'Arry's been reading it to me. One toff doing another in; why's that any business of the likes of me?"

"Well, everyone should care if an innocent man is wrongfully accused. It is all of our business that we have a justice system that only convicts the guilty."

Even as Wolf said these words, he could hear how naive and rather pompous they sounded. He was not surprised when he was rewarded with a sharp bark of laughter. "So, you think that saving one toff from the gallows will make everything fair for the likes of me? Would anyone care if I'd been, as you say, 'wrongfully accused'?"

Wolf knew the question was reasonable, and all he could answer was, "My wife and I would care. We have cared in the past when working people, such as yourselves, have been accused of crimes we did not believe they committed."

"You some kind of 'ired snoop then?"

While Wolf didn't love the characterisation, the concept was correct and so he nodded.

For a moment, he thought he had finally won Ellie Perkins over, but then her face hardened again. "So, you're snooping round 'ere to try to blame someone from Southwark instead of this toff?" While that had not been their precise intention, Wolf could see how someone might come to such a conclusion.

Finally, spreading his hands out in what he hoped was a gesture of openness, he admitted, "I am trying to blame the right person, whether they reside in Southwark or Mayfair. If my wife and I come to believe that the Earl of Warwick is indeed guilty, we will acknowledge the fact. At the moment, we have reason to doubt that is the case and came to Southwark merely to pursue one thread in the investigation." He had no desire to divulge more than that and hoped these words would suffice.

"Well, it's not 'im who done it," she answered definitively, crossing her arms in a gesture of defiance.

"And if that is the case, then we will ensure that he is not taken for the villain." Wolf wasn't sure who "him" was but guessed it was the person who had taken the dowager. "However, whether or not this man is guilty of murder, he is now guilty of kidnapping. And if you know anything about it and do not assist me, you will be guilty of hiding the identity of someone who is committing a crime."

"I ain't done nuffink, and I ain't seen nuffink," Ellie said defiantly. "And ain't nuffink you or no peeler can do to prove otherwise."

Wolf realised he may have overplayed his hand. Of course, Ellie was correct; there was no way to prove that she knew anything. His feeling that she did, even her vague talk of a "him" would hardly stand up in a court of law. This was particularly true given that there wasn't even any evidence that the dowager had been abducted. Wolf himself had wondered if this was merely a case of an elderly woman becoming confused. Despite his threats of Scotland Yard, would they really care?

Perhaps his resignation showed on his face because Ellie said, "I've got punters waiting," and turned and returned inside.

Kicking himself for resorting to threats, however obliquely, Wolf considered what he might do next. As he looked up Talbot Yard in the direction in which he believed the dowager had been taken, Wolf thought he might as well do some exploratory investigation. Someone might have seen the dowager being forced down the street. Though would an elderly woman dressed in the disguise of a middle-class social reformer really have attracted much attention?

As Wolf walked down the narrow lane, he considered how long it might be before Mickey D and his men arrived. First, Tabitha would have to return to Chesterton House, which would take some time on a Sunday. Then, Rat would have to get to Whitechapel, and that assumed that he was at home and able to leave immediately. How long would it take the boy to get to the East End from Mayfair? Wolf hoped the Langley carriage was available. If it was, the journey shouldn't take too long on a Sunday.

Would he find Mickey D at home? Luckily on a Sunday, Mickey D's movements were more predictable than on other days. Wolf knew that Angie Doherty insisted that the entire family attended church and then returned home for a family meal. Afterwards, it was Mickey D's usual routine to retire to The Cock for the afternoon to meet up with cronies over a pint of two and intimidate the locals. Rat knew this as well as he did and so Wolf was hopeful the lad would track down the East End gang leader easily enough. Assuming they spent some time gathering men, it should not take more than twenty minutes to get to Southwark by carriage.

Even as Wolf did these calculations, he realised it would be a couple of hours at the least before help arrived. He should use that time to narrow down the area to search. If Tabitha found Bear at home, they should arrive sooner. If he and Tabitha set out in the Pembroke carriage immediately, they could be expected within thirty minutes of Tabitha's arrival home, even allowing time for a telephone call to Langley House. Given this, Wolf decided he had about an hour to gather what information he could before going to the Leather Market to meet Bear and Tabitha.

Wolf reflected on his frustrating conversation with Ellie Perkins. Did the little that she had revealed make it more or less likely that the abduction was a crime of opportunity and that a ransom note would appear at some point? In his gut, Wolf felt that the kidnapping had something to do with Lord Redding's death. However, their appearance in Southwark the day before might have stirred up something criminal that had nothing to do with the murder they were investigating.

Wolf knew that this area, particularly around the docks, was rife with crime, given the amount of illegal trade and smuggling that went on almost as part of the regular course of business. Could their appearance the day before have caused unwarranted alarm in someone engaged in unrelated nefarious activity? It was certainly plausible.

Wolf considered Ellie Perkins' apparent fear of whoever had taken the dowager and thought about the inhabitants of Whitechapel's unwillingness to cross Mickey D. Perhaps whoever this person was had a similar hold on this neighbourhood. If that was the case, then he was even more sure that asking Mickey D for his help was the right thing to do. As much as Wolf hated continually putting himself in the man's debt, the East End criminal was sure to know of fellow gang leaders. After all, Mickey D and the Battersea criminal, Jackdaw, had known each other. And Mickey D had a professionally respectful, if wary, relationship with Tuchinsky.

Thinking of Tuchinsky caused Wolf to wonder if he should have sent word to Brick Lane as well. Perhaps Tabitha would think of it. Certainly, the Tuchinsky family's fondness for the dowager countess rivalled Mickey D's own.

Suddenly, Wolf was conscious that he was too absorbed in these thoughts and not paying attention to his surroundings. He might have missed a clue thanks to his woolgathering. As he came to a standstill and collected his thoughts, Wolf realised he was at the end of Talbot Yard. He looked left and he looked right. The enormity of the challenge of tracking the dowager and his abductor through the dark, narrow streets of Southwark and Bermondsey washed over Wolf.

As he once again considered which direction to try first, Wolf noticed something from out of the corner of his eye. He almost missed it, but the incongruity of the crisp, bright-white paper against the grey, grimy alleyway made it stand out.

Bending to see what exactly the paper was, Wolf picked it up and realised that something was wrapped in it. With a jolt of surprise, he recognised the paper-wrapped cube he held in his hand as the fudge the dowager often carried with her. Of course, she might have dropped it by accident, but what if she didn't? What if she had dropped it to leave a trail as to her whereabouts?

While it seemed somewhat of a fool's hope to rely on one dropped piece of fudge to guide him, Wolf had nothing else to dictate whether he went left or right. The fudge had been dropped clearly to the left of the end of Talbot Yard, and so Wolf turned in that direction to see where it led.

Chapter 21

Tabitha's trip back to Ludgate Hill had been uneventful. Relieved of the need to monitor the dowager's behaviour, Tabitha could enjoy the experience of blending in with everyday Londoners going about their business. No one gave her a second thought; she was just another middle-class woman, possibly going to visit family, perhaps on her way from church.

As with the trip to London Bridge, the omnibus wasn't busy, and she easily got a seat by the window. She looked out as they crossed the bridge and progressed towards the Monument of the Great Fire of London before turning left.

Ever since Wolf entered her life, Tabitha had become aware of the small and proscribed world she had previously lived in. Most of London, let alone Britain, was not wealthy and privileged. People struggled, they starved, and they worked long, gruelling hours. These people did not have the luxury of worrying about social etiquette and manners; they were too busy trying to ensure their children had food to eat and a roof over their heads.

Perhaps more than anything, Tabitha had come to realise the profound absurdity of the lives of many in the upper classes. Their concerns were petty, and their grievances trivial. When their children fell sick, they had immediate access to the best doctors and the most modern treatments. Even Tabitha's abuse at Jonathan's hand, as awful as it had been, was no more than many other lower-class women endured. At least Tabitha had a maid to help her cover her bruises and a soft bed to cushion her sore limbs at night.

Tabitha was so absorbed in her thoughts that she almost missed the Ludgate Hill stop and had to scramble to get off before the omnibus began to move again. More aware than she had been the previous day of the possibility that she was followed, Tabitha tried to look around thoroughly but unobtrusively. Finally, satisfied that no one was watching her, she crossed to where Madison and the carriage were waiting.

Madison was an excellent and careful driver, and Tabitha had never had reason to question his skills. Now, as he helped her up, Tabitha said in an almost apologetic tone, "Madison, please drive as quickly as you can safely. The dowager countess is missing, and we must make haste to get help." The driver nodded and closed the door behind her.

As they set off towards Mayfair, Tabitha considered everything she had to do and the correct order in which to do it. She hoped that she'd find Bear at home, but what if she didn't? Deciding to cross that bridge when she came to it, Tabitha resolved to make telephoning Langley House a priority. Wolf had only mentioned telling Rat to take word to Mickey D, but now Tabitha wondered how Lord Langley himself might help.

Wolf hadn't suggested that they recruit Tuchinsky and her men. However, there was no doubt that as surprising as it was, the unconventional female Jewish gang leader was as fond, if not fonder, of the dowager than Mickey D was. Perhaps that wasn't quite right; it was Tuchinsky's bubbe who felt a reciprocated kinship with the other elderly woman that no one could have predicted. What Tuchinsky felt was an overwhelming sense of gratitude towards Tabitha, Wolf and the dowager, not only for Wolf's part in saving her bubbe's life but for their subsequent investigation that proved that a vicious Whitechapel murderer was not from the Jewish community. Tuchinsky would help if she could.

From her time staying in the Tuchinsky residence when Wolf was shot, Tabitha knew Jews held Saturday as their sabbath rather than Sunday. Did this mean that Tuchinsky would not be found at home but might be out and about? Even if it did, Tabitha had learned how small and tight-knit the East End Jewish community was; it wouldn't be difficult to get word to Tuchinsky and her men.

Should she suggest to Rat that after he picks up Mickey D, he takes a detour to Brick Lane? Tabitha wasn't sure how far it was from Whitechapel to Tuchinsky's neighbourhood, but she did not want to risk the delay. Instead, she decided to suggest to Langley that Rat take his carriage to Whitechapel and that he hail a hackney to the dowager's home and make use of her carriage to recruit Tuchinsky to the search. Satisfied with her plan, Tabitha sat back against the carriage's plush cushions and tried not to let her imagination conjure up dire scenarios for what lay ahead of them in their search for the dowager.

As she tried to keep her anxiety under control, Tabitha reflected on how much her relationship with her erstwhile mother-in-law had changed in less than a year. She never would have imagined they would choose to spend so much time together and have found a place of, if not mutual respect, perhaps mutual affection. Certainly, it had been incredibly touching when the dowager had stood up for Tabitha to her mother, Lady Jameson, a few months before. While Tabitha had to acknowledge with sadness that she did not care if she ever saw her own mother again, she realised she cared deeply about the dowager's wellbeing.

By the time the carriage pulled up at Hanover Square, in front of Chesterton House, Tabitha's nerves were so ragged that she didn't even wait for Madison to open the door for her and was instead bounding up the steps in a most unladylike manner before he'd even descended to the street.

As soon as Talbot opened the door, Tabitha gave him a rushed update on what had happened, asked him to put a telephone call through to Langley House and then find Bear. Thankfully, Lord Langley was at home, and she quickly told him what had happened, leaving out the details of the actual investigation. He agreed to send Rat to Mickey D and to fetch Tuchinsky himself. It occurred to Tabitha to mention that he might want to change his clothes before joining them in Southwark. Still, Langley had been involved in enough of their investigations, however marginally, to understand the need to play down his rank.

By the time she had replaced the telephone receiver in its cradle, Talbot had located Bear, who now stood waiting in the vestibule, Rose

O'Leary by his side. Tabitha wondered why Talbot had found the two private secretaries together, and again, she made a mental note to talk with Bear about Rose. For now, she had more important things to worry about. Without even bothering to move into the drawing room, Tabitha told Bear everything that had happened and all that she knew.

"Give me five minutes to change my clothes, and we can be on our way," he said.

"I will also join you, if you will let me," Rose said, surprising Tabitha.

Seeing the look of surprise on her employer's face, Rose said, "It sounds like you need as many able-bodied hands as possible. If nothing else, I may be useful for running messages between the various search parties."

Tabitha checked her immediate impulse to refuse the help. If she wanted to assert her right to be involved in the search regardless of her gender, why should this not be the case for Mrs O'Leary? Instead, Tabitha thanked Rose and suggested that she, too, change into a dress that would be less likely to draw attention to herself.

With both private secretaries off changing their clothes, Tabitha went into Wolf's study and retrieved their guns. It hadn't occurred to them when they set off that morning that they might walk into a dangerous situation, and so they had gone unarmed.

For Christmas, Wolf had given Tabitha a Derringer pistol with a pretty mother-of-pearl handle as a gift. She put this in one of her jacket pockets and put Wolf's revolver in the other. She knew Bear had a gun of his own and did not doubt he would think to bring it with him.

Barely fifteen minutes after she had descended from the Pembroke carriage, Tabitha re-entered it, accompanied by Bear and Rose. Tabitha had been in such a hurry that her original explanation to Bear had been brief. Now that they had at least a thirty-minute carriage ride back to Southwark, he asked her to tell them in greater detail about their two trips to London Bridge. Tabitha had decided that they didn't have time to go through the charade of getting the omnibus again. It was clear their ruse had been exposed and so they might as well take advantage of the speed a private carriage would afford them.

Bear and Rose listened intently to Tabitha's story. Then, Rose asked the same question that Wolf had considered: was it possible that a criminal had abducted the dowager, worried by their presence in Southwark, but for a reason entirely unrelated to the murder of Lord Redding?

Tabitha pondered the question. "I think it is not only possible but also likely. However, at this point, it is irrelevant. As much as Lord Pembroke and I are committed to trying to secure an acquittal for Lord Warwick, finding Lady Pembroke is our priority. Someone has taken her prisoner, and it does not matter their reason at this point."

Now, Bear asked the question that had been running through Tabitha's head for much of the drive to Mayfair from Ludgate Hill, "Did you notice anyone suspicious in the inn today?"

"I have reflected repeatedly on our time there. To be honest, I wasn't paying close enough attention. The dowager countess was, well, she was being herself, and I was too consumed with worry over that to pay much mind to our fellow patrons. From what I can recall, no one stood out. The only person behaving strangely was the barmaid, Ellie Perkins. And I did not notice that; Wolf did. He was going to go back inside and talk to her. But there could be a host of reasons that she was out-of-sorts that have nothing to do with us."

For the rest of the trip, Tabitha reviewed every detail they had learned about the murder. When she was finished, Rose said hesitantly, "It is not my place to comment on or judge your reasoning, milady, but..." She paused, biting her lip anxiously.

"Mrs O'Leary, I hired you because you are an intelligent, thoughtful woman who I trust to manage my personal affairs. If it was not stated before, let me do so plainly now: I wish to hear your opinions. All of them. If you ever disagree with my judgement, you are free to tell me so."

Rose's face said enough about her scepticism about this statement that Tabitha didn't even wait for her to answer. Instead, she asked Bear, "Have you ever known this to be untrue of either myself or Lord Pembroke?"

Bear confirmed that both Lord and Lady Pembroke were always open to candid observations and assessments from the people around them. He added quickly, "Though when I say Lady Pembroke, I mean this Lady Pembroke. If I were you, I would refrain from speaking in such a manner to the dowager countess."

Rose laughed. "I had already determined that myself. Thank you, milady. In that case, I was just thinking that you went to talk to this Sally Turnbull because it was the only slim clue you have in an otherwise rather barren investigation. Is there any reason at all to think that she, or anyone around her, has anything to do with Lord Redding's murder?"

Tabitha sighed; her private secretary had accurately identified the weakness in their investigative actions over the past two days. "The only things we know that connect Lords Redding and Warwick are that they were classmates many decades ago and that they shared the favours of the same woman. It strains credulity to believe that a childhood animosity, however extreme, might have culminated in murder. And so, we are left with Sally Turnbull's mother."

Again, Rose pointed out the flaw in Tabitha's logic. "Just because those are the only two things you know the men had in common doesn't mean that is all there is. Perhaps they had shared business dealings. You really don't know." They didn't know. It was a truth Tabitha had to acknowledge.

"You are perfectly correct, Mrs O'Leary. As soon as we have found her ladyship, we need to expand this investigation to learn more about the victim." Tabitha paused. "Perhaps you might join us to review what we know so far. Once the dowager is home safely, that is."

Rose blushed. "I would be honoured to be of assistance, milady."

Tabitha caught the look that Mrs O'Leary shared with Bear and the little smile that seemed just for him. What was going on there?

Although it seemed as if they had been driving forever, eventually, they crossed London Bridge and were weaving their way through the narrow streets of Bermondsey. Located just off Weston Street, the Leather Market sat at the heart of London's leather trade. When the City of London banned tanning because of the disgusting smells that were not helped by the use of dog waste to soften the skins, the leather industry moved south of the river to Bermondsey. Even though Sunday was a day of rest, the foul odour hung in the air like a miasma.

Tabitha couldn't even imagine how much worse the smell was when the tanning was actually taking place. And she certainly couldn't imagine spending all day, every day, inhaling the revolting smell up close. The carriage pulled up outside of a modern, quite grand building that proclaimed it was 'The London Leather, Hide and Wool Exchange'. Wolf was nowhere to be seen.

As they sat in the carriage, waiting for Wolf to appear, Tabitha asked, "When you spoke to Andrews, was he able to share any details about Lord Redding's life?"

"Nothing that wasn't already common knowledge. He and his wife were unable to have children. She is now deceased after some years abroad. Her death certificate said the cause of death was dropsy."

Tabitha considered his words. Something was niggling her, but she couldn't quite put her finger on what it was.

CHAPTER 22

The dowager wasn't sure how long she had been alone in the warehouse. It felt like an interminable amount of time, but she realised it was likely to have only been a couple of hours, maybe less. She had done her best to ignore the rats, and, at least so far, they had mostly ignored her. While Bob hadn't done the best job of using the handkerchief as a gag, the muffled sounds that the dowager was able to make hadn't done more than alert the rats and send them scurrying some more.

The one bright spot the dowager could think of was that she had used the facilities just before she had been taken. She didn't need to add soiling herself to her indignities. Though it occurred to her that if her captor didn't return soon, that might be the least of her concerns.

Just as she was beginning to think that her abductor might never come back, she heard a sound ahead, and then he was in front of her. Bob pulled her to her feet roughly and pulled the gag down off her mouth. Then he stood there, contemplating his prisoner. He hadn't untied her hands or feet and so it was difficult to stand. If it wasn't for the fact that she was next to a barrel she could lean against, the dowager feared she might have fallen back to the ground.

While the warehouse was gloomy, Bob was standing in a beam of light that had managed to break through the grease of the windows. The dowager was well-versed in sizing up an opponent. Rarely did she find herself pitted against someone she found worthy of engaging in combat; this time was no exception. Even in the gloom, the dowager was able to get a better look at Bob and realised he was much younger than she had assumed. She also thought he looked familiar, but she couldn't think why. He couldn't have even been twenty. The most striking feature of Bob's otherwise plain face was a pair of very blue eyes with large pupils. The eyes suggested a measure of intelligence, which the dowager was pleased to observe; a stupid man with a gun was far more dangerous than one who couldn't understand the stakes involved.

The most obvious thing the dowager noticed about his face was how suffused it was with anxiety. This was not a cold, calculated killer with a well-thought-out scheme. Instead, the dowager realised at that moment that seizing her had been a spur-of-the-moment decision and that the young man had no plan. She could work with that, the dowager decided. However, the man was pointing a gun at her, and the dowager knew desperate men acted in haste without considering the consequences. She already knew that Bob was capable of acting impulsively. She didn't want shooting her to be his next impulse.

Modulating her voice to be as compassionate as she could pretend to be, the dowager said, "Young man, I do not believe that you intended to abduct me and that it was something you did on a momentary whim. I am not sure what caused it, but it is not too late to undo what you have done."

"How do you figure that?" Bob asked. His tone suggested genuine curiosity at her words.

"If you let me go now, we can pretend that this unfortunate incident never happened. I will tell my companions that I took a stroll up the lane and became lost. I am an old woman, it is believable; they are always underestimating my vigour and mental acumen."

"Who are you?" Bob asked, cocking his head. "You look like some purse-lipped old biddy from the church, but you sound more like the Queen."

"Far be it from me to refute a comparison to Her Majesty," the dowager said regally. "You would not be the first of your class to see the similarities. However, if memory serves me, her pitch is somewhat higher."

Bob looked at her as if he had encountered a new, bizarre species and repeated, "Who are you?"

While the dowager had been persuaded that it was necessary to disguise her aristocratic heritage for the visit to Southwark, doing so had gone against her firmly held belief that the best way to subdue the lower classes was by rendering them dumbstruck with awe and fear.

It took but a moment for her to decide that the Dowager Countess of Pembroke would be a far more daunting foe than Miss Julia Phillips. Throwing back her already quite straight shoulders, the dowager said in a tone that the Queen would have been proud to call her own, "I am the Dowager Countess of Pembroke. You may refer to me as Lady Pembroke, your ladyship or milady."

"You're pulling my leg, right?"

"If you are suggesting I am speaking in jest, I must warn you that while I am revered for my bon mots, I am not known as a prankster. If I were to wear false colours, I assure you I would at the very least assume the rank of duchess, if not marchioness."

The young man shook his head in confusion; what was this old bird prattling on about? He'd almost immediately realised that grabbing her had been a mistake, but now it seemed it might be an even more significant lapse of judgement than he'd realised.

The dowager sensed his consternation at her news and repeated, "Let me go now, and no one will be any the wiser. You may go about your business, and I will go about mine."

This was the wrong thing to say, and as soon as the words were out of the dowager's mouth, she realised she had reminded her abductor about why he had taken her in the first place.

"Why are you poking around in Southwark with those two, pretending to be ink-slingers?"

While the dowager wasn't certain what an ink-slinger was, she assumed the term had something to do with the charade Tabitha and Wolf had concocted for why they were asking questions in Southwark.

Bob continued, "I saw them leave here and get in some swanky carriage yesterday. If you're this so-called dowager countess, who are they?"

There seemed no good reason to continue claiming that Tabitha and

Wolf were journalists, so she confessed, "They are the Earl and Countess of Pembroke."

"I thought you were the countess."

"I am the dowager countess. This is the title one adopts when one's husband, an earl, is deceased and one's son, the new earl, remarries. His wife becomes the countess, and one becomes the dowager countess."

The young man didn't seem interested in a lesson on how Debrett's defined the various categories of rank. Instead, he zeroed in on the only part of the narrative that mattered to him. "So, why are you all slumming it in Southwark?"

Now, the dowager faced a conundrum. Like Wolf and Tabitha, she assumed that this young man was involved in something criminal unrelated to Redding's murder and that he had been spooked that they were poking around and asking questions. Given that, was there any harm in telling the truth?

Finally, the dowager decided to be no more truthful than she must to maintain credibility. "We are private inquiry agents," she explained proudly. "We have been engaged by a client who has been accused of a crime. He claims he is falsely accused."

"You're a private inquiry agent?" was the sceptical answer. "You short of a bob or two or something?"

"If you are asking if I pursue this career for pecuniary advantage, the answer is no. I do it for the intellectual challenge and to be of service to my fellow man." On the spur of the moment, the dowager added the last phrase. She thought it hit just the right note of magnanimity to impress upon Bob how wrong it was to imprison a woman of such nobility and virtue.

As she considered this and called him Bob to herself, the dowager realised that developing a more personal relationship with her captor might help her cause. "I have told you who I am, yet you have not introduced yourself. What is your name, young man?"

Before he could consider the wisdom of sharing his identity, the man she had thought of as Bob answered, "Joe."

Unable to stifle a smile at her success, the dowager said, "Well, Joe, now that you realise why we are in disguise, perhaps you might release me, and we can both be on our way."

Joe narrowed his eyes and pointed his weapon at the dowager again. "What's the crime you're investigating?"

The dowager waved her hand and replied breezily, "Oh, that is unimportant. We came to Southwark on the slightest of gossamer investigative threads." She lowered her voice slightly to a more conspiratorial tone. "If the truth be told, my colleagues were grasping at straws, and I made them aware of it. I have less faith in our client's innocence than they do. However, I have always recognised that I am merely a cog in the machine and that my insights hold no more value than anyone else's." Of course, she didn't genuinely believe that, but the dowager sensed it was crucial to downplay her role in the investigation in Southwark.

During this conversation, Joe had been thinking about what his next move might be. Even on a Sunday, Butler's Wharf and the surrounding docks and warehouses were not entirely empty of workers. And come very early the following morning, there would be men streaming in and out of this building. He'd come here because it was where he worked, and he couldn't think of where else to take the old woman. However, it was a less-than-perfect solution.

He'd left the old biddy here for a while to think about where else he might take her, but he hadn't come up with anywhere better than the wharf, and that hiding place would only be good for a few more hours. What to do? Maybe he should do as she suggested and release her. Was it possible that she would just go on her way and not immediately report her abduction to the nearest police officer?

While Joe knew little about the aristocracy, he shared the average common man's opinion that things worked differently for toffs than they did for them. He could imagine that if he found the nearest bobby and told him he'd been taken prisoner and then released, he'd be greeted with nothing more than a chuckle and a "Then get on your way and thank your lucky stars." Joe expected that a dowager countess, particularly one who seemed on familiar terms with the Queen, might be able to appeal to a far higher power than a high street bobby.

Why had he taken her in the first place? At the time, Joe had wanted to know what the toffs were really doing in Southwark and thought that the old woman was the best way to get information. Well, now he had it. Or at least some of it. Did it still make sense to hold her? His mother's lament throughout his childhood and beyond was that he was impetuous and didn't think about the consequences of his actions. Joe could only imagine what she would have thought of the pickle he seemed to have got himself into.

The voice kept saying, "You have to kill her now. You know you do." The voice kept getting louder, and now, one of his headaches was coming on. Joe had tried to quieten the voice and then, when he couldn't, ignored it. Could he really kill this old woman? "Yes," said the voice. "You have a gun. Just pull the trigger, and it'll all be over. You can dump her in the Thames, and no one will be any the wiser when her body finally washes up downriver somewhere."

"No, no!" Joe said out loud to the voices in his head.

"No, what?" the dowager asked.

"Just do it," the voice said in a commanding tone. "What other options do you have?"

Joe hated it when he couldn't control the voice. It had got him into so much trouble over the last couple of years. But he also knew that it was futile to try to fight it; the voice always won. And so, he closed his eyes, pulled the trigger, watched the old lady crumple to the ground, then turned and ran. He knew he should have gathered up the body and thrown it into the Thames, but he couldn't bring himself to touch the corpse.

Just before the gun went off, Joe yelled a name. The dowager's last thought as she collapsed was, "Wait, I think I know who he is."

Chapter 23

Wolf had followed the trail of two pieces of fudge into Bermondsey. He'd made a few false turns, and only when no more fudge turned up had he double-backed and tried other routes. When he initially found only the first piece of fudge, he told himself that, even if the dowager had dropped it, perhaps it was merely an accident. However, it was all he had to go on, so Wolf continued to search until he found the second piece at the start of a narrow lane leading into the heart of Bermondsey.

He would have liked to have kept on searching, but a glance at his pocket watch told Wolf that he'd been searching for longer than he realised and needed to meet Tabitha and, hopefully, Bear at the Leather Market.

Wolf wound his way through the various tanneries and warehouses of the leather district and finally found Leather Market Street and what was commonly referred to as The Exchange. The Pembroke carriage was very conspicuous in this gritty working-class neighbourhood, and he could see the curious gazes of passersby. As Wolf hurried towards the carriage, he was relieved to see Bear was with Tabitha and intrigued to see Mrs O'Leary.

Wolf opened the carriage door and was met by Tabitha's anxious and expectant countenance. "Did you find her? Did Mrs Perkins know anything?"

"No and no," he said. As Wolf saw his wife's face fall, he quickly added, "But I think her ladyship left us a trail."

"A trail of what?"

Wolf couldn't help smiling. "A trail of fudge."

"Excuse me? What is a trail of fudge?" Tabitha asked in a bemused voice. Wolf explained.

"So, where did this trail lead?" Bear asked when he was finished.

"Well, there was no time to continue to follow it because I needed to come and meet you. We can take the carriage to the last place I found a piece, then carry on from there." Turning to Tabitha, Wolf asked, "Were you able to get hold of Langley and Rat?"

"I was. And I asked Lord Langley to go and ask Tuchinsky for help while Rat fetches Mickey D."

"Good thinking. The same thing occurred to me after you left, so I am glad you thought of it as well."

"What direction does this trail of fudge seem to lead in?" Mrs O'Leary asked in a quiet voice, still nervous about her right to be involved.

"Well, it started to take me into the heart of Bermondsey. We told Mickey D to meet us by the new Tower Bridge, and so far, that seems to be the direction they were headed in." Wolf paused and considered what he'd said. "I want to make sure we are making the most of whatever manpower we end up having. I cannot believe Mickey D will be here for at least another forty-five minutes, if not more, no matter how fast Langley's carriage went. I think we need to divide and conquer but also be thoughtful and strategic."

Everyone nodded in agreement. Turning to Rose, Wolf said, "Mrs O'Leary, I assume you are here because you wish to be of assistance."

"Indeed. Please use me however you see fit."

"Thank you. In that case, I think we should drop you by Tower Bridge to wait for Mickey D while we go back to the last place I found a piece of fudge."

To Wolf's surprise, Bear interrupted him. "That's a pretty rough area, Wolf. We can't just leave Rose, I mean Mrs O'Leary, there alone."

Surprised, Wolf caught Tabitha's eye, and she lifted her eyebrows just enough to alert him to her suspicions.

"What do you suggest then, Bear?" he asked.

"Mrs O'Leary and I will wait for Mickey D and his men. I assume Tuchinsky has been told to meet in the same place. You and Tabitha drop us off and then take the carriage to wherever you found the fudge and try to follow the trail. When Mickey D and Tuchinsky arrive, we will see if we have any more information to help them begin to search."

It all seemed somewhat awkward to Tabitha. When she considered how having a telephone installed had enabled them to stay in much quicker and more efficient contact with the dowager and Lord Langley, she wondered whether there would ever be a time when the innovation was ubiquitous, perhaps even available publicly.

It seemed Mrs O'Leary had a similar worry to Tabitha. In a very no-nonsense voice, she suggested, "Why don't Bear and I stay in one spot, and you can all use us to relay information between the various groups."

"That is an excellent idea!" Tabitha said, causing her private secretary to blush deeply. "I assume Rat will come with Mickey D."

"I do not imagine the lad will be content to be merely a messenger boy," Wolf agreed. "Particularly if he knows that Lady Pembroke is in danger." Rat and the dowager seemed to have developed a mutual affection, which those around them found quite baffling. That the dowager, who was the epitome of snobbery and elitism, should be so fond of, even have respect for, a boy who less than a year ago was a Whitechapel urchin and pickpocket was something neither Tabitha nor Wolf could get over.

Wolf continued, "Are you thinking the boy could run messages between the various search parties?"

"I am. He does not know these streets, I assume, but he is a bright boy and a fast runner. I think if we implement Mrs O'Leary's idea and utilise Rat in this way, we can try to cover as much ground as possible while coordinating between the various groups."

With a plan in place, they told Madison to take them to Tower Bridge. The bridge, finished only four years before, was still a source of wonder for Londoners. It had been designed for its pointed arches, towers and decorative stonework to echo the architecture of the nearby Tower of London. The towers, while an architectural splendour, also housed the engineering marvel of the bridge's hydraulic machinery, which worked the drawbridge, allowing the flow of river traffic to all the docks while also connecting the two riverbanks of the Thames. Before its construction, London Bridge had been the only way to cross the Thames east of the city. Tower Bridge had significantly reduced traffic congestion.

As they approached the bridge, Tabitha looked out of the carriage window eagerly. She hadn't seen the bridge before and had only ever previously seen photos of it in the newspapers. The reality took her breath away.

Previously, Tabitha always thought of bridges as nothing more than functional. Perhaps the only exception to this had been when they had visited Edinburgh, and she had taken the train across the majestic Forth Bridge as it traversed the Firth of Forth. Its red-brown steel trusses had formed an intricate, almost delicate, lattice pattern in the sky. This bridge had a very different feel to it. The Cornish granite and Portland stone it was built out of had somehow been constructed to seem very old. The bridge had an almost medieval splendour about it, even though the bridge was only four years old. All in all, it was very impressive.

As it happened, Wolf was the only one of them who had ever seen Tower Bridge before, so they all exited the carriage and admired the structure.

"It opens up so the boats can go through, does it?" Mrs O'Leary marvelled after Wolf explained what he understood of how the bridge worked. "Whatever will they think of next?"

A new century was almost upon them, and as the pace of engineering innovation seemed to increase exponentially with every passing year, her question gave them all pause. What would they think of next?

The mechanical marvel that was the horseless carriage, or motor car as people were starting to call them, first appeared on the streets of London a few years before. While it was still a rare sight, Wolf realised it was more common than it had been. He even contemplated purchasing one, though he hadn't mustered up the courage to suggest this to Tabitha yet. Would there come a time when there were more motor cars in London than horse-drawn carriages? When Wolf considered how common and popular train travel had become, it became more believable that the new century would bring its own transportation miracles.

As fascinating as Tower Bridge was, particularly as the drawbridge went up while they watched, everyone realised that time was of the essence. Tabitha and Wolf re-entered the carriage and made their way back to where Wolf had found the last piece of fudge. In the carriage, Tabitha handed Wolf his gun. He smiled, grateful she had thought to bring it.

Unfortunately, given the labyrinthine nature of the alleyways and narrow streets of Bermondsey, and Wolf's unfamiliarity with the area, it took them at least thirty minutes to find where his search had left off. He took the unconventional approach of exiting the carriage and sitting up top with Madison so he could more easily comment on what looked familiar and direct the driver. Wolf could only imagine what the dowager would say if she could see the Earl of Pembroke sitting on top of his own carriage next to his servant. But needs must.

When they eventually found the spot, Wolf directed Madison to do his best to drive alongside them as they followed the trail the dowager had left. Of course, some streets were so narrow that the large Pembroke carriage could not squeeze down them. Then Madison had to do his best to navigate to where he thought the street would lead and meet them there. The entire enterprise wasted time they didn't have, and Tabitha and Wolf were both frustrated by their slow progress.

Finally, they had now found four pieces of fudge and realised they were headed back towards Tower Bridge.

"Do you think Mama has been taken to somewhere around the docks?" Tabitha asked.

"Well, if you remember, originally, I posited that the areas around Butler's Wharf and the warehouses of Leather Market were two likely places to hold someone prisoner."

Tabitha winced at his use of the word prisoner, and Wolf took her hand and squeezed it. "We will find her," he promised.

By the time their search had led them back to where they'd begun, Shad Thames by Tower Bridge, Rose O'Leary confirmed that Mickey D and some of his men had arrived with Rat. He'd been quickly followed by Tuchinsky and three of her men, arriving with Langley. Hoping to cover as much ground as possible, Tuchinsky had taken her men to Jacob's Island, where there were more wharves and warehouses.

"Mickey D and his men decided to go to the other end of Shad

Thames and work back," Bear explained. "But it's rather like looking for a needle in a haystack. There are so many warehouses, and we don't even know that this is where she's been taken. What if we're barking up the wrong tree entirely?"

Wolf was happy he had good news to share about that last question, at least. "We believe this is where they came from. We followed some more pieces of fudge, and they pointed away from Leather Market and in this direction."

Tabitha asked a question that had been bothering her for some time, "Are any of these warehouses even open? How will they possibly search them otherwise?"

Wolf chuckled. "I am sure it is not the first time that some of these men have broken into buildings around these docks, and it will not be the last. But it is a large enough area of packed buildings and so there is a lot to cover. Tabitha, we should continue to search for more of her ladyship's trail. That may help to narrow the search significantly."

Chapter 24

Tabitha considered how far they had walked from The George Inn. Of course, they had not walked the most direct route but had instead gone around in circles and sometimes doubled-backed on themselves. Even so, it was a long walk. She knew the dowager hadn't brought her walking stick with her that day and worried about how the old woman had managed to trudge such a distance.

"If she has been brought here, do you think that means that whoever has taken her works around the docks?" she asked Wolf.

Wolf considered the question. "I think he must. After all, while it is quiet, it is not even entirely abandoned here on a Sunday. Why would someone choose this location if not for familiarity?" As he said this, Wolf looked around at the dreary, almost foreboding docks with their grimy streets and huge, hulking iron cranes.

While most of the workers had taken the sabbath and there were fewer carts, there was some activity. Men were by the river shouting, and a few shipments were being moved on and off the docks. Ships were still moving up and down the Thames, and some lightermen were moving goods off some ships that had docked by Butler's Wharf.

"Though, if he works at the docks, I imagine he realised that they would not be entirely empty, even on a Sunday," Tabitha observed. "Perhaps that speaks to someone acting in the moment rather than with a well-thought-through plan." As she said these words, Tabitha wasn't sure if she thought this boded well or ill. Someone with a plan would be less likely to make silly mistakes. Someone acting on impulse might be more likely to act erratically and perhaps even dangerously.

"You are right, of course. Let us see whether we can get any information out of any of the men here."

"If they had seen one of their own with the dowager, do you think they would have noticed? And even if they did, will they say anything to us?"

It was a good question, and Wolf didn't have an answer to it. He had little experience with dockworkers, but from what he did know, they were a loyal bunch and distrustful of outsiders. Particularly fancy outsiders. Whether they would reveal anything in general, it seemed even less likely they would to Tabitha and Wolf, who, even in plainer clothes, would seem fancy to these men.

Up ahead, they could see a worker in an oilskin coat talking with an older man with a thick, muscular neck and the weatherbeaten skin of someone who has spent many decades out by the water, rain or shine. They were pointing at a barge that the lighterman must have just moved into the wharf.

"Stay here," Wolf told Tabitha. "I think these men will be even less inclined to talk if a woman is present."

Tabitha bristled at the unfairness of this yet knew Wolf was correct. She watched as her husband approached the two men. Tabitha saw the surprise and then derision on their faces as he began to speak to them, and she could imagine the sarcastic, dismissive tone they were answering him in. She saw Wolf point at a few of the warehouses around, then saw the men shake their heads; nothing about this exchange looked promising.

Wolf walked back towards her, and his face told Tabitha all she needed to know. "I am not sure if they know nothing or will not say, but there was precious little to be had from either of them. The only thing I could get out of them is that all these warehouses are usually locked on a Sunday. Apparently, only the foreman has the keys."

Hesitating for a moment, Wolf then said, "I have never been involved in investigations around the docks; they're too far from Whitechapel.

However, I know dockers are known for often turning a blind eye to smuggling as long as they get a cut. Some gangs even control specific warehouses."

"Are you suggesting our kidnapper is involved with a gang of smugglers, and that is how he has access to one of these warehouses?" Tabitha asked in alarm. While it had occurred to her previously that the dowager had been taken because their questions had worried someone engaged in criminal activity, that it might be someone involved with gangs of smugglers somehow seemed far more dangerous.

Wolf shrugged. "I am not suggesting anything more than that there are the people who officially have keys to these warehouses, and then there are others who might know how to gain access in a more unofficial capacity. Let us walk around and make our way down Shad Thames. There are enough workers on the wharf side, even today, that I cannot believe our kidnapper would take the risk of someone asking questions."

Tabitha agreed, and they turned back the way they had come, then cut down a very narrow passageway onto Shad Thames. There was something very bleak and intimidating about the narrow street, lined with vast, soot-covered warehouses on either side. Even on this quite sunny day, the iron walkways crisscrossing the street up above gave the area a dark and gloomy feel. When they had first walked down Butler's Wharf, Tabitha's senses had been rather overwhelmed with the combination of odours of rotting wood, damp ropes and saltwater. At least here, a little way from the water, the smell was less unpleasant and ran more to exotic spices, tea and coffee, even if this combination had an unfortunate underlying whiff of fish and tar.

The cobblestones were thick with the mud and filth. After a few steps, Tabitha realised it was futile to try to pick her way through the grime. Interspersed between the warehouses were dark and foul-smelling side alleys where pipes dripped, empty barrels were abandoned to rot, and rats gorged themselves on the decomposing fruit that had fallen off wagons.

Unlike the wharf, this street was eerily quiet, and Tabitha shivered. If this is where the dowager had been brought, it must have been a very unpleasant few hours for the elderly woman.

Suddenly, Tabitha and Wolf heard footsteps behind them. They turned and noticed a man with thick, grey hair approaching. As the face came into view, the bright blue eyes, thick neck, and oft-broken nose announced Mickey D. While Mickey D was known for his charming, roguish grin, he wasn't smiling now. When he saw he'd been recognised, Mickey D raised his chin in a subtle greeting.

Mickey D didn't speak until he was very near to Tabitha and Wolf. While the docks weren't his territory, London's criminal network was close-knit, and the East End gang leader didn't need word of his chummy relationship with a bunch of toffs to become any more widely known than it already was.

"Wolf!" he said in greeting. "M'lady," he said in a far quieter voice.

"For the purposes of this expedition, why do you not call me Tabitha," she suggested. Mickey D nodded at this. "Have you discovered anything, Mr Doherty?" she asked hopefully.

"Nothing so far. Most of these warehouses have better-than-average locks, which makes sense. Don't mean my men can't get in, but it slows us down. Then, we have to go quietly; don't want to spook whoever's taken Lady P. But, so far, we've found sweet Fanny Adams."

"And what about Tuchinsky and her men?" Tabitha asked eagerly, even though it was obvious that they would have heard if anyone had discovered anything.

"Bugger all!" The passionate frustration behind Mickey D's words said more about his affection for the dowager than anything.

Hearing the hardened gang leader almost get choked up brought the gravity of the situation home to Tabitha. She gripped Wolf's arm and begged, "We must do more. She could be anywhere?" As she said those words, a gunshot rang out.

Before they could even determine where the shot had come from, a warehouse door opened, and a young man ran out. It wasn't clear he had even seen them; such was his haste.

"Oy!" Mickey D yelled out. The young man turned his head, saw them and then, with his eyes wide with fear, he took off in the opposite direction. Of course, they didn't know this was the man who had taken the dowager, but there was no time to consider this. Instead, Mickey D said, "Wolf, you follow him. Tabitha and I will see what's in the warehouse."

Wolf had taken off before Mickey D could even finish his sentence. It had been a long time since he'd had cause to chase anyone, and Wolf silently cursed how he'd allowed himself to be seduced by regular, decadent meals, good claret, and a comfortable carriage. The man had a decent lead on him already. If Wolf had any chance of catching him, he'd have to exert himself in a way he hadn't in a long time.

Watching her husband run off into the gloom of Shad Thames in search of a man who may or may not be the one they were searching for, Tabitha made to go into the warehouse he had just exited.

As she turned towards the open door, Mickey D put a hand on her arm and said in a gentle, almost avuncular tone, "Ah, don't do that, child – you'll only bring yourself grief. Let me go first. You wait here."

Until he said these words, Tabitha hadn't really considered what she might find inside the warehouse. Now, she turned panicked, stricken eyes towards Mickey D, suddenly filled with the urge to throw herself at his chest and weep.

Tabitha took a deep breath; she couldn't fall apart now. Whatever they found in that warehouse, the dowager would need her to be strong and capable. "You may go in first, but I will accompany you," she said determinedly. Mickey D didn't argue. Instead, he pulled a revolver out of his waistband, and Tabitha took her gun out of her pocket. The implication was clear enough: they didn't know what they were walking into.

Inside the warehouse, it was so dark it took a moment or two for Tabitha's eyes to adjust. Once they had, she realised that there was a figure lying prone on the dirty cement floor.

"Mama!" Tabitha gasped, pushing past Mickey D.

The dowager was lifeless. The pungent, acrid smell around them was evidence enough that a gun had been discharged.

Mickey D was already on the ground next to the dowager, who had her hands and feet bound. He picked something up off the ground and held it up for Tabitha to see. "Well, the good news is that this is the bullet."

"Why is that good news?"

"Because if it's on the floor, it's not lodged in Lady P. My best guess would be it hit something, probably her corset."

"If the bullet did not enter, then what is the matter with her?" Tabitha moved to his side and knelt next to the old woman. Lying motionless on the grubby floor of the gloomy warehouse, the dowager looked very frail and every one of her many decades.

Careful not to move her too much, Mickey D lit a match that he pulled out of his pocket. "There's a small pool of blood by her head." Tabitha gasped. "She must have hit her head as she fell."

Mickey D blew out the match and felt for a pulse. "She's still breathing." He turned his head to look at Tabitha. "Lady P isn't one to go down without a fight. But we've got to get her to a doctor. I assume she uses one of those snooty Harley Street types."

As it happened, the dowager's personal physician very much fit this description. While the man had the right diplomas on his wall, Tabitha couldn't imagine when he had last dealt with anything as serious as the head wound that the dowager seemed to have.

Suddenly, she realised what she had to do. "We must take her to Brick Lane, to Dr. Abraham Cohen. He saved Wolf, and I cannot think of anyone I trust more."

It was too dark to see Mickey D's reaction to this statement, though Tabitha could imagine. Whatever he thought, what he answered was, "Then let me get Bear to carry Lady P to the carriage, and I'll run to get Tuchinsky to help us find this miracle doctor."

CHAPTER 25

Wolf moved as fast as he could, his boots echoing on the damp cobblestones. Ahead, the figure he was pursuing slipped into the shadows, gaining ground with each step. As his chest tightened from exertion, Wolf vowed never to let himself become so soft around the middle again. He knew that many of his peers maintained their physical vigour in the gymnasiums of their private clubs. His last thought before his quarry vanished from sight was that he and Bear would undertake regular exercise as soon as this case was resolved.

Suddenly, Wolf could no longer see the man in front of him; he appeared to have vanished into thin air. When Wolf reached the last spot where he had seen the figure he was chasing, he realised there was a very narrow alleyway he must have slipped into. Wolf turned into the alley, made even narrower by the clutter of old barrels and discarded ropes. As he did, he caught a last glimpse of a man's back disappearing up a rusted iron staircase.

Wolf assumed the staircase led to one of the elevated walkways connecting the warehouses above the street. Quickening his pace, he climbed it. The iron creaked under Wolf's weight as he ascended, taking two steps at a time. Although he knew the staircase regularly bore the load of many burly workers moving up and down, it felt precarious, and Wolf stepped on each stair gingerly. Upon reaching the top, he gazed down the narrow iron walkway, slick with rain that must have fallen during the night. The railing was rusted in places, and the entire structure appeared even less safe than the staircase itself.

The man had crossed the walkway by the time Wolf reached the top of the stairs. Joe was fast, but his panic also made him reckless. As he ran, he collided with a stack of wooden crates left abandoned on the already narrow walkway. One crate tumbled over the edge, crashing down into the alley below and splintering on the cobblestones.

Wolf barely had time to duck as another crate came hurtling towards him. He sidestepped, his boots slipping on the wet metal, and with a sudden lunge forward, he nearly caught up with his prey, now only a few strides ahead.

The walkway led to another warehouse. The man grasped its iron door handle, pulling with force, but the door was locked. He looked around frantically. A brief hesitation was all Wolf needed.

Wolf surged forward, grabbing Joe's coat and yanking him back onto the walkway. The fabric tore, and with a curse, Joe spun, swinging wildly. Wolf ducked as the punch glanced off his shoulder, driving his weight forward and slamming them both against the railing. The rusted iron groaned. A piece snapped away, clattering onto the cobbles below.

For one terrifying moment, Joe's balance tipped too far back, his arms flailing like pinwheels. His heel caught the edge of a missing slat, and Wolf had a split second to decide whether to let him fall or to pull him back.

He grabbed the man's wrist.

The man he was assisting snarled in frustration: "Let me fall! Better this than the gallows."

But Wolf had already pulled the man onto the walkway and back towards the safety of the building's edge, preventing him from plunging to the stones below. Joe gasped and struggled, but Wolf twisted his arm behind him, pinning him firmly against the cold brick of the warehouse.

"No more running," Wolf growled, pulling out his gun and training it on the young man. Joe had tucked his own revolver back in his waistband after shooting the dowager, but he didn't even try to reach for it now and immediately put his hands up in surrender.

"You are going to go down the stairs in front of me," Wolf ordered. "If you make any sudden moves or try to run, I will shoot. Do you understand?" Looking at the young man in front of him, Wolf didn't feel that he was looking at a hardened criminal. There was a sad, lost look in the man's eyes. "What is your name?" Wolf asked.

"Joe. I didn't mean to kill the old biddy."

Wolf realised he did not know if the dowager was alive or dead. Joe's words weren't comforting.

Joe continued, "The voice kept telling me to shoot her. I tried to ignore it, but I couldn't make it stop."

"Whose voice?" Wolf asked. Yet, even as he uttered the words, he sensed Joe was becoming increasingly detached from reality. As he used his gun to wave the young man down the stairs, it struck Wolf that perhaps this had little to do with criminal activities around the docks and was merely the erratic behaviour of a disturbed mind.

At the bottom of the stairs, Wolf pushed Joe ahead of him as they made their way back down Shad Thames. It occurred to Wolf that the man might try to make another run for it. Though, looking at Joe's slumped shoulders, it seemed he was utterly defeated.

By the time they returned to the warehouse where he had left Mickey D and Tabitha, Wolf found it empty. As he made his way back towards Tower Bridge, he noticed the Pembroke carriage departing. Mickey D remained with a motley collection that appeared to be a mix of his men and Tuchinsky's. Tabitha was not among them, and the female gang leader was also absent.

The men all turned at Wolf's approach. "So, you got the dastard. Good!" Mickey D exclaimed. "No need to hand him over to the police. I'm happy to take him into my custody." As he said this, he rubbed his hands together.

"That will not be happening," Wolf stated in a voice that brooked no dissent. Well, he hoped it brooked no dissent. However, the look on Mickey D's face was worrying; if the man chose to take Joe, there was little Wolf could do to stop him. He had no intention of engaging in a brawl, or worse, a gunfight, with a group of thugs. He also had no intention of willingly allowing Joe to be subjected to whatever rough justice Mickey D had in mind.

Joe's safety was important, but it wasn't the most important thing. "What has happened to Lady Pembroke?" he asked Mickey D.

"She's alive. Not sure how bad it is. She must have hit her head when she fell, and there was a fair bit of blood."

"But she was shot, was she not?" Wolf asked anxiously.

"The bullet bounced off her corset."

Well, that was some consolation, though it sounded as if the dowager was still badly hurt. Mickey D explained, "Tabitha has gone with Tuchinsky to see some Jew quack."

"Dr. Cohen," Wolf said as much to himself as to Mickey D. It was a good idea and one of which one he suspected that even the dowager would approve. As much as she could be a terrible snob, the woman had been very impressed with the doctor who had tended to Wolf when he was shot. So impressed, in fact, that she had openly flirted with the idea of pronouncing him her personal physician.

Wolf assumed that Tuchinsky had gone along to direct them. Noticing Mrs O'Leary standing at the back of the group of men, he caught her eye, and she smiled wanly. He imagined that Mickey D's men reminded her rather too much of her abusive husband.

Mickey D's words had highlighted a dilemma that had already crossed Wolf's mind: there was no doubt the man in his custody was guilty of shooting the dowager. If he found a policeman and handed him over, his word as the Earl of Pembroke – assuming he could convince the man he was – would suffice for an immediate arrest. However, there was still the question of what, if anything, this Joe fellow might have done in addition. Had he targeted the dowager randomly? Had their poking around stirred up a hornet's nest amongst local criminals? Or was this something to do with the investigation they had undertaken into Lord Redding's death? If he handed Joe over to the Metropolitan Police now, Wolf might lose his only opportunity to question the man.

Wolf thought, not for the first time, that he should cultivate some connections in Scotland Yard. While Bruiser, his police contact from his thief-taker days, had his uses, he was only a not entirely honest detective inspector. Now that Wolf was an earl, perhaps he should get to know at least some detective chief inspectors if not superintendents. Of course, it never occurred to Wolf that a man of his high rank might aspire even higher and command the attention of the Commissioner of the Metropolitan Police if he so chose.

Thinking about Bruiser gave Wolf an idea, though. "Mickey, I want you to find Bruiser and have him come to Chesterton House."

Mickey D raised his eyebrows. "Since when was I your messenger boy, Wolf?" he snarled.

Wolf sighed. "We do not have time for this. We must do something with this man, and I do not feel ready to hand him over to some random police officer."

"What's there not to be ready about? He shot Lady P; there's no doubt about that."

Wolf sighed again. "I wish to see if that is all he is guilty of. For once, can you just take my word for something, and do as I ask?"

It was evident Mickey D would have liked to have kept the spat going if only to save face in front of his men. Perhaps he would have, but Wolf added pleadingly, "Please. I am asking this as a great favour and one I will not forget in a hurry." Even as he said these words, Wolf knew he was continuing to dig himself into a bottomless pit of obligation with Mickey D, one he might never claw his way out of at this point.

This was not lost on the canny gang leader either. He adjusted his tone to one more befitting an emperor granting indulgences. "I'll get him, and we'll meet you there." While Wolf had not explicitly invited Mickey D to join them, he recognised that, having been helpful so far, the man was not about to back out now. At least, not willingly. He nodded in agreement with the plan.

Only when this was finalised did Wolf realise neither Langley nor Rat was part of the group. More to the point, Langley's carriage was nowhere to be seen. He asked, and Mickey D informed him that, after dropping Tuchinsky and her group off at Jacob's Island, Langley, Rat, and Little Ian had returned to the Leather Market area to search there. This made sense; at that point, there had been no reason to prioritise one part of Bermondsey over another.

Mickey D said he and his men would head back to Leathermarket Street, find Langley, and send his carriage back to Tower Bridge for Wolf and his prisoner. Then, they would return to Whitechapel to find Bruiser and meet Wolf back at Chesterton House. Wolf didn't bother asking if Mickey D would be able to find Bruiser on a Sunday. If the detective inspector wasn't working, there was an extremely good chance he'd be found in The Cock enjoying one of Old One-eye's excellent meat pies and a tankard of the better-than-average ale.

CHAPTER 26

The carriage ride to Brick Lane was one of the most anxiety-ridden trips of Tabitha's life. After Bear had gently picked the dowager up as if she were no heavier than a kitten, they had met up with Tuchinsky and found the Pembroke carriage. Bear had squeezed himself into the carriage and had taken one of the seats, cradling the unconscious old woman in his arms, while Tuchinsky and Tabitha had taken the other. Neither woman said much; each was too caught up in her concerns for the dowager.

They made an unlikely pair of well-wishers: a countess turned investigator and the female leader of a brutal criminal gang. Yet somehow, they were united in their concern for this sharp-tongued, snobbish, difficult woman.

At one point, the dowager seemed to stir, but she said nothing coherent, and while her eyes fluttered for a moment, they didn't open. Instinctively, Tabitha took Tuchinsky's hand and received a gentle squeeze in return.

"She's going to be all right. She has to be," Tuchinsky said in the tone of voice that could normally cow business associates and even her own men, as it indicated that only total obedience was acceptable.

No one said anything else during the ride to Brick Lane, which thankfully was as fast and traffic-free as it could be.

Tabitha had more familiarity with Tuchinsky's neighbourhood than she would ever have expected. As they drove up Commercial Street, she recognised Spitalfields Market on her left, even though it was shuttered up. As the market came into view, she realised they were close to Brick Lane, where Tuchinsky lived and worked.

While Wolf had been recovering from his gunshot wound, Dr Cohen had always visited him at Tuchinsky's home. Now, it occurred to Tabitha to wonder what facilities the doctor had of his own.

She voiced the question, and Tuchinsky answered, "I think we should take Lady Pembroke to Bubbe and have Dr Cohen visit us there. He has a small surgery in his house, but he's not set up for the long-term care of patients. She'll be more comfortable where Bubbe can take care of her."

Tabitha was not inclined to argue. She had experienced for herself that Dr Cohen was more than capable of providing medical attention wherever he saw his patients, and she couldn't argue about Bubbe's skill as a caregiver.

Not even five minutes later, the carriage pulled up outside of the tailor's shop, which served as a cover for Tuchinsky's more nefarious business operations. It was a matter of only a few minutes more for the dowager to be carried into the bedroom in the flat at the back of the building where Tuchinsky lived with her bubbe and zayde.

She was so distracted by worry that Tabitha didn't notice who Tuchinsky spoke with, but the dowager was barely settled in the same bed that Wolf had recuperated in before the doctor arrived. Like most Jewish men Tabitha had met, the old, stooped-over doctor with the long white beard wore one of the funny little caps on his mostly bald head. He shuffled into the room, carrying his black medical bag.

It seemed Dr Cohen had already been informed of what had happened because he didn't ask Tabitha any questions. Instead, he merely muttered a greeting as he removed his stethoscope from the bag and examined the dowager. Carefully, he parted the hair that was matted with dried blood and looked at her head injury. He pulled up the dowager's eyelids and examined her eyes. As he did so, she stirred again, briefly. Finally, he pulled back the sheet covering the old woman and looked at where the bullet had struck her corset.

Replacing the sheet, he stood up as straight as he could and informed Tabitha in a soothing, heavily accented voice, "Lady Pembroke has a concussion of the brain. Head injuries tend to bleed a lot. However, I think the wound itself is relatively superficial. She is a fortunate woman; if that bullet had been a millimetre or two over, it would have entered between the whale bones of her corset. As it is, it seems to have bounced off entirely and has not done more than slightly tear the fabric. Her pupils are not overly dilated and are the same size, so I don't believe there is significant swelling on her brain."

Tabitha sighed in relief. However, this was short-lived as the doctor continued, "I am worried that she is not lucid. These kinds of brain injuries can be tricky. It may yet turn out to be far more serious."

"What can you do for her?" Tabitha cried; her anxiety ratcheted back up again.

"For the most part, time and rest are her friends. Now that Lady Pembroke is here, I suggest you do not move her at least for a day or two. Regular application of cold compresses should help to reduce whatever swelling of the brain there is. I am going to use smelling salts to revive her, and I suggest you continue to do so if she seems to be falling back into unconsciousness." With that, the doctor removed a small jar from his bag and waved it under the dowager's nose. At first, this had no effect, but then she stirred. With her eyes fluttering open, the dowager muttered something incomprehensible.

The doctor then waved them under her nose again, and this time, her eyes opened and remained open. In a voice that sounded frail and scared, the dowager asked, "Where am I?"

Tabitha rushed to her side and took her hand. "Mama, you have been hurt, but the doctor is here with you now."

The dowager turned her head slightly, looking at Dr Cohen, and winced. "Try not to move, Lady Pembroke. I am going to bandage your head because you have a small wound there." The dowager didn't reply, but her eyes registered understanding. She gripped Tabitha's hand, and the younger woman's heart clenched with sadness at seeing the usually formidable dowager countess laid so low.

During all of this, Bubbe had stood quietly in the doorway. Now, she came forward, went around the bed and took the dowager's other hand. "I will take care of her, doctor."

Dr Cohen smiled. "There's not much that your chicken soup can't cure, Mrs Tuchinsky."

Bubbe nodded and smiled at the doctor's wisdom.

When Wolf had been shot and was recovering in this same room, Tabitha had spent many nights sleeping in the armchair by the bed, watching over the invalid. While she did not doubt that the dowager would receive all the care she needed from Bubbe and Dr Cohen, Tabitha decided she was prepared to stay with the old woman for as long as necessary.

Turning to Bear, who had gently put the dowager on the bed and then retreated to a corner of the bedroom, Tabitha said, "Bear, please inform her ladyship's household of what has happened. Ask her lady's maid, Withers, to pack a back of necessities to send with you. Then, please return to Chesterton House and ask Ginny to do the same for me. I will stay here for a night or two at least." Turning to Bubbe, she added, "If that is acceptable to you, of course, Mrs Tuchinsky."

"Bubbelah, you are always welcome in this house. Now, let me go and send one of the boys to buy a boiler so I can start the soup. I know how much Lady Pembroke enjoys Brick Lane beigels, so I will also make sure we get some. And, of course, I will make a batch of the rugelach she loves."

While the dowager didn't seem ready for so much food, Tabitha knew Bubbe showed her love through her cooking. She was happy to let the old Jewish grandmother return to her kitchen to begin cutting vegetables for the alchemy that would become her chicken soup.

Dr Cohen did not stay much longer. He left instructions for the dowager's care and said he would return that evening. Of course, if her condition changed, Tuchinsky knew where to find him.

Tuchinsky herself had been quiet throughout the doctor's visit, but now, as he left the room, she came to stand by Tabitha as she looked down at the dowager's pale face.

"She's one of the toughest old birds I know." This was a significant statement coming from Tuchinsky, a woman who had somehow risen to the position of a gang leader in the harsh, male criminal world. "She's not going to be taken out by a bang on the head." With that, she turned and left the room.

Tabitha found she had tears in her eyes at the other woman's words. Less than a year ago, she had anticipated a visit from the dowager countess with trepidation, perhaps even fear. Tabitha wasn't sure when those feelings had so thoroughly changed into filial affection. If she was honest, it was more than affection. Amazingly, Tabitha loved the cantankerous, challenging woman. And even more amazingly, she suspected the feeling was reciprocated.

Bear had gone, Bubbe was in the kitchen, and now Tuchinsky had left Tabitha alone with the dowager. A few minutes later, she returned with the cold compress that the doctor had ordered and then exited the room.

Sitting on the bed, gently applying the compress to the dowager's forehead, careful to avoid the newly applied bandage, Tabitha whispered, "Do not worry, Mama. I am here and am not going anywhere."

The dowager's eyes had been open, but they had not seemed to register much for the past few minutes. Now, they moved to look at Tabitha, and a weak, raspy voice said, "Thank you, my dear. You are a good daughter."

Tabitha's eyes filled with tears, and she took a deep breath to get her emotions under control. Then she continued to apply the compress to the head of the woman who had somehow, without her realising, become more of a maternal figure to her than her own mother had ever been.

Chapter 27

Wolf wasn't sure Mrs O'Leary would be comfortable riding in a carriage with Wolf and his prisoner. However, he couldn't think of an alternative, so she returned to Chesterton House, sitting on the seat opposite the one Wolf shared with Joe. Wolf kept his gun in his hand, but something about Joe's defeated slump of his shoulders indicated he would not be putting up a fight.

It wasn't until the carriage pulled up on Hanover Square that Wolf considered how he was going to parade this man into his vestibule, in full view of his neighbours and then his servants. What was he to do with him until Bruiser arrived? He could hardly serve Joe tea and crumpets in the drawing room.

Finally, Wolf decided the situation called for as much discretion as possible and called to Madison to pull the carriage around to the back of the house so they might enter through the kitchen door. While he could imagine the look of surprise on his servants' faces as their master walked in through the back with a man at gunpoint, they had become somewhat inured to such situations over the past year. They were accustomed to their master donning ragged old clothes and stealing out of the house at all hours. They were even used to Tabitha joining him in some disguise or other.

As it was, Wolf was sure that Bruiser's arrival in the company of Mickey D would set the servants' tongues wagging. Somehow, whenever Mickey D visited Chesterton House, he seemed to do so with none of the staff being any the wiser. Wolf couldn't imagine the rather stocky Bruiser being willing or able to jump through whatever window Mickey D usually utilised.

Stopping by the kitchen door, Wolf had a thought, "Mrs O'Leary, first, I must thank you for your help today and apologise for subjecting you to such a carriage ride home."

Rose smiled. "Your lordship, I have been subjected to far, far worse. It was my pleasure to help in whatever small way I could."

"I have one more favour to ask of you. Would you precede me and our guest into the kitchen and alert cook and the other staff? I have no wish to startle them by barging in with a drawn gun." Rose willingly agreed to do this and slipped in through the kitchen door.

A few moments later, she popped her head back out. "They have been warned. Talbot was in the kitchen and suggested that one of the footmen, Charlie, might help you with your guest. When I told him that the detective inspector was meeting you here, he asked if you wished to take this gentleman into your study. If so, Charlie could remain with you in the room, just in case."

Wolf considered the pandemonium that might ensue if Joe suddenly took it into his head to attempt an escape from within Chesterton House and realised that Talbot's suggestion was a sensible one.

There was one additional precaution he wished to take. "Would you be so good as to ask Charlie to bring some rope with him?" Rose's head disappeared behind the door. Then, a few moments later, she opened it for Wolf to enter with Joe.

While the servants had some idea of the investigative work that their master and mistress involved themselves in, this was the first time that an actual criminal had stepped foot in Chesterton House – well, besides Mickey D, of course. They stood in the kitchen, staring at Wolf and his prisoner, not attempting to hide their curiosity. Wolf did his best to ignore their open-mouthed gaping as he and Joe made their way through the kitchen and up the stairs into the passageway that led to the main part of the house.

Wolf's study was towards the back of the house, so he didn't have to take Joe through much of the downstairs, which was for the best. While Mrs O'Leary had warned whichever servants happened to be in the kitchen, Wolf would prefer not to startle a maid who was busy going about her work.

In the study, Wolf indicated Joe should take a seat on the chair in front of his desk. While the other man obeyed his command, Wolf got the distinct impression that Joe had less and less idea of where he was and what was happening. It didn't bode well for the interrogation Wolf wished to perform once Bruiser arrived.

Taking a seat behind his desk while keeping his gun aimed at Joe, Wolf wondered how to proceed. As he was pondering this, there was a knock at the door, and the footman, Charlie, entered, holding a long piece of heavy rope. The fashion was for tall, broad-shouldered footmen, and Charlie was no exception. He looked more than able to help restrain Joe if necessary.

"Charlie, would you please bind this gentleman's hands and feet and tether him to the chair." With a nod, Charlie began doing as he was asked. Joe seemed barely to register what was happening to him and sat so limply on the chair that Wolf feared he might fall off before Charlie had a chance to tie him to it.

It was tempting to begin the questioning while he waited for Bruiser, but Wolf resisted the urge. It was going to be hard enough to get anything sensible out of Joe, as it was. The odds of getting it and then having him repeat it for Bruiser were slim to none. He would have to be patient.

Deciding that there was nothing to be gained by sitting there, staring at Joe, Wolf stood, handed the gun to Charlie, and told him to watch the prisoner.

Now, Wolf was at a loss for what to do while he waited. Finally, he decided that his time would be well spent in the parlour, writing notecards with what they had discovered during their visit to Sally Turnbull.

Usually, because of her superior handwriting, Tabitha was the one to write up the notecards. Sitting with a pile of blank ones in front of him, Wolf considered what they had learned that day. In truth, it seemed as if it were far longer than a few hours since they had first descended from the omnibus and made their way to Sally Turnbull's house. As he thought about how many hours it had been, Wolf realised how hungry he was. After ringing the bell for Talbot to bring tea and biscuits, Wolf settled back to his task.

What had they learned? There had been no time to discuss any of Sally's revelations. The plan had been to return to Mayfair after their lunch at The George Inn, but then the dowager had disappeared. Now, Wolf considered the conversation with Sally. One thing Wolf was sure of was the poor woman's deformities were due to her mother having syphilis while she was with child. He had seen similar perversions in the features of children born to prostitutes in Whitechapel.

Just as he was considering what this meant, if anything, Uncle Duncan entered the parlour. Actually, staggered in would be a more accurate description.

"Ach, sorry, lad. Didnae think anyone was in here. Jane and Lily are busy in the drawin' room wi' their wummin's clatter, so I needed a wee bit peace for my afternoon kip."

As the man turned to leave, Wolf stopped him. "Mr MacAlister, would you join me? There is something I think you might help me with."

From the look on Uncle Duncan's face, he was less than keen to put off his nap. However, he turned and came and sat opposite Wolf. Then, he had a thought and rose, moved to where the decanters and glasses were and poured himself a hefty drink. Wolf indicated he would not join him in an alcoholic beverage, to which Uncle Duncan merely shrugged his shoulders.

Seated back, but with his drink in hand this time, he asked. "So, what is it, laddie?"

"When you were at Boodles and managed to get some members talking about Lord Redding, did they say anything else besides the name of the mistress that the Earl of Warwick and Lord Redding had in common?"

Wolf knew it was a long shot; Uncle Duncan had been drunk at Boodles and was drunk now. However, the man's ability to function while three sheets to the wind was quite impressive. Then, Wolf considered Uncle Duncan's earlier words and realised that he hadn't told Jane or Lily about what had befallen the dowager. Immediately chagrined, Wolf determined to tell them as soon as he finished talking to Uncle Duncan. He feared that if he left the man now, Uncle Duncan would either be too drunk or napping by the time he returned.

Cognisant that he needed to waste no more time than absolutely necessary before relaying the news about the dowager, Wolf pressed on. "Did anyone perhaps mention anything more, well, more personal?"

He was worried that he was being too oblique and would have to speak in far blunter terms. Luckily, after a moment's thought, Uncle Duncan replied, "Nothin' that comes tae mind. Well, aye, there were the rumours – folk said the man had the Shirra Pox. But that's hardly worth mentionin', is it now?"

Wolf had to prevent himself from groaning out loud and telling Uncle Duncan that it was entirely worth mentioning. Instead, he forced himself to be polite and then made his excuses so he could rectify his failure to speak with Jane and Lily sooner.

When he found Jane and her daughter in the drawing room, Wolf realised he had no idea what to say to them. Until the doctor had seen the dowager, he neither wanted to worry Jane and Lily unnecessarily nor raise false hopes.

Finally, he decided to err on the side of caution and said nothing more than the dowager had experienced a fall and had received a nasty bump on her head.

"Why did you not bring her back here?" Jane asked anxiously. "Is Mama at her home? I should go to her."

"Err, well, actually, it was decided that it would be for the best to take her to see a doctor with whom she is quite familiar and who works in another part of town."

This story may have taken in Jane, but Lily narrowed her eyes suspiciously. "What friend and what other part of town? Grandmama does not have friends who live anywhere other than near here." Then she paused, considering what she'd said and asked, "Is she with that Jewish family who lives in the East End?"

Wolf was surprised that Lily had paid enough attention to their investigations even to know that much, but apparently, she had. He confessed that was where the dowager was.

"And Mama was willing to go and see this doctor rather than her personal physician?" Jane asked incredulously.

Realising that he would have to tell a white lie, Wolf said, "Lady Pembroke had no complaints about the choice of doctor."

"When will she be returning home?" Jane asked. Wolf then had to admit that he did not know and that Tabitha had gone with the dowager while he had returned to Chesterton House with a suspect. He almost slipped and said, "The man who shot the dowager countess", but he caught himself in time.

Jane was concerned, and Lily was distrustful that they were being told the entire story. Wolf assured them he would find out more shortly, though, in truth, he wasn't sure how he was going to do that.

Luckily, he was saved from having to continue the deception by the shrill ring of the telephone, followed by Talbot's arrival in the doorway to the drawing room. "Lord Langley for you, milord."

Assuring Jane and Lily that he would let them know more as soon as he knew it, Wolf rushed out of the room.

Chapter 28

Langley had no new information and was merely calling to see what Wolf knew, which was not much. However, it provided him with a reason to escape the uncomfortable atmosphere of the drawing room. Once he had replaced the telephone receiver in its cradle, he decided he would not willingly be drawn back into the conversation with Jane and Lily, at least for the time being.

Wolf was a kind and caring man, but he kept his feelings close to his chest and struggled with overt displays of sentiment. One thing he appreciated about Tabitha was her ability to express herself openly while maintaining control over her emotions. In contrast, Wolf had a feeling that Jane might be one of those women who dissolved into a fit of weeping very quickly, and he had no idea how to handle that. At the very least, he saw no reason to test his ability to manage a hysterical Jane until he knew more about the dowager's condition.

Now that the parlour, drawing room, and his study were ruled out as spaces for quiet contemplation, Wolf decided to stroll through the garden. He enjoyed being in nature but had never paid much attention to its composite features. However, as Wolf wandered around the quite sizeable Chesterton House grounds, he realised that the garden had a far more interesting collection of plants and trees than it had previously. He assumed Lily was responsible for the gardener's new innovative botanical approach.

As he wandered along the winding paths that made the garden seem larger than it was, lingering by the small fishpond and eventually sitting near the sundial, Wolf contemplated their current case. By this stage, he was so accustomed to considering clues alongside Tabitha as they exchanged ideas, he felt almost bereft doing so alone.

As he remembered their conversation with Sally Turnbull, Wolf considered the obvious question: was she Redding's child? And if so, what did that mean? Of course, Caroline Turnbull might have been the one to give Redding syphilis after she had passed it to her unborn child. That the three people shared a disease proved nothing about a timeline. He thought about the fancy lady Caroline had visited with her daughter and about the downturn in the Turnbull's fortunes five years before.

Suddenly, Wolf had an idea. He sprang to his feet, hoping that the previous day's newspapers were still in a pile on his desk. While he would prefer not to return to his study until Bruiser arrived, Wolf had to confirm his hunch.

Wolf's first thought on entering the study was that he should have clarified that the footman, Charlie, was allowed to sit while he watched his charge. As it was, the young man was standing ramrod straight, not even leaning on a wall, while he silently kept guard.

As for their prisoner, Wolf might have almost thought him sleeping, such was his lack of movement. As Wolf walked into the room and moved to behind his desk, Joe didn't even look up. Instead, he seemed almost carved from marble, such was his stillness. Wolf caught Charlie's eye and cocked his head questioningly. The footman replied with a little shrug of his shoulders.

Wolf sat down, relieved to see that the pile of newspapers had not been touched. As efficient as Mrs Jenkins, the housekeeper, was, she respected that the earl's study was the one space in the house that wasn't subject to quite the same high standards of tidiness that she insisted on elsewhere. Wolf picked up the newspaper from the top of the pile and opened it. He knew that he had seen something in one of the many articles about Redding's death, but he couldn't remember which one.

Patiently going through each newspaper from that day, going backwards to the day that Clarence was arrested, Wolf finally found what he was looking for: the Daily Mail had written a few lines about Lord Redding and had noted that his wife was deceased. Wolf's elation at having this confirmed disappeared as he continued to read that Lady Redding had died six months before. Disappointed, he almost stopped reading in frustration, but then a word caught his eye: Switzerland. Lady Redding had spent the last almost five years of her life abroad, in Switzerland.

While polite society might do nothing more than raise eyebrows at one of its members' removal to Switzerland or perhaps Italy, the Daily Mail imagined that its readers needed this detail to be explained more plainly. Wolf read the paragraph more carefully. "Lady Redding was removed to what we imagine to be a sanatorium for the insane almost five years ago. Sources tell us the baroness' behaviour had become increasingly erratic and involved long periods of paranoia and hallucination."

Given the salaciousness of this titbit, it was surprising that there were no insinuations about the cause of Lady Redding's insanity. Regardless, it was clear to Wolf this must have been a symptom of syphilis. The timing confirmed his theory that Lady Redding was the fancy lady who Caroline and Sally Turnbull had visited when the latter was a child. He suspected the money that Sally saw pass between the women that day had been the first in a series of payments that continued until Lady Redding's insanity had seen her committed to an asylum by her husband.

If Wolf was correct, then it seemed highly likely that Sally was Lord Redding's child. Had he known? Of course, even if he had known, would he have cared? It was the rare man of high birth who gave a toss for his by-blows, even ones that resulted from an ongoing relationship with a mistress.

Wolf had heard enough of his peers discuss such situations to under-stand that as far as most men of his rank were concerned, it was a given that any kept woman did what she must to avert or then deal with preg-nancy. It was not the man's responsibility to prevent conception or support an out-of-wedlock baby.

Then, Wolf remembered Sally Turnbull's comment that the fancy lady hadn't been able to have children. He knew any apparent barrenness or repeated bearing of lifeless babies was now understood to be a possible symptom of syphilis.

Is this what happened? Had Caroline Turnbull's singing career been brought to a halt by the same ravaging disease that afflicted her child, and left motherhood elusive for Lady Redding, the wife of her former benefactor? Did Caroline throw herself on Lady Redding's mercy only to discover the charity ended once the lady was firmly in the grip of insanity?

Wolf pondered the events of the day. If he was right, did the man before him have any link to this tragedy? He studied Joe's youthful features and concluded that the man was likely no more than nineteen or twenty, possibly even younger.

Working off a sudden hunch, Wolf said sharply, "Mr Turnbull, I have a question to ask you about your sister, Sally."

The young man jolted upright, suddenly alert. Well, that was confirmation of one thing, at least.

Whatever Wolf had been about to say was interrupted by a knock at the door, followed by Talbot's entrance, with Bruiser and Mickey D in his wake.

Wolf neither desired nor demanded that people who knew him before he ascended to the earldom stand on ceremony with him now. This was a good thing, given that both Bruiser and Mickey D only ever referred to his title disparagingly.

Unlike Mickey D, Bruiser had never visited Chesterton House, and he looked around him, awed by the grandeur. "You've done all right for yourself, Wolf," Bruiser said admiringly but also with a tinge of a sneer, luckily, after Talbot had left the room. Wolf could only imagine what Charlie would make of his master being talked to in such a way. Of course, Tabitha and Bear both referred to him as Wolf, but that was quite different from a rather rough-sounding policeman doing so in this manner.

Wolf was saved from having to answer by Mickey D, who observed, "I've never come in the front door before. Very fancy. Even your lackey's livery is flash togs. And what is wrong with that fancy manservant? It's like he's got a rod up his rear end."

Out of the corner of his eye, Wolf could see Charlie doing his best to smother a grin at this disparagement of the butler.

"Perhaps you might refrain from a critique of my servants so we can address the matter at hand. Did you explain the situation to Bruiser?"

Mickey D nodded.

"Yeah, he told me that this napper had taken that old countess. From what I gathered, he snatched her from beside a privy in the alley behind The George in Southwark." Bruiser wore such a smirk as he said this that Wolf worried that inviting him there had been a mistake.

He replied, "That is the gist of it."

Bruiser continued, "And you had Mr Doherty bring me here because you wish to turn the lad over to a rozzer but also want to understand if he's part of whatever you're nosing around in?"

Given that this was framed as a question, Wolf answered in the affirmative. He then added, "However, since he has been here, I have ascertained that he does, in fact, have a connection to our investigation. What I do not know is how material that connection is."

Throughout this, Joe had returned to his lethargic state and seemed unaware that he was the topic of conversation. Now, Bruiser approached the chair and slapped the young man around the head. "Hey, we're talking about you."

Looking over at Wolf, he asked, "What's the matter with him? Is he daft or just a tad touched? Perhaps he's away with the fairies." Bruiser chuckled at his own words.

While the words were blunt and unkind, it was a valid question, and Wolf didn't have an answer. Joe Turnbull, if that was indeed who he was, had sufficient presence of mind to run after shooting the dowager and certainly understood the consequences of being caught. His comment regarding the gallows made that clear. However, there was the talk about the voices he heard telling him to shoot, not to mention the almost dreamlike state he seemed to have fallen into.

What was the best course of action now that the detective inspector was here? Wolf was saved from having to decide immediately when the door opened again, and Bear walked in.

All eyes turned to the enormous man. Well, all eyes except Joe Turnbull's. There was no need for anyone to ask the only question that mattered. "Her ladyship is alive and, according to the doctor, is likely to make a full recovery. Apparently, the bullet ricocheted off her corset and the bump to her head was not as severe as the amount of blood had indicated."

Wolf breathed a sigh of relief. Looking over at Mickey D, he saw that even the hardened criminal was touched by the news.

Bear continued, "Dr. Cohen has said that Lady Pembroke should not be moved, at least for the time being. Tabitha is determined to stay with her for as long as necessary and has sent me back here for clothes for them both." He then added with a smile, "And Mrs Tuchinsky is busy making chicken soup."

Although this news reassured Wolf, he felt uneasy about his wife sleeping in an armchair on Brick Lane for days. He hadn't had a say when she did this during his recovery, but they were not married then. He also knew that Tabitha would not appreciate this display of husbandly protectiveness.

Finally, Wolf realised that the issue of Tabitha's residence in the Tuchinsky home was not the most pressing one he had to deal with, and so he turned back to the matter at hand.

CHAPTER 29

All attempts to break through to Joe Turnbull had proved futile. When he spoke, he would only repeat, "I know, it's a secret. I remember." Finally, Wolf and Bruiser had become almost equally frustrated, and Wolf had suggested that Bruiser arrest the young man and take him away. At this point, he was guilty of abducting and shooting the dowager, if nothing else.

While it was frustrating to feel like a significant piece of the puzzle was just beyond his reach, Wolf wasn't sure what else he could do.

Bear had already visited the dowager's home and retrieved some belongings for her. Nothing more than Bear's rather terrifying size and visage had prevented Withers and the dowager's devoted butler, Manning, from insisting on returning to Brick Lane with him.

With Bruiser, Mickey D, and Joe Turnbull gone, Bear waited in the study with Wolf while Ginny packed a bag for Tabitha. As he waited, he and Wolf sipped fine brandy in companionable silence. Wolf knew he ought to seek Jane and Lily out to provide them with an update, but he was putting off the inevitable scene. He had done such a good job of minimising the dowager's injuries initially that even the relatively positive news he had to share now would seem significant as if the woman were in greater danger rather than less.

"Would you mind if I took you through everything we know so far?" Wolf asked.

"Missing Tabitha already, are you?" Bear teased.

Wolf smiled but couldn't deny the truth in his friend's words. He then walked Bear through everything they had learned from the moment that Charlotte and Fiona had interrupted their breakfast days before. He ended with his conjectures about Sally Turnbull's parentage, the role Lady Redding had played until she was dispatched to Switzerland, and his final hunch that Joe was Sally's brother.

Bear let him speak without interruption; this was one of the many qualities that Wolf appreciated in his friend.

When Wolf was finished, Bear still said nothing for some time. He sipped on his drink and contemplated the narrative Wolf had laid out for him.

Finally, he put his drink down on the table next to him, leaned forward, resting his arms on his knees, and asked, "So, who do you think the Earl of Warwick is trying to protect and why?"

That was it! Wolf believed that the answer to those two questions would unlock this entire investigation.

After contemplating this for a few more minutes, Wolf articulated what didn't sit well with him. "Under normal circumstances, I would say that he was protecting Caroline Turnbull and her children. She had meant something to him once, after all. Joe Turnbull is a violent, deranged man. Perhaps Clarence suspected Joe had tracked his father down and killed him because of the disease he bequeathed to them, which ultimately killed their mother."

"So, you think this was in revenge for his mother's death? Can we even be sure that Redding gave Caroline the disease and not vice versa?"

"That is not even the most challenging part of this puzzle. Caroline Turnbull fell on particularly hard times five years ago. Clarence has always struck me as a decent and honourable man. If he had found out about his former mistress' descent into such extreme poverty, would he not have tried to alleviate it? After all, if we are even somewhat on the right track, it seems more of a sacrifice to face the gallows for a crime he has not committed than to spare a few banknotes occasionally."

Bear stood and said, "I really should get back to Brick Lane. It is getting late, and I want to make sure that Tabitha and her ladyship have what they need."

These words jolted Wolf's conscience; he still had said nothing further to Jane and Lily. Talbot had suggested that, under the circumstances, they forgo any formal dining plans for the evening and, instead, food be laid out in the dining room so people could eat at their leisure. Since Wolf had never enjoyed formal dining, and he and Tabitha often avoided it when they had no guests, he was happy to agree. Talbot had brought some sandwiches into the study, which Wolf and Bear had munched on as they chatted.

Now, Wolf realised he had been extremely neglectful in leaving his guests to worry for longer than they might have to. It also occurred to him that any assurances might come better from Bear, who had been in the room when the doctor examined the dowager. Explaining this now to Bear, his friend agreed to postpone his departure until they had spoken to Jane and her daughter.

Fortunately, both women were soon found in the dining room with Uncle Duncan. As Wolf revised his statement regarding the dowager's injuries, occasionally turning to Bear for Dr Cohen's precise words, he noticed Jane biting her lip anxiously, with tears welling in her eyes. However, the mild-mannered woman did not chastise him for his delay in providing the update on her mother.

Instead, she pushed her chair back from the dining room table, stood and said in a voice filled with barely controlled emotions but also unexpected determination, "I will join Mr Bear on his trip to Brick Lane."

Wolf wished Tabitha were here to manage this delicate situation. What was the correct way to handle it? If he allowed Jane to go to Brick Lane, would her presence be a help or a hindrance? The dowager did not conceal her low opinion of her daughter. Would she even welcome Jane's presence at her bedside?

Apparently, his conflicted feelings on the matter had made themselves apparent on his face. Jane approached him and put a gentle, but again, firm, hand on his arm. "I am more than capable of controlling my emotions around Mama and quite aware my presence may not be welcomed, at least initially. Nevertheless, I will attend my mother in her time of need."

Wolf and Bear exchanged glances. There was nothing more to be said. In fact, if Jane was going to Brick Lane, the question arose whether it made sense for Bear to go as well. Now that Wolf thought about it, perhaps he should be the one to accompany his cousin. Despite Jane's brave words, Wolf couldn't imagine how she might react when faced with the brutal reality of the East End, particularly at night. As soon as he thought this, Wolf realised it was the right thing to do and informed Bear and Jane of the slight change in plans.

Uncle Duncan had been quiet during this conversation, seemingly absorbed in his food and claret. Now, he raised his head as if suddenly awoke from a stupor. "Aye, of course, I'm at yer disposal, if need be, lass."

Wolf couldn't imagine anyone less appropriate for this situation than the irascible, already quite inebriated old man, and so he politely declined.

"Aye, aye. But mind an' pass on my best tae the bonnie lassie." Assuming that Uncle Duncan was referring to the dowager, he assured the old man he would do so while being sure it was the last thing he would tell the dowager.

Within ten minutes, Wolf and Jane were seated in the carriage and on their way to Brick Lane. It took another three minutes for Wolf to realise that he had never been alone with his cousin and did not know what to talk about with her. Fortunately, she hadn't yet asked for any details about how her mother had hit her head, and Wolf didn't want to broach any topic that might change that. He knew it was cowardly, but there it was.

Finally, it was Jane who broke the awkward silence. "I am sorry that you and Tabitha have been drawn into this wretched affair on behalf of my family. This should be a time of newly wedded bliss when you are able to focus on each other and sweet Melody."

Wolf shrugged his shoulders. "We had our time in Corfu, which was wonderful. In truth, we, well, Tabitha at least, derive a great sense of intellectual challenge and purpose from these investigations."

"You do not?"

Wolf considered Jane's question. When he had first inherited the title, he had been determined to abandon everything from his previous life as a thief-taker. Well, everything except his old partner and dear friend, Bear. Over time, as he had been forced and then persuaded to take on investigations, Wolf had come to realise this was a skill set that he could employ for the betterment of the people around him. If he so chose. He and Tabitha had decided that they would take on cases where a genuine injustice had been committed and where they believed they were in a position to help right a wrong.

So far, the person wronged had usually been a member of the lower orders who did not have the access to legal and investigative redress as their so-called betters did. Wolf comforted himself with the thought that their willingness to take on these cases helped right a genuine societal imbalance, which he and Tabitha were the beneficiaries of merely because of an accident of birth.

That their client in this case was another aristocrat didn't sit quite as easily with Wolf. However, the knowledge that the Earl of Warwick's arrest had negatively affected the lives of Lily and Tobias, two young people Wolf cared for deeply, provided a sweetness that eased any disquiet he felt.

Now, as Wolf considered Jane's question, he realised that his claim that any sense of purpose derived from the investigations was felt only by Tabitha was untrue. Acknowledging this, he added, "And regardless, you and Lily are family. While I cannot promise that we will achieve the desired outcome, I can promise that Tabitha and I will do all we can to help uncover the truth."

Jane seemed content with this answer and smiled gratefully. Luckily, Jane also seemed content to ride in silence. As with Bear, this quiet did not feel uncomfortable and gave Wolf time to think. As he stared out of the carriage window into streets dimmed in the twilight, he had two realisations: Sally Turnbull needed to be told about her brother's arrest, and so did Clarence.

Apart from anything else, the Earl of Warwick had now spent three days and two nights in Pentonville Prison. Wolf wouldn't blame the man if his resolve to take the blame for a crime he didn't commit weren't sorely tried by the experience. It was one thing to commit to a noble gesture and quite another to have to endure the extreme deprivation that gesture entailed. Perhaps Clarence might be more willing to cooperate with their investigation by the time Monday morning rolled around.

A larger question was whether he would be at all swayed by the news of Joe Turnbull's arrest. The young man would be tried and convicted for the attempted murder of the dowager. Even though her survival ruled out the gallows, Joe would be imprisoned for a very long time. Was it possible that he was the person Clarence was trying to protect?

That was the question to which Wolf continually returned. Had Clarence somehow discovered the gruesome fate that his former mistress had met and the dreadful consequences of the ravaging disease she had transmitted to her children? Did he consider it the honourable thing to protect one of those children, regardless of the cost? Perhaps. Yet, there were too many aspects of this conclusion that didn't quite add up.

Again, Wolf wished he could discuss these questions with Tabitha. The dowager's sickbed in the Tuchinsky residence was hardly the place where he could easily and discreetly have such a conversation with his wife.

<h1 style="text-align:center">CHAPTER 30</h1>

When Wolf and Jane entered the Tuchinsky kitchen, it was to find the family, plus Tabitha, seated around the table eating some kind of meat stew that smelled delicious.

"Bubbelah, it is so good to see you," Bubbe cried as she pulled Wolf into an embrace. Whatever ceremony the old Jewish grandmother had ever stood on with Wolf had disappeared once he had been shot while saving her life and had recuperated in her home.

Bubbe showed her love by feeding those around her. Almost before Wolf knew what was happening, he was being swept onto Bubbe's now vacant chair, and a bowl of the stew was set down before him.

Jane seemed quite bewildered by everything that was happening to her. When Wolf had brought her through the tailor's shop to the abandoned workroom behind it and then up the stairs to the Tuchinsky residence, she hadn't commented, but her eyes widened in increasing surprise.

Wolf wondered what his mousey cousin had envisioned when they had talked of Brick Lane and the Tuchinsky family. He suspected that the sheltered, privileged woman had no frame of reference to imagine much beyond perhaps a middle-class residence in a pristine neighbourhood. Brick Lane, even in the relative quiet of the evening, wasn't that. In fact, without the bustle of the vendors and the constant foot traffic, the street felt quite intimidating.

Luckily, Bubbe's warmth and hospitality sufficed to calm Jane's nerves. As the old woman put food in front of her, Jane attempted to refuse, saying she had already eaten that evening. Wolf could have told her that, in the Tuchinsky household, having already eaten was not considered a reason not to eat again.

Tuchinsky herself tried to save their guest's blushes. "Bubbe, if Lady MacAlister has already eaten this evening, I am sure she does not want cholent."

"She's too skinny. She needs fattening up. All these grand ladies do. They're all skin and bones. Eat bubbelah, eat."

Sighing, Tuchinsky gave Jane a look that said, "I tried."

In fact, Bubbe was correct; Jane would eat. Good manners were too well ingrained in her not at least to take a few mouthfuls of the stew.

"It is delicious," Jane admitted, sincerely.

"Bubbe makes cholent on Shabbat but there is often enough for the rest of the weekend as well." Jane didn't know what Shabbat was but nodded her head as if she did.

When she had taken another spoonful, she asked meekly, "Would it be possible to see my mother now?"

Tabitha answered in a kind but firm voice. "Jane, Mama has just fallen asleep. She was awake and quite lucid for an hour but then became very drowsy. Why do we not let her rest for now. I am worried about disturbing her so soon after she dropped off."

It was not in Jane's nature to argue, and so she said no more on the subject.

"Tabitha, we have brought you some clothes. I do not know what Ginny packed, so if you need to stay longer, I can return with more things," Wolf explained.

At this, Jane sat up a little straighter. "Tabitha, while I very much appreciate your willingness to stay here with Mama, it is my responsibility and indeed my duty to do so, not yours."

Tabitha's first instinct was to assure Jane that was not the case and that she was happy to remain at the dowager's bedside. However, a quick glance from Wolf made her rethink this; what would it mean to the dowager when she awoke to discover that her daughter was not the one mopping her brow? As challenging as the relationship between mother and daughter was, perhaps this was an opportunity for Jane to demonstrate her worth. The charitable thing to do was to allow the woman to be of service to her mother.

While Tabitha had doubts about Jane's stamina and ability to cope with any crisis that might occur, she didn't doubt Bubbe and Tuchinsky's capability. She knew that both women were more than competent enough to handle whatever arose. Moreover, Tabitha could see Wolf was restless and sensed he wished to speak to her privately.

Putting her spoon down, Tabitha stood and said, "Mrs Tuchinsky, thank you for your hospitality and for taking in her ladyship. If it is acceptable to you and your family, I will leave my cousin, Jane, in my stead, and I will return home with my husband."

Bubbe and Tuchinsky both assured her that Jane and the dowager were welcome to stay for as long as necessary. Zayde nodded along as the women spoke. The old man knew better than to inject his opinion, whatever it was.

With that settled, Wolf was eager to be on their way. As much as Bubbe looked forlornly at his only half-eaten food, she was persuaded that he would have other opportunities to eat at her table, particularly while the dowager was a patient under her roof.

As they prepared to leave, Tabitha looked at Jane concernedly. Was the woman really prepared to sleep in an armchair in the home of a family she didn't know in the East End of London? Jane seemed to interpret the look correctly and put on the brightest, most confident smile she could. Regardless of how she felt about what she had volunteered for, Jane was determined to do her duty and see this through. Tabitha returned the smile, proud of her meek cousin-in-law.

A very short time later, Tabitha and Wolf were settled in the Pembroke carriage. Wolf had asked Madison to hold off driving until they had a few minutes to talk. Wolf used the time to tell Tabitha about the attempted interrogation of Joe and about his own deductions that he was Sally's brother.

"Yes! He is," Tabitha confirmed. "When Mama came to, this was one thing that she told me. Honestly, given the bang she has had to the head, I was not entirely convinced that she knew what she was saying. But now you have said it as well, I am sure she was speaking lucidly. Apparently, Joe implied as much to Mama before he shot her."

"Then he did not abduct her ladyship for some random, unrelated reason. That would be too much of a coincidence," Wolf asserted. "He must have overheard or been told about our visits, followed us yesterday and then waited for a chance to learn more. Lady Pembroke's use of the facilities provided him the opportunity he had been looking for."

Wolf paused. "Though, given the man's evidently disordered mind, I wonder how much of this was planned and how much resulted from Joe jumping at shadows." Wolf checked his pocket watch. It was now early evening. Was it too late to take a detour to Southwark?

Voicing this question, Wolf added, "I am sure that Sally Turnbull rises early. However, she should be told that her brother has been arrested. I doubt she knows. And perhaps the shock of this will lead her to disclose anything she knows about her brother's involvement with Redding."

Tabitha shared Wolf's concerns about the hour but agreed that they had little choice. They knew once Monday morning came, it would be even more challenging to track down Sally Turnbull and talk with her. With this decided, Wolf called Madison, and they set off.

On a Sunday evening, the drive was as speedy as it could be, and soon enough, they pulled up outside the dilapidated house in Southwark. While most of the house was dark, there was a light shining through the window that Wolf thought was Sally Turnbull's room.

Turning to Wolf, Tabitha asked, "What do we say?"

Wolf considered the question. "Well, the first thing to tell her is that her brother has been arrested for kidnapping and shooting her ladyship. Given that we saw him running from the scene and that Lady Pembroke is sure to be able to identify Joe as the man who snatched her, there seems little doubt that he will be convicted."

"Exactly. If he is going to be convicted for a crime that will not send him to the gallows, what incentive does Sally have to share any additional information that might make her brother's sentence worse?"

Wolf had been considering this question during their ride from Brick Lane. "There is all the difference in the world if her brother is judged as criminally insane. In that case, regardless of the severity of the crime, he would get sent to an asylum such as Broadmoor rather than prison."

"Is that really any better?" Tabitha asked sceptically.

"Well, I do not know the details. However, from what I understand, Joe would be treated far better at Broadmoor than as a member of the general inmate population. He would not be subject to hard labour and would receive medical attention at least. While he would be held there until deemed well, which, of course, might be the rest of his life, that might not be a bad thing given his condition."

"I still do not understand why Sally would have an incentive to be honest with us," Tabitha admitted.

Wolf was tempted to smile at his wife's naivety. Instead, he took her hand and answered, "Someone like Joe Turnbull does not have the wherewithal to ensure that he is properly defended in court; we do."

"Are you suggesting we offer to ensure that her brother has appropriate counsel for his defence if Sally cooperates to help clear Clarence's name?"

"That is precisely what I am suggesting," Wolf confirmed.

Tabitha considered this plan. It felt wrong to be bribing the young woman. Shouldn't Joe Turnbull have the right to appropriate counsel without his sister having to play Judas? Yet, even as she thought this, Tabitha realised this was yet another example of the world being very different for those with status and money. If she were accused of such a crime, she would be given the benefit of the doubt at every turn. She would gain access to the best legal minds and have the most lenient punishment possible handed down to her. That was if she ever got to the point of being tried and convicted. More likely, her family would be able to shuffle her off to the Continent and sweep everything under the rug.

Of course, this was precisely the kind of preferential treatment of the upper classes the newspapers were railing against, and which made them so gleeful that Clarence seemed to be treated as the common man might be with some kind of comeuppance to balance against all the years of injustice.

Chapter 31

Wolf was concerned about waking the entire household and rapped on the door as gently as possible. When there was no answer, he rapped a little more loudly. After a few moments, they saw the dingy curtains at the window on the ground floor tweaked open as someone attempted to see who was at the door. Tabitha and Wolf waited for a few more moments and finally heard footsteps and the door handle being turned.

The door opened just a little, and Sally Turnbull looked out at them in confusion. "Why have you returned, and at this hour?"

"Miss Turnbull, this is something which would be better discussed inside," Wolf suggested.

When the young woman wasn't persuaded, Wolf added, "It is about your brother, Joe."

Sally became visibly alarmed at Wolf's words. "How do you know about Joe? What has happened?"

"Miss Turnbull, please allow us to enter so we may explain everything," Tabitha suggested gently.

Sally Turnbull nodded and fully opened the door to allow them to enter. Tabitha and Wolf followed her into her room. An oil lamp was on the small table, which must have been the light they had seen from outside. A book was resting by the lamp.

Sally took the chair she had evidently just vacated; Tabitha took the other one. Wolf continued to stand.

"So, what do you have to do with my brother?" Sally demanded. Her face was hard, and her tone cold. Assuming that Sally didn't know that Joe had been arrested, she clearly believed she had other cause to worry about her brother.

Wolf then explained everything that had happened since they had left Sally earlier that day. While the young woman didn't interrupt, she was clenching her jaw, and her fists were balled up tight.

When Wolf got to the part of his narrative where the shot rang out, the tension in Sally's face was painful to observe. As he described seeing Joe Turnbull flee the scene of the crime, the young woman's hand flew to her mouth, and she gasped. Finally, Wolf described chasing and then catching Joe before handing him over to the police.

"How did you know he is my brother?" was the first question out of Sally's mouth.

It seemed the simplest explanation to give was that the young man had revealed as much to the dowager before shooting her.

"And the woman he shot, she's alive?" Sally asked. Tabitha interpreted her tone while asking as showing more concern for what the situation might mean for her brother than for the dowager's survival.

"She is alive and appears to be stable. The bullet missed her, but she hit her head badly when she fell. She is an old woman, and this kind of injury is particularly dangerous at her age," Tabitha explained.

"Then Joe isn't guilty of murder?" Sally pressed.

"Well, he is not guilty of murder in this instance," Wolf replied, with emphasis on the last two words.

"What do you mean by that?" Sally asked sharply.

Not wanting to reveal more than necessary, Wolf asked a question of his own, "Why do you think your brother would want to abduct our friend?" Neither on their first visit nor this one had they revealed their true identities. Wolf wasn't sure why he hesitated to do so, but he continued to speak of the dowager in these vague terms.

He was very curious to hear what answer Sally would give. How had Joe known they were asking questions about his mother? If Wolf had to guess, it would be that the landlady, Ellie Perkins, had told him or that Joe had overheard their initial conversation in The George. Was it possible Sally was ignorant of the fact that her brother had followed them and seen the Pembroke carriage? The more Wolf considered this question, the more he realised that Sally's suspicions that they were not researching a book about her mother had only arisen as they had spoken to her that morning. Surely, if Joe had told his sister what he had seen the day before, she would have been immediately suspicious.

As cold and hard as Sally's tone had been, now it seemed one of genuine bemusement as she admitted, "I do not know why my brother would target your group. You said your friend was taken while you were eating in The George. That's his regular haunt now. He started going there when Ma got really bad, and he'd come to visit. Do you think he overheard you talking there after speaking with me?"

"Possibly," was all Wolf acknowledged. "The question remains: why would Joe be so worried about what we were asking you?" It occurred to Wolf to mention how Sally herself had become far less helpful as soon as she realised why they were asking questions. First, he wanted to see what Sally admitted to without prompting.

That was if she admitted anything. From the look on the young woman's face, she would refuse to be drawn on the question.

Finally, Wolf lost all patience. "Miss Turnbull, is it possible that the reason Joe was worried was because he was the one who killed Lord Redding?"

Whatever Sally expected him to say, it didn't seem as if that was it. She looked genuinely shocked at his words. "Why would you think such a thing? Joe wouldn't hurt a fly."

"Miss Turnbull, it is quite evident that is not true. An old woman fighting for her life after being shot gives the lie to your words. Your brother abducted her, held her captive and then shot her. Those are not the actions of someone who wouldn't hurt a fly."

With her eyes blazing in anger, Sally Turnbull jumped out of her chair and spat, "He was not like that before. It is this sickness; this sickness that man passed to our mother and that we are also inflicted with. Joe was always a lovely, gentle boy until the pox took his senses just as it took our mother's voice and my face."

Leery of further enraging the young woman but cognisant that she was more likely to let the truth slip in a moment of passion, Wolf added, "That man is your father, Lord Redding. Am I correct?"

A look of pure hatred came over Sally's face. "He was no father, merely the man who bedded our mother until his appetites took him elsewhere, leaving her with child and infected."

It didn't seem like the right time to posit that Caroline Turnbull could have given Redding syphilis rather than the other way around.

Sally continued raging. "I knew none of this until my mother died. She told me everything on her deathbed. How she had gone begging to this Lord Redding when she could no longer perform on the stage and that he'd turned her away with a callous disregard for any of us."

Tabitha thought about what Sally had just admitted. "Your mother confessed the truth of your parentage a week ago before she died, then mere days later, Lord Redding was murdered. You can see why we might suspect your brother, who has already shown himself to be violent, of being the killer."

As she said these words, Tabitha had an epiphany. Speaking her thoughts out loud before she'd had a chance to consider their wisdom, she said, "Unless you were the one who tracked Lord Redding down and confronted him that night."

The fear in Sally's eyes at this conjecture said all they needed to know. Whether she had gone merely to challenge Lord Redding or with the expectation of attacking him, they might never know. Wolf considered the work the woman did in the leather market preparing the hides and did not doubt that she might have found a knife in her pocket opportunely. Certainly, that a young woman walking the streets of London alone at night might want to ensure she had a way to protect herself made sense.

After witnessing how quick Sally was to anger at the mention of Redding's name, it wasn't hard to imagine how she might have been similarly enraged at her father's refusal to acknowledge her as his daughter or, perhaps even worse, his scornful acknowledgement.

"Is that what happened, Sally? Did Joe know what you had done and followed us out of concern for you?"

Again, Sally's face said all they needed to know. Instead of answering that question, she replied, "I didn't know he'd followed you. I was at work later than usual and haven't seen him for days."

Then, before they could ask anything more, Sally made a sudden movement and turned the small table over, sending the oil lamp flying. Tabitha managed to jump out of the way of the splattering hot oil in time, but the curtains immediately caught fire.

Wolf didn't even think before reacting. He leapt forward and grabbed Tabitha away from the flames.

"Get out of here before the entire place is in flames," he yelled as he pushed her towards the door.

"Wait, where are you going?" Tabitha screamed.

Even as Wolf pushed her out the door into the hallway, he was running up the stairs to the storey above, yelling at the top of his voice, "Fire, fire. Get out."

Tabitha was tempted to follow him, but she realised Wolf would be too distracted by ensuring her safety, and that wouldn't help the situation. Instead, she would make sure that Sally Turnbull was safe and then try to alert the London Fire Brigade. Tabitha thought she had seen one of their red alarm boxes further up Borough High Street. If nothing else, she could try to find someone to send to the nearest fire or police station.

Tabitha turned, prepared to re-enter Sally Turnbull's room, but it was ablaze, and she realised it would be suicidal to go back in. As it was, she didn't have long before the fire moved beyond that room. Was Sally still inside? She must be.

Resigned to her inability to help Sally Turnbull, Tabitha realised that there were other lives she could help save and ran out of the house. Wolf's warning of fire had aroused at least some of the building's inhabitants, and a woman and man ran out of the room next to Sally's, pushing past Tabitha to get to safety.

Out on the street, Tabitha ran past the Pembroke carriage to where she remembered seeing the firebox. Luckily, it was where she thought it would be, which wasn't far. Tabitha reached the box attached to the cast-iron pillar just past where the gates to The George stood. Tabitha yanked down the handle attached to the box. She heard a metallic clunk as an electrical pulse was triggered that travelled to the local fire station.

Tabitha had no idea where the nearest fire station was and how long it might take them to reach her. Given this, she was amazed when, within a few minutes, she heard the clanging of bells to alert residents to make their way on the road. Quickly, a crowd gathered at a safe distance from the burning house, watching the blaze take hold. The window to Sally's room was lit up by the flames within. But how fast was the fire spreading within the house?

The clanging of the bells was getting closer, and before she knew it, a steam-powered pump drawn by two galloping horses was almost upon them. Firefighters in their blue wool tunics and brass helmets jumped off the truck and ran to a small iron plate that was almost flush with the pavement. Removing the plate, they fed the end of a large hose into it, with the other end attached to the steam-powered truck.

As fascinated as Tabitha was to see the firefighters in action, all she cared about was whether Wolf had got out of the house safely.

CHAPTER 32

As Wolf reached the first floor of the house, he continued to yell "Fire!" at the top of his lungs.

Doors opened, and people stumbled out; some had clearly already fallen asleep.

"Fire, there's a fire downstairs. Get out as quickly as you can. Leave everything behind and just ensure that your family is safe," Wolf advised.

Despite his warning, he saw one woman disappear back into her room before reemerging, carrying a large leather satchel. The cantankerous woman who had yelled out of the window the day before appeared in a doorway.

"Oy, wot you about? Aren't you the toff who came by yesterday looking for Sally? Now you've set fire to the 'ouse? Lord 'elp us!"

"I did not set fire to this house. Miss Turnbull knocked over an oil lamp," Wolf explained in exasperation. There was no time to stand arguing with this woman. There was only one thing he wanted to know: "How many people live in this house?"

"Three on this floor, Sally and the Coopers below. Oh, and there's a girl that does for us upstairs in the attic."

Wolf didn't stay to hear any more. Instead, he looked around for a staircase leading to the attic. Smoke was already filling the hallway, and he didn't know how long they would have before the flames spread. The only thing that was likely slowing it down was the dampness in the walls that had caused the black mould.

Spotting a narrow staircase further down the hallway, he pulled his cravat up over his mouth to prevent inhaling the smoke that was billowing upwards.

As he turned to make his way to the stairs, the woman he'd been speaking with cried plaintively, "This 'ouse is all I've got. I can't lose it."

Wolf had no time to commiserate with the landlady. Instead, he said brusquely over his shoulder, "And if you do not leave immediately, you will lose your life as well."

It seemed his words were taken seriously, as the woman nodded and then ran downstairs, coughing loudly as she breathed in the acrid fumes.

Glad that she hadn't argued any further, Wolf bolted up the narrow staircase. At the top, there was a closed door. Hoping that the door wasn't locked, Wolf tried the door handle and was relieved that it turned easily. The door opened onto a narrow attic room, sparsely furnished with a small bed and a chest of drawers. A young woman lay sleeping in the bed. Apparently, she was sleeping so deeply that she hadn't heard the commotion downstairs.

Wolf approached the bed, hoping to wake the young woman but not startle her too much. That hope was dashed as he stepped on a creaking floorboard. The young woman—really, she was more of a girl—woke with a start, took one look at the man approaching her bed, and screamed.

"Don't kill me," she cried. "I'm a good girl I am. I ain't seen you 'ere, I promise. If you're stealing from Old Ma Brown, I don't care. She ain't never done nuffink for me that I should stop you."

"I am not a thief, and I am not here to hurt you. A fire has started downstairs, and we need to leave this house as quickly as possible."

"A fire! I'm going to burn, I am." The girl jumped out of bed, clutching the thin blanket off her bed and pulling it in front of her to protect her modesty.

"You will not burn. Not if I have anything to do with it. But we need to leave immediately." Even as he said this, Wolf could smell smoke. Had the fire reached the first floor of the house already? Even if it hadn't, would they be able to escape out of the front of the house?

"Stay here," Wolf ordered. "I just want to take a look down the stairs before we try to leave that way."

The terrified girl nodded her compliance. Wolf retraced his steps back down to the first floor. The landing was filled with smoke. He could only hope everyone had managed to escape already. What was clear was that he and the young maid could not leave down the main stairs. Was there any other way to get out of the house?

Returning up the narrow staircase, Wolf immediately closed the door behind him as soon as he was in the room. Whatever tiny amount of time this bought them, they had to take it. The room had a small window. Wolf crossed to it and looked out. There was a building behind this one that did not have an attic. Because of this, it was possible to drop out of the attic window onto its roof. Well, Wolf could do that easily enough. Would this young woman be able to follow suit?

Then there was the question of what they should do once they were on that roof. Wolf decided they had no choice but to go that way and make of it what they could.

He explained the plan to the young woman. "No. I can't jump out of the window. I'm dead afraid of 'eights, I am. Makes me sick even standing on a chair."

Summoning every bit of patience he could, Wolf said gently, "We have no choice. What is your name?"

"Missy. Missy Palmer."

"Well, Missy Palmer, what about we do this?" As he said this, Wolf grabbed her sheet off the bed and tied one end to the iron bed frame.

"I ain't going to climb down no sheet!" Missy protested.

"Missy, would you rather climb or jump?" Even as he said this, Wolf could see the smoke coming under the door. "Missy, we do not have time. We must leave now. I will go first and will be there to catch you, I promise."

Missy stared at him wide-eyed but didn't protest any further. Wolf didn't want to take the chance of tearing the sheet before Missy had a chance to use it. Instead, after throwing the free end of the sheet out of the window, he jumped out of it, tucking and rolling as he landed. He gave thanks for the many times he and Bear had given chase to some criminal or other, and he'd perfected that manoeuvre.

Standing, he looked up at the window where Missy's pale, anxious face stared down at him. Wolf tugged on the end of the sheet to ensure that it was tied tightly enough. Of course, even as he did this, he wondered what he would do if it weren't.

"Missy, I need you to hold tight to the sheet, then climb out of the window, wrapping your legs around the sheet as you do so."

"I can't do it. I can't," Missy sobbed.

Wolf realised that time was running out, and he had to stop being gentle with the girl. "Missy, do as I say now!" Wolf yelled.

In service since she was nine, Missy was so accustomed to obeying orders she did as she was directed. Before she knew it, she was clinging to the makeshift rope.

"Good girl," Wolf cried. "Now, climb down as slowly as you need to. Remember, I am down here and will catch you."

At a painfully slow pace, Missy made her way down the rope. Luckily, she was a skinny, small girl and the sheet held under her weight.

When she was only a foot out of Wolf's reach, Missy cried out, "I can't hold on anymore more, I can't."

"Then let go, Missy. I will catch you. I promise."

The next moment, the girl was falling. Wolf held out his arms, hoping he could fulfil his promise. Missy landed safely in his arms, a little winded, but besides that, no worse for wear. Wolf put the girl on her feet. Then looked around. He walked to the edge of the roof and looked down. The house whose roof he was now standing on had a room on the ground floor which jutted out beyond the second storey, probably a kitchen. Again, he could jump down easily enough, but could Missy?

Wolf couldn't imagine persuading the frightened young woman to leap from one roof to another. Instead, he looked at the sheet she had just climbed down. Would it hold his weight if he climbed up it? He would have to take the risk.

"Missy, I am going to climb back up, undo the sheet, and jump back down. Then we will find somewhere to tie it and repeat what you just did down to the next level."

"I can't do it again. I can't! I just can't. Please don't make me do it," Missy pleaded.

"Missy," Wolf said firmly but kindly. "The alternative is that I leave you on this roof."

"Don't leave me," the terrified girl cried. "Please don't leave me."

"Then you will have to do what I say." Missy nodded reluctantly.

Of course, it was all very well saying that he was going to climb up the sheet. Yet again, Wolf was reminded that he was not in the fine physical form he had been in until his fortunes took a turn for the better. Hoping for the best, he grabbed the sheet and pulled himself up. There was no doubt this wasn't as easy as it would have been a year ago. Still, Wolf persevered and managed to drag himself up to the window frame above. More importantly, the sheet held his weight.

By the time he swung his legs over the ledge and climbed back into the room, it was filled with smoke. Again, covering his mouth with his cravat, he untied the sheet from the bedframe as quickly as possible. Then, he repeated his jump out of the window. This time, he didn't land as smoothly and felt a jolt of pain shoot through his ankle.

Standing up cautiously, Wolf tested whether he could put weight on his leg. He winced. It was painful, but he could stand. Hobbling over to the edge of the roof, he looked for something he could tie the sheet to. There was a rusty iron bracket attached to the roof. Would it hold? There wasn't any other option, so he tied the sheet onto the bracket.

Now, he had to jump again to the roof below. Aware that his ankle was bad already without landing on it again, he braced himself, then jumped, making an extra effort to tuck and roll as he landed. Even so, Wolf winced as his ankle came into contact with the roof.

Standing as best he could, Wolf looked up at Missy. He would still promise to catch her but wasn't as sure he could follow through on that assurance. He promised it anyway and just prayed that Missy wouldn't lose her grip this time. Luckily, she was more confident, having already climbed down once, and she made it all the way to the bottom unaided.

Now, they were only one storey from the ground. Wolf looked up at the sheet. He was not at all sure that the bracket would hold his weight if he attempted to go back up the sheet rope. Even if it could, his ankle was not up to making the climb again. Limping to the edge of the roof, he looked down. Right below where he stood, there was a costermonger's cart parked for the night. With all its goods sold for the day, the cart was full of empty hessian sacks. Wolf wasn't convinced the sacks would provide a thoroughly soft landing, but he turned to Missy, determined to convince her it would.

"We will hold hands and jump together," he assured the girl. The terror in her eyes was evidence that she wasn't persuaded, but at this point, she had put her safety in his hands entirely. The girl came and joined him at the edge of the roof and put her small hand in his.

"On the count of three, we jump," Wolf told her. "One, two, three!"

The landing on the hessian sacks was better than it could have been but worse than Wolf had hoped. In particular, his ankle was throbbing.

"Are you all right?" he asked Missy.

When she didn't answer immediately, Wolf was worried Missy was seriously hurt. Then, a small voice answered, "Is it over?"

"Yes, Missy, it is over, and we are safe."

After helping Missy down off the cart, Wolf attempted to assess where they were and in which direction they needed to go to get back to Borough High Street.

As he looked around, Missy said softly, "It's this way, sir," and pointed down the street. Realising he should have asked her to begin with, Wolf let Missy lead as he hobbled along beside her.

Three turns later, they came out just north of The George Inn on the high street. Looking down towards the house they had escaped from, Wolf could see the fire brigade busy trying to extinguish the blaze.

In a moment of terror, Wolf realised he had no idea if Tabitha was safe. In the panic of trying to alert the house's residents, he hadn't had time to worry about his wife. Now, he scanned the crowd of people intently regarding the spectacle of the burning house, desperate to see the only person he cared about at this point. Wolf walked towards the crowd, becoming more anxious by the moment.

Suddenly, a beloved voice called out, "Wolf, Wolf, over here."

With unbelievable relief, he saw Tabitha standing next to Madison. While she had a few hairs out of place, Tabitha seemed unharmed. Wolf rushed to his wife's side, oblivious to the pain in his ankle. Sweeping her up in his arms, Wolf held Tabitha so tightly that he almost squeezed the breath out of her.

"You are safe!" he whispered into hair that smelled of smoke.

"Are you hurt?" she asked. While Wolf had ignored the pain in his ankle, it was apparent that he was limping.

"It is nothing serious. I will tell you about it on the drive home." Then, he realised he had lost Missy. Glancing around, he spotted the young girl standing on the edge of the crowd, unsure of what to do next.

Wolf gestured to her to join them. Having saved the maid's life, Wolf didn't feel he could just abandon her now. Once the fire was quelled, there would be no house to return to as a maid. Making up his mind on the spot, he said something to Tabitha. She smiled and answered.

When Missy reached them, Wolf introduced her to Tabitha and asked, "Missy, would you like to come and work in our house?" Missy Palmer had worked nowhere grander than the house on Borough High Street. While she did not fully understand what was being offered to her, the girl had a sharp mind. She realised she had no home or job anymore. Moreover, Wolf was her saviour, and she would willingly follow him to the ends of the earth.

Smiling at the young woman, Tabitha made a decision of her own. "Missy, do you like small children?"

"Got nine younger brothers and sisters I 'ave," Missy assured her.

"Would you like to work as a nursery maid?" While they already had Kitty helping Mary, Tabitha suspected that the twin boys were quite a handful and that it wouldn't be a bad thing to have an extra helper in the nursery.

Missy smiled and gladly accepted the job.

Wolf realised he hadn't yet asked an important question. "Did Sally Turnbull survive?"

Tabitha shrugged her shoulders. "I am uncertain. However, I do not believe she escaped that room. I cannot imagine how she would have."

"Well, we have our answer about who killed Redding either way. I will have Langley speak to the Home Secretary tomorrow on Clarence's behalf.

CHAPTER 33

The following morning, Wolf was up with the dawn and making telephone calls as early as was seemly. When he was finished, he found Tabitha in the breakfast room with Lily. From the look on the young woman's face, it seemed that whatever Tabitha had told her about their adventures the previous day had given Lily hope; she was brighter than Wolf had seen her since Clarence was arrested.

Both women looked up expectantly as Wolf entered the room. "What did Langley say?" Tabitha asked. Before Wolf had a chance to answer, she added, "Has he spoken to the Home Secretary? Is Clarence being released?"

Wolf sat and poured himself a cup of coffee. "Langley has spoken with the Home Secretary. He did so immediately after he and I spoke, in fact. However, it is not all good news, I am afraid." Lily's face fell. Wolf put up a reassuring hand. "It is not all bad news either. It is just more complicated than we hoped because we do not have Sally Turnbull to offer as the culprit."

"But she confessed to you; Cousin Tabitha told me she did," Lily protested.

"And who witnessed that confession?"

"You each did!"

Wolf sighed. He hadn't expected this conversation to be easy, and it had already exceeded his expectations.

Anticipating what the issue was, Tabitha suggested, "Is the problem the current climate and what it would mean to accept our word?"

"That is precisely the problem," Wolf answered gratefully. "This is exacerbated by Clarence's continued refusal to provide an explanation for what happened that night. Sir Matthew believes that if he were to release the Earl of Warwick merely on the say-so of the Earl and Countess of Pembroke, then the newspapers would make hay while the sun shines and pronounce this yet another example of aristocratic privilege. Even worse, it will seem as if arresting and jailing Clarence was just a charade to placate the masses before the inevitable sham story was rolled out to justify releasing him."

Wolf could see tears forming in Lily's eyes. He hastened to add, "However, I have a plan. Well, it was Langley's suggestion, actually. What the newspapers need is a new story of aristocratic comeuppance to focus on instead."

"What is he suggesting? That we create some kind of spectacle ourselves?" Tabitha said half-jokingly but also nervous about what Wolf was going to suggest.

"Actually, he suggested we focus their journalistic thirst for blood on a more deserving source: Lord Redding."

Tabitha furrowed her forehead, confused but fascinated by where this line of thought was going to lead.

"The other telephone call I made was to Andrews." Correctly foreseeing Tabitha's next question, Wolf explained, "Yes, apparently, The Westminster Gazette has a telephone and has had one for some time. Bear discovered this when he went to visit Andrews, who asked why he kept coming in person rather than using that contraption to communicate. Honestly, I am still so uncomfortable using it myself that it never occurred to me that was an option but apparently, it is."

"Anyway, Langley's idea was that I offer Andrews a scoop: the possibility of sitting in as Clarence finally confesses to the truth, or at least to the aspect of the truth he is party to."

"Cousin Jeremy, I rarely consider myself slow on the uptake, but I have absolutely no idea what you are talking about," Lily exclaimed. "How is this Andrews going to help save my wedding?"

Tabitha patted Lily on the hand, hoping to calm the young woman. "I believe the plan is that The Westminster Gazette will write a front-page article that redirects the ire of the general public away from Tobias' father and instead toward Lord Redding, a man who was a very public moraliser and yet, not only kept a mistress, but then abandoned the children he fathered with her after inflicting a ravaging disease on them and their mother."

Addressing Wolf, Tabitha asked, "Is that the long and the short of it?"

Gratefully, he acknowledged that was precisely the plan.

Tabitha smiled ruefully, "So, we will hang Lord Redding out to dry, posthumously, in order to save Lord Warwick."

"Well, I am not sure I would use quite that characterisation. One man is guilty of, if not crimes against the law, crimes of morality, and the other isn't. And to boot, Redding was a very vocal crusader against the very sins he was busy committing. Moreover, Redding has no wife or children living against whom this black mark would cast a long shadow. As far as we know, he has one living child, Joe Turnbull, who is already caught up in this saga. Yes, doing so will taint Lord Redding's memory, but perhaps that is not a bad thing."

"Indeed," Tabitha agreed. "Perhaps it might even make other aristocratic and wealthy men who treat their by-blows similarly take stock!"

"We can only hope."

Tabitha assumed she knew the answer to her next question but wanted to make sure. "Is Andrews amenable to writing this story as you have suggested?"

Wolf laughed. "Amenable is an understatement. He is champing at the bit to meet me at Pentonville. We should both change into our best bib and tucker and proceed with all due haste. While this is not normally something I advise, the more diamonds, the better. We want to ensure Warden Featherstone's complete cooperation in this matter and need to ensure we strike an appropriate amount of awe in the man."

Tabitha stood up. "Then let me go and get into my Sunday best. Well, in this case, Monday best. I have a new silk Worth gown, which will be suitably awe-inspiring. And while Warden Featherstone was treated to my ruby pendant for our last visit, this time, I will deign to drape myself with the extremely ostentatious diamonds that Jonathan insisted I wear frequently. I banished them after his death but will have Ginny resurrect them for this occasion."

Thirty minutes later, bedecked in silk, jewels and furs, Tabitha joined Wolf in the drawing room.

"Is it too much?" she asked self-consciously.

Her husband laughed as he approached and took her hands in his. "Well, under normal circumstances, I prefer your more restrained and refined style. However, given the task at hand, you look magnificent. From what I know of the warden, one look at those diamonds alone will ensure utter compliance with our request. Shall we be off?"

Traffic was terrible that Monday morning, and it took an age to drive to Pentonville. Finally, the carriage pulled up outside. Andrews had beaten them to it and was waiting outside for them impatiently. Tabitha had never met the journalist, though she had heard a lot about him during their investigations. She was eager to meet the man himself.

If Tabitha had been asked what she expected in Andrew Andrews, she would have said: in his mid-thirties, slight, keen intelligence. Well, she was right about the last of those guesses. What she didn't expect was that the man whose parents had so little imagination that they called him Andrew Andrews would be well into middle age, portly, with a balding pate and very yellow, crooked teeth. The man was rarely seen without a cheroot in his hand or mouth. In fact, as he stood and waited for Tabitha and Wolf, one was dangling from his lips.

As they alighted from the carriage, the journalist hailed them. "That took long enough, Wolf. Think you can keep a working man cooling his heels now that you're a toff?" The joking tone took the bite out of the man's words. Wolf ignored the comment and went to shake Andrews' hand. Then he turned and introduced Tabitha.

"Mr Andrews, I am delighted to meet you finally," Tabitha said, extending her hand.

"The notorious Countess of Pembroke," Andrews said with a wry smile before taking the proffered hand.

Notorious? Was that true, Tabitha wondered with alarm. She was aware that their investigations had not entirely escaped society's notice.

However, she had long assumed that this was mostly due to the dowager's insistence on advertising, even bragging about her involvement to all and sundry. It had not occurred to Tabitha that her own involvement might be almost as renowned.

Society shut its doors very firmly to Tabitha when Jonathan died. While her reinstatement as the current Countess of Pembroke had meant that those doors were now flung wide with welcome, Tabitha made little effort to socialise with the men and women who had shunned her previously. Now, as she considered this apparent notoriety, Tabitha decided she no more cared what those people thought of her investigative role than she did when they gossiped about and judged her for Jonathan's death.

Now, replying to Andrews, she merely smiled and gave a slight incline of her head in acknowledgement of his words.

"Shall we go in?" Andrews suggested. "I assume that you have reason to believe that we will face no obstacles to speaking with his lordship."

Wolf assured him they would be welcomed into the prison by the warden.

As Wolf had promised, Warden Featherstone was delighted at their return. He remained hopeful that Wolf would give a glowing report of his management of the prison to the House of Lords and the Home Secretary. Wolf had been vague enough in his promises to do so previously that the warden continued to hold out hope that each visit of Wolf's was finally in the service of such a report.

While Warden Featherstone continued to fawn over him yet again, it occurred to Wolf that it would be beneficial to future investigations if he, in fact, gave a favourable report to Sir Matthew at some point. He never knew when he might need a warm welcome at the prison and imagined that even the obsequious Warden Featherstone might eventually reach the end of his tether if such a report was not forthcoming.

"Milord, what an honour it is to see you again. Might I hope that this time it is to make a report lauding the work I do here?" Given that Wolf had foreseen that these would be some of the first words out of the man's mouth, he wasn't surprised and made some vague sounds that might be interpreted however the warden wished.

"Superb, superb," Warden Featherstone murmured, evidently choosing to give Wolf's indistinct mutterings the best possible interpretation. "What can I show you first? And if I might ask, who is the gentleman accompanying you today?"

As Featherstone said this, Wolf was struck by an idea of how he might both justify speaking with Clarence again and explain Andrews' presence. "Warden Featherstone, as it happens, I have asked my good friend Mr Andrews to join me today so that he might view your exemplary establishment for himself. Mr Andrews writes for The Westminster Gazette and is particularly interested in prison reform."

At this, Andrews shot Wolf a look of surprise. This was news to him. Not that he was uninterested in prison reform, but he didn't have any plans to write about it in the near term.

Warden Featherstone was taken aback by this news. "Prison reform, you say? That assumes that there is something to reform."

Immediately, Wolf realised he'd made an error in judgment by focusing on that particular topic. Pentonville was one prison that reformers often cited as particularly harsh in its treatment of prisoners.

As Wolf cast about for a way to salvage the situation, Andrews spoke up and said smoothly, "Indeed it does, Warden Featherstone. In fact, while so many of my colleagues are riding the same wave of the need for reform, I am interested in representing the other side of the story: the absolute need for whatever methods are in place in the current penal system. I am interested in explaining to the public that no unnecessarily harsh treatment takes place somewhere such as Pentonville and that any and all routine practices are justified."

While Wolf silently gave thanks to the man for jumping in and saving the situation, he was aware he had now made a rod for his own back if such an article didn't appear in The Westminster Gazette at some point soon. Given the newspaper's well-known liberal bias, would they be inclined to publish such a piece, even if Andrews was inclined to write it? Wolf decided this was a problem for another day and nodded along eagerly with Andrews' explanation.

"Excellent, excellent," Warden Featherstone exclaimed gleefully. "Then how should we begin?"

"While I am sure that Mr Andrews will require an extensive tour of the facilities and interview with you, we will start with the Earl of Warwick."

Featherstone looked startled at this suggestion. It was hard for the man to understand why their most infamous resident in the penitentiary would be relevant. What positive things about his time in the prison would an earl have to say?

"Warden Featherstone, when we last spoke to the earl, he mentioned the good treatment you have afforded him." Tabitha didn't add that such treatment was merely in deference to Clarence's rank and almost certainly not indicative of how the average prisoner was treated.

Luckily, Warden Featherstone latched onto her comment. "Indeed, indeed. His lordship would indeed have nothing but good things to say of his stay here, given that he is a prisoner, after all. Let me take you to my office and have the earl brought up."

Wolf smiled in gratitude at his quick-thinking wife.

As they followed Warden Featherstone to his office, Andrews leaned in and whispered to Wolf, "An extensive tour of the facilities and an interview with the warden? You are really going to be in my debt for this one, Wolf!"

Chapter 34

While Tabitha and Wolf had last spoken with Clarence, Earl of Warwick, less than four days prior, the change in the man was shocking in such a short time. The already ill-fitting prison garb now seemed to hang off a frame that was skin and bones. When they had seen him last, Tabitha had thought that Clarence looked as if he had aged ten years overnight. Now, after another such three nights, she would have said he looked twenty years older than he was. He looked like a very old, frail man. Even if he was being afforded preferential treatment, Pentonville was hardly a pleasant sojourn by the looks of things.

When he saw his visitors were Tabitha and Wolf, Clarence smiled wearily. "Has a pardon arrived from Sir Matthew?" he asked hopefully.

While Wolf was sorry to have to disappoint the already suffering man, he was also happy to use this as an opportunity to encourage Clarence to cooperate with them.

Answering in the negative, Wolf continued, "However, we have a plan." The glimmer of hope in Clarence's eyes was sad to witness. Gesturing towards Andrews, Wolf introduced the journalist. "He is interested in writing about Redding's death for The Westminster Gazette."

"Why did you bring one of those muckrakers here?" Clarence asked accusingly. "I can only imagine what he and his fellow so-called journalists have been writing about me."

"Your lordship, I am interested in the truth and in exposing Lord Redding," Andrews asserted.

"What do you believe the truth is?" Clarence asked Andrews warily.

Tabitha answered in Andrews' place. "We know that Sally and Joe Turnbull are Redding's by-blows, and that Sally confronted him for abandoning their mother as she became sicker from the pox he had inflicted on all three." Clarence seemed stunned by this statement, but Tabitha didn't give him a chance to respond. "And finally, we know Sally killed Redding. Perhaps by accident, perhaps intentionally. The one thing we do not know now is why you are shielding her."

Having spent days carefully hiding this information, Clarence sat back in astonishment. He had so many questions he wished to ask, but the first words out of his mouth were, "Has Sally been arrested?"

Wolf realised someone had to break the news of what had happened to Clarence and decided that it was for him to deliver the final blow. "We went to confront Sally with what we knew. In the altercation that followed, she upset an oil lamp, which set the house ablaze. We do not believe she survived the conflagration."

Clarence's hands flew to his mouth in horror at Wolf's words. But there was still more bad news to deliver. "In the course of our investigations earlier yesterday, we were overheard by Joe Turnbull, who then abducted the dowager countess and shot her. Luckily, the bullet bounced off her ladyship's corset. However, the impact of it caused her to fall, and she hit her head very badly, though not fatally. Joe is now in police custody."

"So, this has all been for nothing?" Clarence waved, spreading his arms to encompass the horror of his time in Pentonville Prison.

"How did you know Sally had killed Redding, and, more importantly, why were you prepared to go to such lengths to protect her? We know Caroline Turnbull was once your mistress. However, this seems like extreme lengths to go to for even a former lover."

Clarence seemed shocked at their knowledge of his relationship with Caroline Turnbull. Yet, that was not the part of the story he began with. "I first met Redding at Eton. For reasons I have never understood, he took against me immediately and made it the principal mission of his life for the next three years to torture me by any means possible. Much of it went beyond mere bullying and traumatised me as a boy. Redding was older than me and the year he moved on from Eton was the happiest time I remember there."

Tabitha and Wolf both made genuinely sympathetic noises. "You can imagine my horror when I began my time at Oxford to find that not only was Redding also there, but that he was a fellow scholar at Christ Church College. I hoped that having had a year to mature and with far more interesting things to take up his time as an Oxford man, I would be beneath his interest. Unfortunately, such hopes were in vain."

Clarence paused, his eyes suddenly unfocused, as he seemed swept back in time. Finally, he continued his narrative. "His utter disdain for, one might almost say, hatred of me seemed to increase as we grew into manhood, particularly after my brother died and I became the heir. He seemed to feel a need to crush any happiness I ever found. Particularly any love I found."

Tabitha and Wolf exchanged glances; was this story finally going to get around to Caroline Turnbull?

It seemed it was not, at least not yet. "Redding had inherited the barony while he was still at Christ Church and quite a fortune along with it. My brother did not die until some years after I left Oxford. Before that, I tried to make my way in society, unsure of what to do with my life. In truth, I was somewhat lost. During that time, I met the most beautiful girl, Angelina Bartlett. We fell in love almost at first sight. I believe that even as a second son, her father would have allowed the marriage. However, Redding saw an unmatched opportunity to ruin my happiness and stepped in and offered for her. He was a rich baron and had the superior suit, at least then."

"So, he married Lady Redding merely to spite you?" Tabitha asked incredulously.

"Indeed."

Tabitha couldn't conceive of how mean-spirited one man would have to be to do that to another. What kind of loathing could someone carry such that they would tie themselves to a spouse merely to hurt a nemesis?

"That is hardly the worst of it, though."

How much worse this story was going to get?

"Two years later, my brother died, and I became the heir. Of course, there were many clamouring to be my wife then. Yet, I never forgot Angelina and could not bring myself to marry." Clarence now looked apologetically at Tabitha as he continued, "However, I am a man. I am sorry for speaking of such things in front of you, Lady Pembroke, yet it must be said if the story is going to be complete."

Tabitha acknowledged his words. "I am no shrinking violet, Clarence. Say what you must."

"One evening, I attended the theatre and became entranced by the woman on the stage. While what I felt for Caroline was no match for my love for Angelina, she was a beautiful, vibrant woman and helped my heart heal a little. Marrying her was out of the question, and she knew that. Yet our time together was special in its own way. But my father died suddenly. I became the earl and knew I must grow up and marry. I met Fiona at a ball. It was her first season, and she was young and shy. She was also beautiful, gentle and kind, and I offered for her before the season was over. It goes without saying that I then ended my friendship with Caroline."

Did it go without saying? Certainly, it hadn't sounded so from the way Fiona had talked about her husband's marital indiscretions. Why had Clarence's wife made such assumptions, and did he realise she believed he had continued to keep a mistress? This was not the time to ask such questions, but Tabitha made a mental note to return to this once Clarence was a free man.

"When I was still with Caroline before I met Fiona, Redding had come sniffing around her yet again, determined to steal what was mine. However, Caroline made it clear she had no interest in him. Or at least she did until I married. Then, her need for a new patron trumped any distaste she had for Redding and his evident competition with me."

Clarence looked thoughtful as he considered his own words. "I never really understood why Redding was still interested in Caroline when the opportunity to take her from me was no longer there. Though she was a beautiful woman with the voice of an angel, and I do not doubt she was able to use her wiles to reignite his attention, at least for a time."

Wolf needed to clarify the timeline, at least for Andrews' sake. "So, at some point, before he met Caroline Turnbull, Redding became infected with the pox which he passed to both his wife and mistress?"

"Indeed. Of course, I knew nothing about such things at the time. I did my best to avoid Redding as much as possible and went about my life. It was always painful when I saw Angelina in society. Yet I hoped she was happy, even though it seemed she would not be blessed with children."

This story was long, and they still had not come to any part that seemed relevant to their investigation. Wolf was tempted to hurry Clarence along. Before he had a chance, the timeline jumped forward, and they finally seemed to be at a relevant point.

"Six months ago, I was approached by a solicitor representing Lady Redding. I knew she had died, of course. Like everyone else in society, I had heard rumours she had lost her senses and had been sent to the Continent to recuperate."

Tabitha didn't know how to ask her next question delicately, so she just asked it, "Did you ever guess what her affliction was?"

A look of such sadness washed over Clarence's face that Tabitha wished she hadn't asked the question. "There was gossip, I am sure, though I never paid heed to any of it. However, in her will, she left a letter written to me while she still had some of her faculties. She told me of the disease her husband had inflicted on her that left her barren and was now taking her mind. She also told me about Caroline Turnbull, who had visited her some years before with two children in tow, twins, a girl and a boy, who she claimed were Redding's. Caroline was already suffering some acute symptoms from the same disease, and she feared that at least one of her children was as well. She told Angelina that she had lost her ability to support herself with her voice and begged for help."

So far, this lined up with the story Sally Turnbull had told. She hadn't mentioned that her brother had also visited Lady Redding, but besides that, the two stories matched closely enough.

Wolf remarked that Sally Turnbull had told them of this visit, though, at the time, she hadn't understood who they were visiting. "She told us that Lady Redding gave her mother some banknotes and she believed she must have continued sending money for some years, at least until she left the country."

"Indeed," Clarence continued. "It seems that Angelina had left instructions for the money to continue to be sent, but perhaps an overeager steward had considered himself obliged to double-check the arrangement with Lord Redding. However it happened, the money stopped."

"Did the solicitor know any details?"

"Just that the money had ceased to be paid when Lady Redding went abroad. He only told me because he was honour-bound to confess the money had stopped some years before at Lord Redding's instructions after I read Angelina's letter to him. Angelina begged me to continue to take care of the children after her death and shared the last known address she had for Caroline. She felt a deep obligation towards the innocents her husband had sired, infected, then abandoned to their fate.

"Of course, I immediately began to look for Caroline and her children, weighed down by guilt that I had not given a thought to Caroline in all those years."

"Had you any reason to believe she had fallen so low?" Tabitha asked, hoping the answer was no. She liked Clarence and had been happy at the thought of uniting their two families. She didn't want to think that Lily was marrying the son of a man who would be so callous.

"In truth, I had lost track of Caroline many years before. After I lost Angelina and before I met Fiona, I became something of a rake: gambling, drinking to excess, and more. I will spare you from hearing the details, but I was lost until I met Fiona. Even my time with Caroline was one of reckless disregard for the honour of my family and my good name. Marriage was the making of me, and I put aside all connections to that prior life."

Tabitha remembered the dowager speaking of Clarence's rakishness as a young man when they were searching for Tobias in Brighton. Apparently, Charlotte had worried that there was a familial predisposition to youthful indulgence.

"I took my duties as an earl and as a husband seriously and no longer patronised music halls and the like and so did not know what had become of Caroline. When I read Angelina's letter, I made every effort I could to track down the Turnbull family, but with no success. Then, on Thursday, I was making my way into White's when I was stopped on the street by a young woman. While many of her features were grotesque, there was something about her eyes that immediately reminded me of Caroline."

"This was Sally Turnbull, I assume," Wolf asked.

"Indeed. Of course, I did not realise that immediately. She asked me if a man called Lord Redding was a member. It seemed she had been turned away by his butler and had discovered that men of Redding's ilk were usually members of gentleman's clubs. White's was the third club she had gone to since her mother had died. Most members had refused to talk with her as they entered, but she had been persistent enough that she had learned where he was not a member. Little did Sally know that, not only had she finally come to the right place, but she was also asking the one person most interested in her and her story.

"At what point did you realise who she was?"

"I asked why she was looking for Redding and for her name. She was hesitant to tell me both but eventually I persuaded her. As soon as she told me her name, I realised who she was and why she was asking for Redding. I took her across the street to a cafe. She was a sorry sight, and looked as if she could do with a square meal. I did not reveal that I had known her father, but I did promise to be her messenger to Redding if she told me why."

"And that was when you found out that Caroline had recently died?" Tabitha asked. "We know it was only days before Redding's death and that she had told her daughter her full parentage on her deathbed."

"Indeed. I am not sure what Sally wanted from Redding; I am not even sure that she knew. But she wanted to look the man in the eye and proclaim herself his daughter and chastise him for abandoning them to such a gruesome fate."

"So, is that what you argued about?" Andrews asked.

"Yes. I left Sally on the street and found Redding in White's. At first, I tried to reason with him. I thought he might have no idea that he had left Caroline with child, let alone that he had left her and her babies infected with the pox."

"But you knew he had stopped the money for Caroline, did you not?"

"Yes. However, I only knew what the solicitor knew, which was nothing more than that. He might have stopped the money for many reasons. It was unclear what Angelina's payments implied in his mind." Neither Tabitha nor Wolf believed Redding was innocent of the knowledge of what he had done to Caroline, but was there a glimmer of hope that he had not known that he was taking food out of his desperate children's mouths when he stopped that money?

That hope was immediately dashed when Clarence continued, "We argued, and it became horribly clear that he had known exactly who the money was for and why. Yet he had stopped it anyway."

"What an unfeeling man he must have been!" Tabitha exclaimed, shocked at the harshness the man showed towards his own children.

"All I had the chance to say was that he needed to do the right thing by his children now. That it was the honourable thing to do. I never even had a chance to tell him that Sally was waiting for him outside of White's before he stormed out of the room and then out of the club. I am sure he had no wish for any more of his dirty laundry to be aired in public. I followed him out of White's, and we argued and then came to blows on the street."

"Hence your rather dishevelled appearance when you arrived for dinner," Tabitha observed.

"Indeed. I realised I was late for your soiree and did the best I could to straighten my clothes, but it seems it was not a good enough job."

Tabitha had one last question: "Why are you so sure that Sally Turnbull killed Lord Redding?"

"Because I saw her follow him as he walked away from me. I should have done something about it, but as I said, I was late for dinner. Shame on me."

CHAPTER 35

Tabitha and Wolf left Andrews in Warden Featherstone's office. The journalist was resigned to having to go through the motions of pretending to be interested in interviewing the warden and touring his facilities. After again reminding Wolf of just how much he owed him for seeing this charade through to the end, Andrews promised he would give Featherstone no more than an hour of his time and that the story would be in the evening paper.

As they rode back to Mayfair in the carriage, Tabitha wondered at the story they had been told. "I am not sure what is more amazing, that Clarence would take the blame for Redding's murder in order to protect a woman he barely knew, or that he had the hubris to believe he could do so because there would be no serious repercussions for him."

"Well, in all fairness, until recently, he was probably correct. It could and would have been swept under the rug. And as for protecting Sally Turnbull, he had been asked to do so by his first great love. That can be a powerful motivator."

Tabitha knew she shouldn't ask, but she couldn't help herself. "If Arlene came and asked you to do something like this under similar circumstances, would you?" Tabitha knew she was allowing herself to be controlled by the green-eyed monster, yet talk of first loves inevitably made her think of Wolf's.

Wolf had been sitting opposite her in the carriage. Now he moved to sit next to Tabitha and took her hand. "What I felt for Arlene has no comparison to what I feel for you, my love. You need never fear that my feelings for her continue to have any hold on me."

Angry at herself, yet unable to stop, Tabitha said in a small voice, "Yet you did not seem as sure in Brighton, and that was not so long ago?"

"Where is this coming from, Tabitha? How can you possibly doubt the depth and completeness of my love for you?"

Tabitha shrugged. "It was hearing Clarence speak of Angelina, Lady Redding, and how she was the true love of his life and how he married Fiona only after that love was denied to him."

"Which is absolutely nothing like our story, is it? If I had wanted to reunite with Arlene, I had every opportunity to in Brighton. She made no secret of her willingness to pick up where we left off. And yes, I will admit, there was a moment, a tiny fraction of a moment, when nostalgia for what had been blurred my senses. Then that moment passed, and I saw Arlene and what I had believed I felt for her for what it was: nothing compared to what I knew I felt for you. While I was not sure then if you felt anything for me in return, I knew where my true love lay."

Even hearing this, jealousy pricked at Tabitha again. Yet she knew she was being unreasonable. She had been holding Wolf at arm's length even before they arrived in Brighton. When, in a moment of abandon, he had kissed her at the end of their investigation, Tabitha still could not acknowledge her feelings for him. If she had felt conflicted, why was he not allowed a moment of confusion?

Determined to put her absurd doubts aside, Tabitha moved the conversation back to the investigation. "Do you really believe that one newspaper article will suffice to change Sir Matthew's mind?"

"We will see. Andrews is an excellent journalist and a compelling writer. I do not doubt that he will make the story compelling and melodramatic. As it is, with no more details emerging, the articles about Clarence were losing steam. There are only so many times the newspapers can retell the same story before people become bored and look elsewhere."

"So, you believe that the mere novelty of Andrew's piece will attract attention? I hope you are correct."

"I know I am. And then there is the fact that people love to see a prig exposed. An aristocratic prig who sermonised from his ivory tower while being as debauched as the most base-born amongst them, well that will be irresistible. One who was then killed by the illegitimate child who he spurned and would have seen starve to death; well, that seems almost too good to be true. As much as Andrews tried to play on my guilt at leaving him to Featherstone's clutches, he knows he owes me for giving him this scoop. It will make his career. Clarence may have to spend one more night in Pentonville, but Langley assured me that will likely be his last after this article hits the newsstands."

"I hope you are right."

"The Home Secretary needs a sacrificial lamb so that the government can show that it metes justice equally to all men. How much easier is it if that particular lamb is already deceased? I think that Sir Matthew will leap at this opportunity to achieve his ends far more cleanly than he ever could by prosecuting the Earl of Warwick."

By the time they arrived back at Chesterton House, Bear had gone to Brick Lane and returned with news of the dowager's continued improvement. "Dr Cohen thinks she should be able to return home by tomorrow."

"She must come here," Tabitha insisted.

"You know that Manning and Withers between them will fuss over her as much as she needs, probably more," Wolf assured her.

"Even so. I would feel far better if she stayed with us for at least a night or two. Withers can join her. Why even Manning can if he does not trust our care." Wolf realised it might end up coming to that, but he let Tabitha have her way.

The hours until the evening papers appeared on the street corners felt like days. Tabitha and Wolf tried to occupy themselves, but nothing made time move any more quickly. Wolf had asked Bear to loiter near the nearest newsstand so that they could be sure of getting The Westminster Gazette as soon as it was available. Accordingly, just before three o'clock, Bear set out. Tabitha and Wolf sat in the parlour while he was gone, but on hearing the front door open and close, they both leapt up and rushed out to meet him.

Bear hailed them with a newspaper in his hand. "It's a good thing I went early; they're flying off the newsstand like hotcakes." Then, impersonating a newsboy, he cried, "Extra! Extra! Read all about it. It was the bastard daughter who did it. Earl is innocent of holier-than-thou baron's murder."

"Is that what the headline says?" Wolf asked, reaching for the newspaper.

"Close enough."

Wolf led the way back into the parlour so he could reach the article out loud. When he was finished, Tabitha exclaimed, "Andrews really is good. It is hard to imagine that Sir Matthew will be able to ignore that. Particularly if it gets picked up by the other newspapers."

"I think it is a case of when, not if. Now they have the scent of a new trail, they will be like bloodhounds for the rest of the story. I appreciate Andrews was vague about the identity of who Joe Turnbull shot. The more we can keep our names out of this, the better."

"Definitely," Tabitha agreed. "You would imagine that with one of Redding's illegitimate children already in prison for attempted murder and kidnapping and the other supposed dead in a recent fire, there will be enough juicy details for the other newspapers to track down that this story will stay on the front pages for days. The scandal of such a moralising man behaving in such a manner will be fodder for many headlines to come."

She paused. "I do feel sorry for Joe Turnbull. I know he is guilty of taking Mama and of shooting her. It is no thanks to him she is not dead. However, it seems likely that it is that terrible disease that made him lose his senses, and that is no fault of his."

"While we never had the chance to make the offer to Sally, I will do as I was prepared to offer to do: pay for him to have the finest legal defence possible," Wolf promised. Tabitha smiled lovingly at her kind and generous husband.

It was only an hour later when Talbot knocked on the parlour door and announced Lord Langley. Lily had joined them in the parlour and now she jumped out of her seat and ran towards their visitor.

"What has happened? Has the earl been released?" she demanded.

"Lily, let Lord Langley enter the room and take a seat before we bombard him with questions." Despite her words, Tabitha was as eager to hear what Langley had to say as Lily.

"To answer your last question, Lady Lily, the earl has not been released. However, I have every reason to believe he will be no later than tomorrow." Addressing Tabitha and Wolf, he continued, "I received a very terse telephone call from Sir Matthew. He had read your journalist's piece and wanted to know what we were playing at."

"Why would he assume we had anything to do with this?" Wolf asked, genuinely bemused.

"Well, this morning, I told him a story about a confession to you by Sally Turnbull and asked him to release the Earl of Warwick. Then, no sooner has he refused than a story appears on the front page of an evening newspaper detailing that confession and more about Miss Turnbull and her altercation with her father. It was not difficult for him to guess at the provenance of such an article."

Wolf shrugged his shoulders. "Does it matter if he believes we are behind it in some way?"

"Probably not," Langley acknowledged. "Sir Matthew is many things, but he is no fool. He knows that this version of the story will catch fire like dry kindling. He also realises that it ensures that there is still an aristocrat held accountable, even if not by the authorities. It helps that Sally Turnbull is presumed dead, so the government does not have to waste time or manpower trying to find her. With Joe Turnbull already in police custody, it is a rather tidy outcome from his perspective. He may rant and rave about your interference for a short while longer, but I do no doubt he will see the wisdom of closing the door on this particular murder inquiry."

Everyone was delighted with the news, no one more so than Lily. She insisted on telephoning Tobias to tell him the news, even though everyone warned her to err on the side of caution and not raise Charlotte, Fiona and Tobias' hopes prematurely. Lily ignored their words and rushed out of the room to place a telephone call to her betrothed.

"Will you stay for dinner, Langley?" Tabitha asked. "I feel we owe you more than a fine rack of lamb, but that will have to do for now. Cook is making Eton Mess for dessert. Rather apropos when you think about it."

"Should I telephone Langley House and have Rat join us?" Langley asked.

"What a delightful idea. He has not been here in far too long."

EPILOGUE

The following morning, Clarence was released from Pentonville and the dowager left Brick Lane to continue her recuperation at Chesterton House. She arrived just after lunch in a bath chair Bear had obtained from somewhere.

Tabitha and Wolf waited by the front door as Bear lifted the bath chair with the dowager in it up the steps and into the house. A rather weary-looking Jane followed him through the front door.

"Mama! It is so wonderful to see you out of bed. How are you feeling?" Tabitha asked.

"Better, better, I suppose. Mrs Tuchinsky's chicken soup really has quite amazing medicinal qualities. Dr Cohen assures me he has witnessed it perform miracles over the years."

"We have your room all ready. Bear will carry you up, and we can bring you a tray whenever you are ready to eat."

"While I appreciate your hospitality while I get back on my feet, Tabitha, I will not be treated as if I am in my dotage. I have spent quite enough time in bed over the last couple of days and I do not intend to eat my meals from there as if I am my decrepit Aunt Sophia. Mr Bear may wheel me into the parlour where you all will tell me about the investigation."

Tabitha wanted to argue, but a quick shake of Jane's head told her it would be futile. Indeed, as Bear took the handles of the bath chair and pushed the dowager into the parlour, Jane whispered, "She will not be dissuaded from this and is determined not to be treated like an invalid, even though she is one."

While she might not want to accept being treated like an invalid in some ways, the dowager was happy to make the most of it in others. No sooner had she ordered that Bear move her usual armchair so that her bath chair could be wheeled into its location than she demanded that Talbot bring her a cup of tea and that Jane find a particular book from the library to place on the table beside her.

As everyone else was obeying their orders, Tabitha and Wolf sat and waited for the pandemonium to ease. Withers and Manning had been waiting for their mistress in her assigned room. However, once alerted to her new location, they both hurried down and fussed around her like a pair of mother hens. The dowager enjoyed every bit of attention.

Finally, though, even she had enough and said, "Withers, stop clucking around me. And Manning, get a hold of yourself. I am not dead yet and have no intention of being so for many years to come. One of you fetch me a shawl, and the other rectify Talbot's oversight in bringing me ginger biscuits rather than shortbread."

With her devoted servants dispatched to their tasks, the dowager turned to Tabitha and Wolf and said, "From what I heard being called from the newsstands as we drove here, it seems there have been some developments in the case which you need to bring me up to date on."

Lily had joined Tobias at the Warwick London home to welcome his father, but she had telephoned just before the dowager had arrived to say that the family wished to call at Chesterton House to give their thanks in person. Given that they might arrive at any moment, Tabitha and Wolf were eager to tell their story before their guests arrived. They didn't want to risk that the dowager might react to aspects of it they'd prefer Clarence and Fiona not overheard.

Jane returned with the book requested by the dowager, placed it on the table, took a chair, and moved it right next to the reluctant invalid.

"There is no need for you to hover like that, Jane. I am not about to expire if you are not by my side." While the dowager's words were no more charitable towards her daughter than ever, Tabitha noted that there was far less acid in her tone than usual. One might almost imagine that the words were said with a surprising gentleness. Almost.

Tabitha and Wolf then told the dowager everything from the moment they had discovered that she had disappeared to the Home Secretary's eventual capitulation early that morning.

"Well, well. It seems you have been very busy in my absence," she noted almost ruefully. "I am glad that my deduction about Mr Turnbull's identify proved to be such a pivotal clue." Tabitha almost pointed out to the dowager that she had said, to Tabitha, in fact, that Joe Turnbull made clear his identity unprompted. She had deduced nothing. Luckily, Tabitha thought better of it before she spoke. Instead, she let the dowager claim far more credit than was her due.

"I must say, Jeremy, it was clever of Maxwell to suggest that you force Sir Matthew's hand in that manner. Then, he always was a clever little boy, even if it was in an annoyingly clever-clogs fashion much of the time." This was said with a sniff and in a mean-spirited tone that Tabitha was glad Langley didn't have to witness.

Tabitha realised that the true source of the dowager's petty irritation was that the case had concluded without her. She had hoped that the woman could rise above her usual self-absorption to be happy for her dear friend Charlotte's family and, more importantly, for her granddaughter.

As she thought this, Tabitha realised that the topic of the wedding needed to be resolved before Lily and Tobias arrived. She decided to act as if the dowager had never proclaimed that the wedding could not go ahead, even if Clarence was absolved of all guilt.

Adopting a nonchalant tone that did not hint at her concerns on the subject, Tabitha said, "And the best news is that the wedding will proceed as planned. In fact, Jane, isn't Hamish arriving for dinner?"

The dowager narrowed her eyes. "I am sorry if I was ambiguous previously, but this wedding will not be proceeding as planned. In fact, it will not be proceeding ever. I thought I had been quite clear on how tainted the Warwick title will continue to be for some time. Clarence chose to embroil himself in this mess, and now his son will pay the price. I will not allow my granddaughter to shackle herself to such a family. This is my last word on the matter."

Before either Tabitha or Wolf could debate the subject with the dowager, a quiet but resolute voice piped up. "Mama, while you may be the matriarch of the family, this is not your decision to make. I am Lily's mother, and Hamish is her father. He and I spoke on the telephone this morning before he left Scotland, and we are of one mind: Lily should marry Viscount Tobias if she wishes. This is the last word on the matter."

Everyone looked at Jane in astonishment, no one more so than the dowager. Tabitha bit back a smile at the woman's amazement at her daughter's words.

Then, with one of her signature harrumphs to indicate that she wouldn't capitulate too easily, the dowager said, "It seems you are growing a backbone after all, Jane. Just make sure you redirect it in the future. I do not appreciate being overruled."

Despite her tone, the dowager's use of the word "overruled" was evidence that she realised she had lost this battle. And just in time.

Talbot entered the room and said, "The Earl of Warwick and his family are here, milady. Should I ask them to wait in the drawing room?"

"We are all to be family soon enough, Talbot. Bring them into the parlour. It seems we have a wedding to finish planning!"

~

Do you want to attend the wedding of Viscount Tobias and Lady Lily? Find the link at sarahfnoel.com for a bonus chapter.

~

Want a sneak peek at book 10, An Enigmatic Woman? Keep reading...

At last, Tabitha and Wolf can relax and settle into newlywed bliss... or so they think.

Just as they prepare to leave London for a quiet summer at the Pembroke Estate, an unexpected—and rather cryptic—invitation arrives. The notoriously flamboyant Henry Cyril Paget, 5th Marquess of Anglesey, has personally requested their presence at Plas Newydd, his ancestral estate, accompanied by a desperate plea for their investigative skills. Intrigued, the couple agrees to a detour—with the ever-formidable dowager in tow, of course.

But upon their arrival, it's not just the marquess' lavish theatrics and eccentric indulgences that catch them off guard. Another guest is in residence—none other than Empress Elisabeth of Austria, "Sisi" herself, who has taken refuge at Plas Newydd after receiving chilling threats against her life.

Now, Tabitha and Wolf must unravel the danger that lurks within the marquess' gilded world—before their most illustrious charge becomes its next victim.

Afterword

Thank you for reading A Patient Woman. I hope you enjoyed it. If you'd like to see what's coming next for Tabitha & Wolf, here are some ways to stay in touch:

SarahFNoel.com
Facebook
@sarahfNoelAuthor on BlueSky
sfnoel on Instagram
@sfnoel on Threads

If you enjoyed this book, I'd very much appreciate a review (but, please no spoilers).

ABOUT SARAH F. NOEL

Originally from London, Sarah F. Noel now spends most of her time in Grenada in the Caribbean. Sarah loves reading historical mysteries with strong female characters. The Tabitha & Wolf Mystery Series and its spin-off, The Continental Capers of Melody Chesterton, are exactly the kind of books she loves to curl up with on a lazy Sunday.

Visit Sarah's website (sarahfnoel.com/) to join her mailing list, connect with her on social media, and see what's coming next!